TONY HARTE AND THE BOYS FROM AVONDALE

D. R. POLLOCK AND C.W. POLLOCK

TONY HARTE AND THE BOYS FROM AVONDALE
Copyright © 2022 by D.R. Pollock

ISBN
978-1-957895-78-9 (Paperback)
978-1-957895-79-6 (eBook)
978-1-957895-77-2 (Hardcover)

TABLE OF CONTENTS

PART II

PREFACE

When my father retired, he sat down and wrote his memoirs. He did it as a novel, changing some names to protect the questionably innocent. The pages were a series of stories, most of which I had heard growing up.

Since names became an issue early in the writing, let us explain. My father was born in a tuberculosis Hospital in Colorado in November 1909 and was christened Henry Loyal Harte. His mother passed away when he was about two years old. Wilbur and Mildred Pollock adopted him and had his name legally changed to Claude in memory of birth mother Claudia. His middle name was changed to Wilbur after his adoptive father. He really did not like being called "Claudie" and went by his nickname "Tony" for most of his life.

Having recently published a historical novel, *Koa Kai*, I decided to take on the challenge of writing a novel based on my father's manuscript with the ability to include some stories I had heard growing up that my father choose to ignore in his writing.

So, while this is a story of Tony Harte, it is also the story of his friends and lovers during the exciting years of the roaring 20's and the depression plagued 30's.

Most of the story takes place in Chicago, a town known for machine politics and famous gangsters such as Al Capone and Bugs Moran. This was the background where our hero and his friends were trying to make it in the big city. All of this happens later on in the story, but first we need to get the hero through school.

Claude, and we will call him this for awhile, attended Avondale School. As the story unfolds, many of his friends and cohorts also attended Avondale, a boy's school located northwest of Chicago, Illinois. Edward Cap' Bagley bought the Avon farm in 1897 and founded the school as an orphanage for homeless urban boys. By 1920 this self-sustaining community had moved beyond an orphanage to a boarding school, the Avondale School for Boys.

Claude's stepfather, Wilbur, had an early job as bandmaster of the school around 1900. Wilbur's education was an agriculture degree from the University of Wisconsin. His goal was to get rich growing pecans and citrus fruits. He and a number of his friends moved south to pursue their dreams. They settled in Irvington, Alabama, a small town southwest of Mobile. The second Great Galveston storm of 1915 wiped out most of them, many of whom returned to the North in defeat. Wilbur decided to stay and build a nursery business. He would live in Irvington for the rest of his life.

When Wilbur's wife Mildred died in 1922, he made a tough decision: rather than try to run a business and care for his only son at the same time in this backwoods setting, he would send his son north where he would receive a proper education and be looked after by his wife's sister Amy and her family, who lived in Grayslake, Illinois, a few miles from the school.

CHAPTER 1

AVONDALE

It was hot and humid as usual that late August day in 1923. Irvington was always like this in the Summer. Wilbur and an entourage escorted Claude, dressed in his Sunday best, down to the little whistle stop train station. To complete Claude's outfit, Wilbur presented him with a jaunty little hat which complemented the suit coat. Claude looked in the mirror in the waiting room and was impressed with his worldly appearance.

The group assembled to see Claude off included not only his father but also Aunt Mariah, the woman who had been Claude's nanny since the Pollocks adopted him. Mariah was a voodoo woman and a freed slave, having been a child at the end of the Civil War. Also, there was Asa, Wilbur's trusted field hand for the past twenty years. There was a small group of kids and local men who came down to the station because it was rumored, they could see the train stop, as this would be the most exciting thing to happen in Irvington in quite a while.

The Gulf Mobile & Ohio passenger trains rolled past here a couple of times a day, but they only stopped at the little station if the signal was set, alerting the engineer there was a passenger waiting. The smoke from an approaching locomotive could be seen from several miles away. Then the headlight of the locomotive could be seen. This heightened the excitement among the crowd. Kids jumped out onto the tracks to look straight down the right-of-way at the approaching beast. They would then jump back to the safety of the little platform. The locomotive let out a long blast of its whistle, causing the lad of the bold local boys to scurry off the tracks. The engineer engaged the bell before reaching the platform. The locomotive chugged by the platform, blowing steam on the crowd before coming to a complete stop and blowing off excess steam.

There were hugs and kisses and promises to write. Then Claude grabbed one of his suitcases and Wilbur grabbed the other and handed them to a uniformed steward. Claude climbed on board waving goodbye to the only people he had even known. He found the first available seat on the station side of the car and continued to wave.

The conductor signaled to the engineer and after a long and short whistle, the train began to roll out of the station.

Claude sat back in his coach seat for the first time and caught his breath and for a moment had a sinking feeling. He was alone and on his own for the first time in his life. This almost brought tears, but these feelings quickly passed, being replaced by a mixture of fear, sorrow for leaving home, and excitement over this new world which promised to be way different than Irvington, Alabama.

Getting Claude safely from Irvington to Avondale School took some coordination between Wilbur and Oscar Olsen. Several letters went back and forth before the plan was finalized. The dates for Claude's departure and subsequent arrival in Chicago had to be firm. It was decided Claude should arrive in Chicago on a Saturday, so Oscar could be available to round him up in Chicago. The family believed Claude was mature enough to be on the train by himself. The problem was the Gulf, Mobile & Ohio passenger trains arrived in Chicago on Illinois Central tracks at Central Station and the Milwaukee Road, which passed through Grayslake, utilized Union Station, some blocks away from Central Station. It was decided Oscar would meet Claude at Central Station and take a taxi to Union Station to catch the next train home.

On the appointed day, Oscar was sitting in Central Station, but the train coming from the south was two hours late. He had seen a picture of his nephew but figured he would just look for some lonely looking boy of about the right age.

Finally, the train arrived, and Oscar's sighting plan worked like a charm. After a mass of people hurried by him, the crowd cleared enough for him to see a lad dressed in his Sunday fines, dragging two suitcases down the platform. Oscar was not sure how affectionate he should be in meeting a male relative, so he strode up to Claude, held out his hand, shook Claude's right hand with his own and patted him on the back with his left.

Introductions complete, Oscar hailed a porter to take the bags while they walked to the Station's exit. At the taxi stand, Oscar tipped the porter, who passed the bags to a waiting cabby who placed them in his trunk and then held open the rear door of the taxi for Claude and Oscar.

Claude had not said much to this point, so Oscar decided to start some small talk. "So, how was your train trip?"

Claude had not had anyone to talk with for the past day and a half, so he bubbled forth, "It was pretty neat! I saw big cities like Nashville and Louisville, way bigger than Mobile. The conductors looked after me and told me all about their railroad."

Oscar replied, "If you think Nashville and Louisville were big, take a look north of us at downtown Chicago."

"Wow," responded Claude. He returned to his train trip. "We were a couple hours late, because we had to sit while they fixed a de-rail ahead of us."

Oscar said, "We're almost to Union Station. You can tell me more on the ride home."

On the train north, Claude didn't say too much, as he was taking in the big buildings, the topography, and towns spaced every few miles.

At the Grayslake Station, they departed the train and carried the suitcases to Amy's waiting Model T. Oscar had left her car at the station, being more expendable than his own car.

The house in which Claude had been raised had a rickety front porch and a screen door which was used most of the year. Inside was a sitting room, flanked by a bedroom on each side and a kitchen at the rear of the building. Driving from the station Claude observed some large and some small houses. All were built much more substantially than the small houses of Irvington.

After rounding a third of the lake, Claude's jaw dropped as they turned into the driveway of a three-story Tudor style house. "This must be a castle," he thought.

Oscar honked the horn and Amy came bounding out of the front door. She was shorter than Claude's stepmother; other than that, it was easy to see they were related.

As Claude stepped out of the car, Amy was on him with hugs and kisses. She stammered, "Claudie, we are so happy to have you with us. We want you to be a part of the family."

Claude's younger cousin came forward at a much slower pace than her mother. Amy directed, "This is your cousin Dorothy." She gestured toward her daughter, "Dorothy give your cousin a hug." Dorothy did as she was told with some reluctance. Claude responded in return with a half-hearted hug. He was not sure he was up for all this affection and he still did not like being called "Claudie."

Amy wheeled around, stating "I must get back to dinner, before I burn it." Waving at Claude, "Oscar, help Claudie get his bags to his room, so he can freshen up before dinner."

As they entered the guest room, Claude looked around the room for a wash bowl and pitcher, so he could clean up. "Oscar responded, "there is a bathroom down the hall." When Oscar departed, Claude announced to himself, "Dang, this must be a castle, I don't know of anyone in Irvington who doesn't have an outhouse."

Claude washed his face and hands as best he could, still wearing his dress shirt and suit pants. He did not know if he should dress down for dinner or not, so he left on his now quite wrinkled Sunday suit. He laid back on the bed for a few minutes thinking how he had lucked out by getting to be at what must be a castle.

Downstairs Claude followed voices and entered the dining room. He burst into the room where the rest of the family was seated at the table. Oscar was at the head of the table. On either side of Oscar were Amy's parents, who were introduced as Mister and Misses Hannington. Grandpa Hannington had emigrated to the United States as a young man, but his demeanor was that of an older privileged Englishman. Amy was at the end of the table, with Dorothy sitting at her left. An empty chair on the other side, obviously awaiting Claude.

Claude hustled to his seat. "Sorry if I am late."

Amy replied, "Not at all, we have just been seated."

Amy was always a good cook and was known locally for putting on a fine formal dinner, but for this dinner she had pulled out all the stops in celebration of her nephew's arrival.

This was the most majestic room Claude had ever seen. Not only did all the dishes and silverware match, but there was a lace doily under each plate and glass. There was wine in the small glasses and iced water in the large glasses. Candles flickered in their silver candlesticks. On a platter in front of Oscar was a large rib roast, waiting to be carved. Several other bowls containing potatoes and vegetables were spread around the table. Some bowls matched the plates, some were gleaming silver.

Not wanting to spill on his suit, Claude tucked the cloth napkin under his chin. He didn't know why there was more than one fork and spoon, but he picked up the largest fork and the knife and was ready to eat. Seeing the rib roast, he began to salivate like Pavlov's dog.

Amy's conservative English heritage showed in much which she did in her role as a gentile upper class woman. She turned to

Claude, "First of all, one only wears a hat at dinner if they are Jewish."

Claude had no idea what that meant but whipped off his hat and placed it in his lap. "Sorry Ma'am."

Amy continued, "Please put your hat on the sideboard and your napkin in your lap."

Claude quickly complied, thinking there must be a lot more about eating a good meal than he ever could have guessed.

Amy patted him on the shoulder, "We will have to teach you some of the more civilized table manners before we take you out in public." Gesturing towards Dorothy, "Please say the grace."

The dinner was one of the best Claude had ever eaten. The only spoiler was as much as Amy tried not to continually pick on Claude, she could not help but correct his table manners on several occasions.

Claude thought, "I knew I was going to a military school, but I didn't think it would have been at my aunt and uncle's house."

After dinner Claude excused himself early so he could try out his new palatial bed and get some well-earned sleep.

Oscar and Amy drove Claude to the Avondale School on a sunny Sunday afternoon to be there early for the Fall semester 1923. Claude saw a neat row of buildings: a school, a chapel, a dining hall and several dormitory cottages, all facing a medium size lake. Inland from the lake and a distance behind the row of buildings, the tops of barns and other outbuildings were visible.

Oscar stopped in front of Cap' Bagley's cottage. Cap' was the headmaster of the School. Cap' was a short stocky man, somewhere in his late 40s to early 50s. He wore a tan military looking shirt, baggy pants, boots with leggings and a round Smokey the Bear hat. He cut the figure of a World War I cavalry officer. His wire glasses added to his Teddy Roosevelt demeanor.

Oscar introduced Cap' to Claude and then engaged in some olden days small talk about his days as a student at Avondale.

Oscar had been a Cadet here when Claude's Father, was Band Master. After Oscar and Amy departed, Cap' summoned a senior student to show Claude his cottage. Cap' would come over to the cottage later to help with the introductions.

Claude wanted to show his respect to this older student, "Thank ya'll for lookin' after me."

The student responded, "You talk funny, where are you from?"

Claude, "I just come up from Alabama on the train."

The student responded, "I guess I never seen or heard somebody from Alabama."

At the cottage, the upperclassman motioned for Claude to precede him up the steps to the porch of the stone and frame cabin. Claude dragged his two bags while the upper classman held the door. Inside there was a sitting study area on one side of the large room and ten bunks on the other side. In the sitting area were several boys about Claude's age.

The upperclassman announced, "Lads this is your new roommate, Claude. Cap' will be along to introduce him." With that he exited the cabin.

Claude standing alone in the doorway feeling awkward, he tried to greet his new classmates. "Howdy, ya'll, I'm Claude Harte."

The closest boy, Bill responded, "You talk funny, where are you from?"

Claude again replied, "I just come up from Alabama on the train."

Bill, "You sound like the niggers I've heard in Chicago. Are you some kind of a nigger?"

Claude ignored the insult, and was about to respond when Bill interrupted him, "You know Claudie." That did it; Claude hated to be called "Claudie." He dropped his suitcases, took one step forward and punched Bill with a left hook to the jaw. Bill fell back against a chair but was up in an instant and took a right swing at Claude's head. It was on; the other boys started hollering and mostly cheering for their buddy Bill. The two combatants traded blows. When Bill tripped on the carpet and fell backwards. Claude was on him and pounding his head against the floor.

The door swung open and Cap' Bagley strode into the room. All of the observers snapped to attention. He grabbed Claude by the back of his coat and pulled him up. "What the hell's going on here?"

Bill, "We was just funnin' with him, and he got all hostile."

Claude responded, "I ain't no nigger, and I don't like to be called 'Claudie."

Cap' responded, "Oh, I see. First you gentlemen need to shake hands and then Mr. Foy, I believe that owe Mr. Harte an apology. Mr. Harte, at Avondale we do not appreciate such rough behavior. If two students have true differences, they settle it in the ring. If you will accept Mr. Foy's apology, then the issue is ended if not the two of you shall meet in the boxing ring."

Claude not wanting to appear weak in front of his new acquaintances, stated' "I ain't been in a boxing ring, but if that is what it takes around here not to be treated like shit, then let's have it."

Cap', "We try to remain civil around here and not cuss, but we understand your position. The two of you will meet in the gym after tomorrow's classes to settle your differences like gentlemen."

Cap', "You have already met Mr. Foy, let me introduce your other roommates," he said, pointing to the nearest boys, " Mr. Cliff Birdwell, Mr. Bill Maloney, and Mr. Doug Getchel is the cottage master. He will introduce you to the rest of your mates" Gesturing toward Claude, "Please shake hands with your new roommates."

The nine snapped to attention, each stepped forward, shook hands and offering his name and his welcome.

Cap', "Now you two clean up before the dinner bell rings. And for God's sake, try to get along until tomorrow." Just as he opened the cottage door, he once again turned to Claude, "You will be issued your uniforms in the morning."

Claude responded, "Yes sir."

Claude and Bill went to the bathroom to clean up. Doug, as the cottage master, accompanied them to make sure there were no further hostilities. Trying to break the silence Doug said, "Damn you guys sure ugly'd yourselves up."

Looking in the mirror, Claude saw the left side of his jaw was bruised and there was a bit of a mouse forming under his left eye. Bill looked at similar battle scars. As he had ended up on the floor with Claude pommeling him, he had a swollen jaw, abrasions on both cheeks. He felt a lump and blood on the back of his head, from bouncing off the floor.

Claude was not sure what he had let himself in for. Was this going to be a place of violence, or had his temper caused the fight? Where all these Yankees going to make fun of him forever? The dinner bell interrupted his thoughts.

The cottage mates waved at Claude to come along to the dining hall. They formed into a squad and marched to the dining hall. Doug at the lead called out the cadence. Claude at the rear tried in vain to keep in step.

At dinner a couple of the boys tried to make conversation with Claude but knowing little or nothing about Alabama they had little to ask and were careful with their comments, as they did not wish to again infuriate this foreigner in their midst.

Claude had not eaten since he left the train and was famished. He attacked his plate with a vengeance, eating every morsel even the cooked vegetables that he would normally have tried to avoid.

Back at the cottage, the uniforms were waiting for Claude's return. The dress uniform was a navy-blue jumper with matching bell bottom slacks. The hat, a blue tam, was reminiscent of a World War I naval uniform. Doug explained the dress uniform was for special occasions and Sunday morning service at the chapel. The everyday uniform was kakis of which there were three sets along with five sets of underwear. Doug told him how to prepare his bunk and the weekday schedule which included the wakeup bell at

6:00 AM, being in formation by 6:15 AM to march to the dining hall. They would form up and march back to the cottage at 7:00. First class was at 8:00 AM, as Claude was new, there would be a list of his classes pinned on the bulletin board just inside the school building's front door. The cottage would march to class at 7:45 AM.

Claude's first day of classes went well, however he kept thinking about the boxing match that he had agreed to which would be happening right after classes. He still hurt in strange places from yesterday's engagement. He thought to himself, 'He might take a beating this time, since he did not know how to box. He could not back down and be considered a wussy by his cottage mates. He would just have to do what he could and take what was coming.'

The time came, class was out at 3:30 PM and instead of marching back to the cottage, the squad turned and proceeded to the gymnasium. Claude and Bill changed into gym shorts and t-shirts. They proceeded to a grungy ring in the cover of the gym. Cap' Bagley was there to officiate and make sure that things did not get out of hand. Doug helped Claude put on his boxing gloves, while another boy helped Bill with his.

Cap' Bagley preceded the combatants in the ring. He could see that the mouse under Claude's eye had partially closed it and that the side of Bill's jaw was still swollen. Placing a hand in each of the boy's gloves, he calmly stated, "You know that you gentlemen do not have to go through with this fight. No one would question either of your pluck after yesterday's engagement."

Claude did not move he could not back down at this point. Bill, being a bit older and having nothing to prove to his mates responded, "I'll tell you what, if I don't call you 'Claudie' anymore and you don't beat my head on the floor anymore, can we consider it settled?"

His fat eye blinking and watered a bit, Claude touched his gloves against Bill's; and said, "That is agreeable. I look forward to being your friend."

The two went to their respective corners and departed the ring, to be ready for the dinner bell to ring. Cap' Bagley departed feeling good that this potential feud was settled better than he had hoped for. After that, the two combatants became the best of friends, neither wishing to test the other's metal again.

During the following weeks Claude got into his routine at Avondale. He learned to march and participate in intermural sports. He did in fact become friends with his past adversary, Bill Maloney, and his other cabin mates Messrs. Birdwell, and Foy.

Sitting on the front porch of their cottage, after a Saturday morning inspection and parade, Claude and his mates contemplated the fine day and a possible afternoon football game against one off the other cottages. Maloney put a hand on Claude's shoulder and looked at him like a Dutch uncle, breaking the silence, "I been thinking about it. Let me try to explain without pissing you off again. "We got change something, what the hell kind the name is Claude? It can only serve to make you sound less cool than you really are. What do you say we rename you after my favorite uncle, 'Tony'?

Claude's back stiffened at the first questioning of his name, but he relaxed by the end of Maloney's pitch. He sat quietly for a couple minutes and finally responded, "Ok we'll try it and see if it works." So that is how Tony got to be Tony, forever after, except for Aunt Amy who would always call him, "Claudie," much to his chagrin.

Since his father had once been the Band Master at the school, it was assumed that Tony would also be musically inclined. It was deemed that he should join the band, playing the French horn, just like his father. Tony tried to do what was directed, but he had little interest in the French horn or the band. After a couple weeks of uninspired band practice, Tony was looking out the window at the football team's practice. The Bandmaster seeing this, came over to Tony, "Mr. Harte, I get the feeling that music is not your forte, maybe you would be better suited in sports. Feel free to go."

Tony responded' "Yes sir, thank you sir." He bolted for the door heading straight to the football field to find the coach and tryout for the team.

Sports were indeed Tony's forte, he became the Fullback on the football team, he played on the baseball team and ran track. Though he never quite separated himself from the band. As an upper classman, he became the Drum Major. His last year at Avondale he was also the dormitory master of his cottage.

Avondale School was pretty much self-sustaining, i.e., the students spent part of their time working on the farm with crops and livestock, performing maintenance of the building or performing janitorial tasks or kitchen tasks. The time spent working on site helped to offset part of their tuition. Though each student got a taste of all the activities, they could concentrate in areas where their skills and preferences led them. At a time when the majority of citizens did not possess a high school diploma, teaching farming and craft skills was important for students to find a potential career path.

At Avondale only a few months, it did not take Tony long to fall desperately in love with Rhoda Prost. Rhoda's mother was a Cottage Mother at Avondale. For a couple of years Rhoda lived at the school and attended classes with the boys. This proved to be an up-and-down haphazard romance at the best. Her mother was ill tempered and weighed in at 250 pounds, presenting a formidable deterrent to Rhoda and Tony's romance. Add to this the Avondale faculty, plus 105 boys, several of whom were also in love with Rhoda, it appeared to be an impossible romance.

Rhoda at fourteen was a very pretty girl with a well-developed figure for her age, flashing dark eyes, her hair in a Dutch bob and mischievous smile a perfect set of even white teeth which was she was known to use on any sway with wandering hands.

Over the next two years Tony and Rhonda managed an occasional romantic interlude with the help of to their good friends Bill Foy and Bill Malone, who delivered love notes back and forth ranging placed team meeting when chances permitted. The friends could be counted on unobtrusively protect the lovers from found by the elders.

On one occasion, they learned that there had been a staff meeting scheduled for Friday evening Foy and Malone arrange a rendezvous for Tony and Rhonda in the Rose Garden alongside Bagley House. The garden was enclosed by a five-foot-high hedge and was an ideal location for a summer night rendezvous.

Tony and Rhonda had been preparing for their lovers meeting by passing notes indicating the time and place. Both were excited to again be in each other's arms. It had been several days since they had managed a few minutes alone.

The Avondale campus was lighted only by the glow from the cottage windows. Shadows cast by the hickory and oak trees clustered about the campus offered good cover for anyone wishing to get from the Shelter House where Tony lived to the Bagley House and the rose garden. Tony opted for the even safer route along the lake shore and up the bank directly in back of the garden.

As quietly as possible, Tony climbed the steep bank, and then climbed over the wall into the garden. Pausing to catch his breath and peering about in the almost total darkness to catch sight of his beloved. He finally made out a shadowy form at the front of the garden. Rhoda was waiting. Throwing caution to the winds, he rushed forward. A moment later as he tried to clasp all of Mrs. Prost's 250 lbs., and implanted an impassioned kiss on her lips, romance died a sudden death! Mrs. Prost's screams rent the night air, sending Tony fleeing for his life. As he passed Bagley House at a dead run, he saw his beloved Rhoda doubled over in laughter. She had tried to warn him that her mother had found out about their rendezvous but got there too late. It was some time before Tony decided to arrange another meeting and when he did; it was not in that garden.

The rose garden episode was never mentioned by Mrs. Prost to either Tony or Rhoda, but it was noted that Tony and his accomplice Bill Foy, were suddenly on K.P. duty a lot.

Spring came early in 1925, by mid-April the evenings were warm, the air was sweet, and it made young men think of love or at least their version of love, which was trying to get lucky.

Friday after dinner, Tony and his mates were sitting on the dock nearest their cottage. They skipped stones on the lake's glassy water and contemplated the fine evening.

Bill Foy put down his stones and began the conversation. "Tony, on a fine evening like this we should go to Greys Lake or Waukegan and see if there are sweet young things out taking the air."

Tony responded, "Both towns are a few miles away, so we would spend the night getting there and back."

Foy, "But you have access to the truck."

Tony, "You are trying to get me into real trouble this time."

Foy looked at the three other lads, Messrs. Birdwell, and Maloney, and said, "Are you men up for a Hardy Boys adventure?"

They all stood up and surrounded Tony patting him on the back, chanting, "Hardy Boys, Hardy Boys!"

Tony, "You guys are going to get me killed! Cap' will string me up by my nuts if he finds out we took the truck out without permission."

Foy took back control of the conversation. "He'll never know, we'll wait to after dark, roll the old girl down the hill out the gate and away we go. We go for a couple hours, see what's happening in Greys Lake and be back in our bunks by midnight."

The three cheerleaders continued with, "Hardy Boys, Hardy Boys!" They patted Tony on the back and proceeded to the cottage to prepare for the adventure.

Being April, the sunset before 8:00 PM. The adventurers snuck out of their cottage and went straight to the shed behind the dining hall where the Model T pickup was kept. Rather than pushing it down Avondale's main street which went past Cap's cottage, they pushed is behind the cottages to the dirt road that led from the barns. The dirt road met the paved street just before the main entrance. The dirt road sloped downhill, so they hopped on, Tony in the driver's seat, Bill Foy next to him and the other culprits in the bed of the truck. With the clutch kicked in, the truck built up speed as it coasted downhill. Just before the paved street, Tony popped the clutch and the Model T came alive, with only one small backfire.

Living in a quasi-military environment brings restrictions on almost every facet of life. Being off campus on their own brought an elated feeling of freedom, like they had never felt before. No matter what the night brings, this will be one of the most memorable of their short lives. The lads grinned from ear to ear.

The streets of Grayslake were dead, as no one in the small town had much to do outside after dark. They cruised the few streets, finding no available girls or much of anything else. The one policeman on duty drove by but paid no attention to them.

Foy was undaunted, "Let's go by the railroad station, maybe something is happening there."

All was quiet at the station. One station agent was busy with paperwork. There was an 0-6-0 switch engine on a siding on the other side of the tracks, about a hundred yards north of the station. The lads drove to the other side of the tracks. They hopped out of the truck to check it out.

The locomotive was still hot. As they walked by, it gave a hiss from a relief valve. Foy, "Crap, it still has steam, let's climb in the cab and check it out."

They scrambled up into the locomotive's small cab. There were some glowing embers in the firebox.

Birdwell, "Wow this is neat, look there's still some pressure on that gauge."

Foy, "Let's take her for a ride."

Tony, "Shit no, we're already in trouble enough."

Foy, "didn't you ever want to be a train engineer?"

Tony, "Yea when I was on the train up to Chicago, I thought that being an engineer would be the neatest of jobs."

Maloney, "So let's run it down the siding away from the station and then we bring it back here. This looks like the throttle." He moved the horizontal bar and the engines shuddered pushing against its brakes. He gave it more throttle, the locomotive shuddered even more.

Foy and Tony hollered, "Oh crap," in unison.

Birdwell, "This looks like a brake." As he squeezes the top of the handle and pushes it toward the firewall. The locomotive begins to move slowly forward, then increased its speed into the dark night. Next stop Wisconsin or the end of the siding, whichever comes first.

There is an in unison, "Oh shit," as the engine builds up speed.

Foy, "Slow it down."

Maloney, "I'm trying!"

Tony, "How do we turn on the headlight?"

Birdwell, "We can't do that, or they'll know we're here."

Having travelled a couple hundred yards, the steam gauge started down as the remaining pressure was expended.

Foy, "We're saved!"

Down low to the ground was the hand throw that allowed the turnout to be switched to the mainline. It showed its red side meaning that the turnout blocked their access off the siding. Though losing steam and pressure; therefore speed, the momentum of the locomotive slowly crept through the turnout, derailing with its frontend out on the Milwaukee Road's mainline between Milwaukee and Chicago. The engine shuddered badly as its drive wheel left the rails.

Birdwell, "Oh, crap! We've done it now. Let's get the hell out of here."

Foy, "We can't leave this here and cause a train wreck."

Tony, "Let's get the lights on, wherever they are."

Maloney, "We need to get out of here!"

Foy, "We are so screwed it isn't funny, but we can't leave this here to cause a wreck." Foy continued, "Birdwell run up to the station and tell them what's happened. Tony, you go get the truck. Maloney and I will try and find some flares or something to mark the track."

Fifteen minutes later, Tony brought up the truck, having picked up Birdwell along the way. Foy noticed that the southbound signal that they could see had changed from green to red.

The station agent came running down the siding with a bag of flares. Before leaving his office, he took time to call the Grayslake police. He handed a couple flares to Foy who carried them down track a hundred yards before the station agent hollered for him to light them.

The lone Grayslake duty officer arrived with the red light flashing on top of his Studebaker squad car. Seeing the cluster of teenaged boys, he announced, "What have you little shits done tonight?" Shinning his light on the derailed locomotive, he exclaimed, "Oh, crap, you guys are in deep, deep trouble!"

The culprits squirmed into a tighter formation as if that would help their situation.

The officer pointed his nightstick at the pickup truck, "Whose truck is that?"

Tony replied, "It belongs to Avondale School, we were just taking it for a breather."

The officer, "You are all coming with me. I can't fit all you bastards in my car," he pointed his nightstick at Tony, "You know where the police station is?"

Tony nodded affirmatively.

The officer, "You drive to the station. I'll drive behind you, and don't try anything dumb or I'll shoot you ass!"

The five loaded into the truck and Tony drove the three blocks to the Grays Lake police station. Inside, the officer, ushered the culprits into a jail cell, while he called his boss to get help with the finger printing and paperwork.

Police chief, Mike Slaughter, arrived at the station at 10:30 PM. Having known Cap' Bagley for years, he was not in a big hurry to make criminals out of a bunch of Avondale boys out on a lark. He called Bagley, "Cap' I wanted you to know that I have your boys in my lockup."

Cap', "who are they and what have they done?"

Slaughter, "We haven't taken their names and done our paperwork yet, but they somehow derailed a locomotive."

Cap', "You're kidding?"

Slaughter, "Not at all, and the Milwaukee Road is going to be really pissed."

Cap', "It's late and there is little that can be done tonight, so keep them there and I'll come for them in the morning. Being behind bars for the night might teach them something."

Slaughter went back to the holding cell and announced, "I talked to your Headmaster, and he said that I can keep you hooligans. The duty officer will take your fingerprints and paperwork. Then we will spread you into a couple cells with cots. Have a good night."

As he curled up on his cot in a fetal position, Birdwell moaned, "We're so screwed."

As directed, starting at 11:30 PM, the duty officer took the detainees from the holding cell, one at a time. He finger-printed them, gave them some goop to clean their fingers and then led them to his desk for the paperwork. With forms and pen at the ready with a monotone voice, he asked the questions, "Last, name, first name, middle initial, date of birth…."

By 2:30 AM all of the detainees were placed in one of the two cells adjoining the holding area. These cells had three lumpy, smelly cots, one against the back wall and one on either side against the bars to the next cell. None of the five slept much that night, as each pictured, as only a teenage mind can contemplate, the heinous things which might happen to them.

Dim light shined through the dirty, smoke covered glass of the windowpane just beyond the vertical steel bars. The five began to squirm on their lumpy cots with a series of grumbles and groans.

The door from the police station's front room to the cellblock swung open, and in strode a red-haired, round-faced police officer. Cheerfully, he ordered, "Wake awake! Why, look at all the customers I got over night. If you villains will sit up, I'll get you some coffee."

Birdwell, "Oh shit, that's all I needed to hear, someone who's happy to be here."

Thinking of his nighttime worries, "I hope these aren't the kind that buggers young boys."

Foy, "Birdwell I'm sure they wouldn't want your scrawny butt anyway."

After the detainees got up and took turns splashing water in their faces, they settled down for strong black coffee and some kind of porridge.

Cap' Bagley, up at the first bell, cleaned up and put on a fresh uniform. He went to the dining hall and got his cup of coffee. As it was Saturday morning, the students were not in a hurry to eat and leave. Cap' sat down at the table where half the chairs were empty. He addressed the students who were at the table, "So, do any of you know what happened to your colleagues last night?"

There was a uniform reply, "No sir." One of them added, "We saw the empty bunks this morning and we are worried about them. Do you know where they are, Sir?"

Cap' replied, "I don't know the details yet, but it seems there were some kind of shenanigans last night and when I find out, there will be hell to pay!"

He finished his coffee, departed the dining hall, and walked to his Model T touring sedan behind his cottage. As he drove off campus, he noted the pickup truck was not in its shed.

Cap' arrived at the Grayslake Police Station a little after 9:00 AM. Chief Slaughter was already there reviewing the pile of paperwork from the previous night's activity. Cap' held out his hand, "Good to see you Mike, though not under these circumstances. What the heck happened?"

Slaughter, "Near as I can tell, a few of your boys found an engine with some steam, tried to take it for a spin, and derailed it. I'm sure the southbound Hiawatha was really late getting to Chicago last night, so the Milwaukee Road is going to be pissed off. Plus, they have to put their locomotive back on the train and get it off the mainline."

The Chief shifted in his chair, "Legally there are a bunch of things your boys could be charged with, I'm just not sure how tough I should make it. I called the magistrate and was about the go see what he wants to stick them with." He got up and motioned toward the door, "You should go with me, they're your boys."

Cap' silently followed the Chief to his squad car and they drove two blocks and parked at the court side of the City Hall building.

Entering the Magistrate's chambers, they found Judge Henry in dingy overalls as he was about to work in his garden before he got the call from the Chief. Judge Henry started the conversation. "So, what's the problem, Chief?"

Slaughter started, "Let me introduce Captain Bagley, the Headmaster at Avondale School."

Henry, "We've met." Shaking Bagley's hand, "Good to see you Cap'"

Cap', "Likewise."

Henry folded his hands on his belly in a most judicial pose.

Slaughter began the story again, "Last night five of the students from Avondale found a switch engine with some steam and decided to take it for a joy ride."

Henry began to smirk, giving away his judicial pose.

Slaughter, "The locomotive ran over a switch and derailed on the mainline."

Henry giggled a little.

Slaughter, "This could be serious shit." He waved his hand at the magistrate. "We could have had a train wreck in the middle of town." Slaughter's voice rose as he became more frustrated, "These young men are guilty of trespass. I'm not sure if there's a law against stealing a train engine, but there ought to be, damaging railroad property, to name a few. Waving his hands again, "I came here to get your professional advice as to the laws that have been broken."

Henry relaxed and leaned forward with his hands on his knees. He could not stop the smirk on his face. He replied, being as calm as he could, "I'm sorry Mike, I always wanted to be a train engineer, but I never had the guts to try it out like these lads did."

Slaughter, "Judge, this is serious. We could have had a train wreck."

Henry, "But we didn't because these boys saw the problem and ran for help. If they had run away and let an accident happen, I'd be ready to lock them up. He leaned back in his chair, "This was a teenage prank that got out of hand." He turned toward Bagley, "Cap', do you have some appropriate disciplines for your culprits?"

Cap', "Your Honor, I'm sure I can dream up some chores that'll get their attention."

Henry, "Good, Mike. I suggest you let all five out of your lockup and turn them over to Cap'."

Slaughter, "Judge, I'm just not sure letting these boys off Scott free is the thing to do."

Henry, "Mike let me be clear. If charges against these boys come before my court or the courts of my colleagues, they will be thrown out. So, make it easy on all of us and let Cap' take care of his young villains."

Slaughter, "Fine, it's your call, Henry."

The three men stood up and shook hands. Slaughter and Bagley left the court and returned to the police station. Little was said during the brief drive as both men were lost in their thoughts.

Back at the police station Slaughter told the duty officer to bring out the five detainees. As they came through the door they saw Cap' and automatically formed into a straight line in front of him.

Cap' addressed them, "Gentlemen, it seems the system can go easy on first time offenders and dumb shit teenagers." He looked directly at Tony, "Mr. Harte you will drive your crew back to Avondale, place the truck in its shed and don't plan on using it for a while. You gentlemen will clean up, have your lunch and assemble at my cottage at 1 PM. Is that understood?"

In unison they replied, "Yes Sir!"

Driving back to the school, Foy was the first to talk. "Well, I guess we lived, after all, to fight another day."

Foy, "Yeah, we're out of jail, but Cap' looked really pissed. He may bring back flogging."

Birdwell, "I don't think you can flog anyone in Illinois, anymore. Whatever he decides to do with us won't be good."

The crew's brass and shoes shining, stood at attention on Cap' Bagley's front porch as his mantel clock struck 1 PM. Cap' strode out on to the porch, "Be at ease gentlemen."

The cadets relaxed their braced bodies but maintained their line.

Cap' went on, "Gentlemen what you did was serious. There could have been a train wreck and the loss of life. If not for the good will of the judge and the police chief, all of you could've been facing charges which would have brought jail time and a permanent black mark on your names." Striding back and forth across his porch, "Though it appears there will be no legal charges brought against you, there is still the matter of the cost and inconvenience to the railroad, and we don't know yet what they will expect."

He stopped in front of Tony. "Mr. Harte, I am particularly upset with your actions. You have been a fine student and therefore given certain freedom and responsibilities which most of your colleagues do not have."

Tony replied, "Yes sir, I am terribly sorry for what happened. I should never have taken the truck without your permission."

Foy interrupted, "It wasn't Tony's fault, we all goaded him into it. "

The remaining culprits affirmed Foy's statement. "It was our fault Sir. Tony really didn't want to go."

Cap' was silently pleased the lads were willing to fess-up on behalf of their friend, but this was not the time for praise. "That's fine, and you shall all share the punishment." He continued, "It's 1:20 PM. By the dinner bell, the pig sties shall be immaculately clean." Rubbing his chin, "And after dinner, stick around the mess hall to clean up. You gentlemen are the KP crew for some time to come."

They all responded with a quiet, "Yes Sir."

In the evening after doing KP, Tony walked over to Cap's cottage and knocked on the door. Bagley opened the door and invited Tony into the sitting room.

Tony began, "Again, I am sorry for what happened and assure you it will not happen again."

Cap', "If something like this happens again, we might have to institute the firing squad."

Tony, "The reason I stopped by is to tell you my Uncle Oscar is a friend of a manager at the Milwaukee Road. Maybe he can talk to his friend."

Cap', "I'll not have you wandering off campus on your own, but maybe Sunday afternoon we could visit your Uncle."

Tony, "Yes sir, that would be great."

Cap' Bagley and Tony made a visit to Uncle Oscar to enlist his help in gaining the support of Mr. Proctor to sooth the railroad's feathers. Uncle Oscar, having some of the rascal genes similar to his nephew, listened to the matter with as serious composure as he could maintain. Oscar promised to see his friend, Doug Proctor, that afternoon to see what could be done to make the situation better.

In the afternoon Oscar knocked on the door of the Proctor house on the other side of the lake. Being Prohibition, a favorite gift was to bring a sample of one's home brew. Oscar, having become fairly proficient at making beer, had a bucket of ice with six of his best brew.

Doug, "Oscar come on in. It's good to see you. What brings you out on a Sunday afternoon?"

Oscar extended the bucket, "I felt a calling to bring you a couple lagers, and there's something I need to talk to you about."

Doug, "Sure Oscar, come on in. I'll get the opener."

Once inside they lifted the brown bottles toward each other as a toast. Oscar got right to the issue. "Did you hear about the derailment in town on Friday night?"

Doug, "Hear about it? I got a call before dawn to go take a look at it. The Maintenance of Way guys were really pissed at having to roust out a crew in the middle of the night to fix the mess. I heard it was caused by some delinquent kids."

Oscar, "Well Doug that's why I'm here. It seems Claude and some of his friends from Avondale are your delinquents."

Doug, "I heard they were all in jail."

Oscar, "The judge didn't want to press charges so he released them back to Captain Bagley's custody. Cap' came to see me and asked me to visit with you to find out how we can quietly make it right with the railroad."

Doug, "As I said, the M-O-W guys were really pissed. I'm not sure if they will ask management to press charges or not. Let me talk to some people on Monday and see what I can do."

Oscar, "Thanks Doug. Let's have another beer before I go home for my Sunday afternoon nap."

Doug and Oscar commuted to Chicago having had seats together for a number of years. They spoke a little about the issue during the Monday morning ride. On the way home that evening Doug said he had not been able to corner the right people in order to address the problem. It took several days for Doug to see his friends in the Maintenance of Way Department who might lend a sympathetic ear. On Thursday evening he reported to Oscar that he was working on a fix but did not want to say anything until it was a done deal.

On Friday evening Doug explained the outcome: "It seems M-O-W is over their annual budget and after they got over being pissed at the kids, their biggest concern was spending the money to get the locomotive back on the tracks and off the mainline." Doug rolled his head a bit, "so I had a little negotiation with the Regional M-O-W Manager. Though it will be painful for my department, I agreed to take funds from my budget to pay for half the cost of the re-railing and the Milwaukee Road will forget about the incident."

Oscar beamed, profusely shaking Doug's hand. "Doug, this is great! A much better outcome than I had hoped for. You remain the best friend a man could have."

Oscar passed the results on to Cap' Bagley. Cap' passed the news on to the culprits and ended with, "Whenever I decide to let you gentlemen off KP it will be the last time I ever wish to hear of this incident."

CHAPTER 2

GRADUATION AND A JOB

Tony did the tasks as assigned, making the rounds of the farm and school chores. After a year he found he liked working in the dining hall kitchen. He, like most teenagers, liked to eat and learning how to make the dishes he enjoyed seemed like a good thing.

For a period in the summer of 1925, a gentleman who had been a chef on a cruise ship took command of the school's kitchen. There was quite an improvement in the quality of the food served in the dining hall and Tony learned all he could from this maven.

Being an upperclassman at Avondale came with much more freedom than Tony experienced his first years at the school. He never quite separated himself from the band, for as an upper classman, he became the drum major. Also, during his last year at Avondale, he was the dormitory master of his cottage.

He was also given authority over the kitchen crew when the chef was not there. Working in the kitchen also allowed him to drive the Model T pickup truck to nearby towns to pick up groceries and other supplies.

On a cold evening in mid-December 1925, the cleanup crew had finished their post dinner chores, so Tony released them and prepared to lockup for the night. It had been a miserable day, rainy and just above freezing. Now at dark, the rain was turning to sleet. Just as he was about exit and lock the kitchen door, a large man pushed his way through the door. He wore a sopping wet dark pinstripe suit, and was holding a blood-soaked handkerchief against the right side of his neck. In the other hand was a 38-caliber revolver.

The man stuffed the handkerchief in his pocket, grabbed a towel from the sink and held it to his neck. When he did this, Tony saw a two-inch wound on his neck, just under his jaw.

Tony heard other people outside the dining hall. Waving the pistol, the man demanded, "Kid, where can I hide?" Tony pointed toward the pantry. The visitor ducked into the pantry and hid behind a couple of barrels. No sooner had he taken refuge when there was a loud knock on the kitchen door.

Tony opened the door and three men carrying shotguns came in. From their badges it was clear they were the sheriff and two of his deputies.

The sheriff asked, "Kid have you seen anyone strange around here? We're after a punk who got himself out of the Waukegan jail."

Tony glanced over his shoulder and saw his visitor waving the pistol at him to make the lawmen go away. Since the fugitive would have a clear shot at him, he decided to comply, then said, "A guy knocked at the door, but when he heard you guys, he ran off."

The sheriff asked, "Which way did he go?"

Tony replied, "I think he headed toward the lake."

The sheriff turned and hollered to somebody outside the door, "When the dogs get here, take 'em down by the lake."

Turning back to Tony, the sheriff said, "Thanks kid! This is a bad ass we're after. We heard he was involved in a couple of gang killings in Chicago."

A few minutes after the lawmen left, the visitor came out of the pantry, chewing on part of a loaf of bread which was intended for the morning meal. "Thanks kid, you done good." With that the fugitive set off into the night and headed away from the lake.

Tony decided not to tell anyone about this event. Since he was known as a B.S. artist, his buddies probably wouldn't have believed him anyway. Also, if he told the sheriff he might be charged with aiding the fugitive.

After the rose garden event, Tony and Rhonda still managed an occasional romantic interlude with the continued help of their good friends Bill Foy and Bill Malone. In January 1926, the two were stunned and heartbroken when Mrs. Prost announced Rhoda would be attending a girl's boarding school in Iowa. Unable to do anything about this catastrophe, other than pledging undying love for each other, they said sad goodbyes as Rhoda boarded a train for Iowa.

June 15, 1926, dawned bright and warm at Avondale. The 6:00 AM bell woke Tony from a sound sleep. He jumped up and washed, then got busy rousting out those mates in his dorm who were still asleep. This was the last time for him to do this chore as he was graduating today. Hurriedly getting into his uniform, he looked out at the small campus. It was hard to believe by 4:00 PM today he would be a graduate.

There was a lot to be done. The senior class would have breakfast together one last time, then commencement in the chapel was scheduled for 3:00 PM. Tony checked his drum major uniform for his final dress parade at 4:00 PM. It was going to be a busy day.

By noon, the campus was alive with kids, faculty, parents, and friends of the graduating class. There wasn't much time to think about the past years, except they seem to have gone by so quickly. Tony and his two best friends managed a few minutes to chat with Foy. Bill Malone would be going home to Chicago, but they would all get together again later in the summer.

Tony, however, would not be going back home to Alabama, though he had not seen his father since a visit in 1923. He was afraid their relations might be a bit strained as his dad had remarried in 1924. His new wife did not seem too anxious to have a 16-year-old stepson ending up on their doorstep. Tony didn't feel too bad about not going home since Irvington had seemed pretty dull on his last visit. Besides, he was anxious to get a job and become his own man.

In the last three years at Avondale, Tony had been senior captain of the student body, assistant chef, kitchen steward, and town messenger. These various jobs had given him a sense of pride and self-confidence in his ability to accept whatever the outside world had to offer in the future.

In the past six years, his aunt and uncle, taking the place of parents, had visited quite often. Tony spent most holidays and part of the summer with them since they lived only a few miles away in the nearby village of Grayslake.

His aunt and uncle attended the graduation, after which they helped him get his clothes and other things into their car as he was going to stay with them for the summer. A pleasant surprise was an immediate job which had been arranged by his aunt. Amy instructed, "Get a good night's sleep because you start work Monday morning as a delivery boy for the Cook General Grocery Store."

Mr. Cook was a short stocky man with piercing dark eyes, a harsh high-pitched voice, and a no-nonsense approach to the grocery and meat business.

Arriving at the store at 7:00 AM on Monday morning, Tony introduced himself to Mr. Cook. From the conversation which followed, he learned his job was by no means considered permanent until he had successfully concluded a trial of one week. Amy had previously informed Mr. Cook that Tony was an experienced meat cutter, having overseen the job at Avondale for the past two years. Mr. Cook proceeded to outline the duties of a delivery boy which meant sweeping out the store at 7:00 AM, then making up customer orders. All nonperishable items, roots and vegetables first, then butter and eggs last so everything was as fresh as possible before loading the model T Ford truck for the day's deliveries.

Depending on the number of customer stops, Tony would be back at the store no later than 1:00 PM. The afternoon would be spent waiting on customers, stocking shelves, and preparing customer orders for the next day. Store hours were from 7:30 AM to 6:00 PM, six days a week. His salary would be $18 per week which seemed like a fortune at the time.

After the job had been explained, Mr. Cook invited Tony over to the meat block for him to demonstrate his ability with a knife, saw, and cleaver. Mr. Cook brought out a quarter of beef from the icebox and asked Tony to cut a few steaks and a couple of standing rib roasts. As soon as he picked up the butcher knife, Mr. Cook let out a howl which could be heard four blocks away. Besides yelling that nobody could cut meat left-handed, he also screamed about Tony being on the wrong side of the meat block where customers could see a dumb left-hander mangling their favorite cuts. Tony tried to explain, to no avail, he could cut meat and had been doing it quite well left-handed for some time. Mr. Cook was adamant there would be no left-hander in his meat market and that was that.

For a few minutes Tony was sure his new barely started career was down the proverbial drain. Calming down a bit, Mr. Cook knew he needed to let Tony have his week's trial, but also knew he was very hesitant about having a 16-year-old driving his delivery truck and handling his customers minutes later. Tony felt even more insecure when he learned from Elsie, the full-time clerk, that Mr. Cook had hired and fired two 18-year-olds from the job in the last two months.

By 10:00 AM the customer orders had been checked by Mr. Cook and Elsie and loaded on the truck. Fortunately for Tony, Grayslake was quite small and all of today's customers were located in town and around the lake, so the addresses were not too difficult to find. Some customers had charge accounts, but there were also several cash customers, Tony made sure the cash collection was correct. The 1923 model T Ford truck had a wooden body, roll curtains, and was designed for this type of delivery. It ran quite well, and Tony drove carefully. This was no time for an accident.

Arriving back at the store on Main Street at about 3:00 PM and able to report the day's deliveries were complete, Tony turned over to Mr. Cook the day's cash receipts along with the signed copies of the charged orders. After checking out the cash and receipts, Mr. Cook was relieved to find everything was in order. He even managed a weak smile when he ordered Tony to get to work behind the counter helping Elsie wait on customers, and when not busy, he could start putting up the next day's orders. By quitting time, Tony realized he had done a good job and was happy nothing, so far, had gone wrong on his first day, except for the meat cutting incident.

Excitedly regaling his aunt and uncle with the day's events at dinner, Tony was shocked to learn not being accepted by Mr. Cook as a meat cutter would cost him part of his salary, since the $18 per week had been based on his aunt's assuring Mr. Cook, he could function at the meat block. The other delivery boy only got $15 a week. Tony would certainly have to do an outstanding job the rest of the week, or very possibly lose the rest of his salary before even getting paid for the first week.

With this disturbing thought in mind, Tony reported to work the next morning determined to please Mr. Cook if it was at all possible. Fortunately, the rest of the week passed without incident and the routine became easier. The customers seemed satisfied with his service, and some evidently told Mr. Cook so. Saturday night came, payday at last! Tony's hands shook as Mr. Cook handed him $18 in cash. Not only that, but his boss was also pleased with his work and said so, almost smiling.

Several small lakes were located within a 10-to-15-mile radius of Grayslake and the store. During his first week on the job, additional orders had been called in by summer residents from Gages Lake and Sand Lake. In 1926 there were no shopping centers and only a couple of small chain stores such as A&P and

National T in the general area. Shopping was, therefore, a time-consuming chore for those having summer cottages on the lakes.

Tony decided it might be a clever idea to solicit some extra business for the store simply by calling on other residents in the areas where he already delivered supplies to the few customers who phoned in their orders to the store. Practically all prospective customers were delighted with the idea. Tony would take their orders and deliver them the next day. Besides, a lot of these people did not have telephones in their cottages. Within the second week, the lake business had more than doubled. By the third week it became necessary to make two delivery trips every day. Mr. Cook couldn't believe the full loads of groceries and meat orders which left the store. He even got into the habit of laughing as he totaled the receipts each evening. Needless to say, Tony was somewhat of a hero, and as a reward, Mr. Cook insisted his lunch was on the house and let him take the truck home at night so he would not have the mile and a half trek back and forth to the store. For the first three weeks on the job all had gone well. Tony had been very careful with driving and paid strict attention to the business. But then it happened. Driving out of the village one morning with a full load on board, including two cans of kerosene, Tony let his eyes wander momentarily when he saw a pretty girl walking down the street. Twenty seconds later his gaze was brought back to earth by a resounding crash. Eggs and other groceries flew all over the truck. To make matters worse, the tops of the two kerosene cans popped and splattered their contents all over the boxes of groceries. Scared and shaken and looking through the steam of a busted radiator, Tony discovered he had plowed into a laundry truck. Fortunately, neither driver was hurt so both jumped out to survey the damage. Tony's cargo was a mixed-up mess. The other guy was lucky. After all, what damage could be done to laundry? The laundry truck sustained the least damage, only a broken radiator hose, and no discernible damage to the front end. This wasn't the first or last time a pretty girl would cause Tony a problem. As he and the other driver, Joe, tried to straighten out the mess, the girl walked by to take in the scene and listen to the poor excuses Tony had to offer for the accident, like watching a girl, and driving on the wrong side of the street. With a large giggle, the girl took off.

In a few minutes, with the radiator hose back in place in Joe's truck and water from a nearby house, the laundry truck was ready to roll again. Joe and Tony agreed since no serious damage was done to the trucks, neither would mention the accident to their respective employers.

Tony spent the next hour trying to sort out the orders, discarding broken eggs and the inspection list which was contaminated by the spilled kerosene. This done, he drove the truck back a few blocks to the Grayslake garage to get the broken headlamp and slightly bent fender fixed. It was possible he might get going on his route since Bill Cannon ran the garage and knew Tony quite well. He was sympathetic and went right to work on the truck. Within an hour or so the truck looked quite acceptable, except for a noticeable dent in the right front fender. Tony could offer his boss some reasonable explanation for the dent after securing Bill Cannon's promise not to mention the garage visit to Mr. Cook if at all possible. Tony started back on his route. Realizing he was already two hours or more behind on his regular schedule and somehow, he would have to buy groceries to replace those broken and damaged by the kerosene, he remembered a farm stand on the highway and managed to get the produce he needed there.

Arriving back at the store two hours later than usual and with another route to cover that afternoon, Tony hustled to get back on the road. Mr. Cook eventually figured out Tony was hustling more orders as he made no mention of how late he had returned. In the following weeks, no mention of the accident was ever made at the store.

The weeks passed quickly. It was already the middle of August and Tony realized he needed to make some important decisions and soon. Should he go back to school or continue working? Despite his long hours, Tony managed some interesting dates with some of the local fairer sex.

One Saturday evening at dinner with the Olsens and Proctor, unexpectedly answers to his concerns came quickly with decisions being made which would affect Tony's life for the next few years. Tony had a great deal of respect for both his uncle Oscar and Tom Proctor. Both were successful businessmen: Oscar in the steel industry and Proctor with the Chicago Milwaukee and St. Paul Railroad. During dinner, Proctor brought up the subject by asking "Tony, do you want to continue your job as a grocery clerk, go back to school, or look for something better?"

Thoughtfully Tony replied, "Mr. Proctor I'm not a very good student and even though I like the store job, I'm sure it doesn't offer much of a future. Besides, while I've always wanted to be in the movies or vaudeville, I also would like to get started on some job with a future."

Proctor smiled, "Though I swore I wouldn't bring it up, it's obvious you have an interest in trains."

Tony squirmed in his seat.

Proctor's reply stunned Tony for a moment, "That's history and we should all forget about it. What I want to know is would you like to work for me? I'm going to need a new office beginning in two weeks. You can have the job if you want, but the pay is only $15 per week."

Before Tony could answer, his uncle cut in saying, "Son, think about this. Mr. Proctor is very particular about the people he hires, and you should feel proud of his evident interest in your future."

Remembering his uncle had been with the Milwaukee Road for several years and had also started in Mr. Proctor's office as a clerk, Tony quickly came to a decision and replied to Proctor's offer. "Mr. Proctor, thank you. I'll try to do a good job. Only one thing, I should give Mr. Cook a week's notice."

Offering his hand to seal the new relationship, Mr. Proctor replied, "No problem, Tony. I'll get you set up to start a week from Monday and arrange for your monthly train pass so you can join your Uncle Oscar in commuting to Chicago. Our offices are in Union Station."

Hardly able to believe what had happened so dramatically to change the course of his life, Tony chatted happily with those present about his new job and how to break the news about leaving to his current employer, Mr. Cook. In spite of his gruff exterior, Mr. Cook had been a pretty good employer and friend, but if Mr. Cook was to get a replacement for him, allowing for a couple days of breaking in on job, Tony realized he would have to face Mr. Cook soon, like Monday morning.

Arriving at his usual time on Monday, Tony found Mr. Cook busily cutting meat for the day's orders. After good mornings were said, Tony placed himself near the door in case a hasty exit was necessary and blurted out his announcement, "Mr. Cook, I'm quitting my job here on Saturday."

Looking like he'd been hit with his own meat, Cook dropped the Ray's Cleaver on his foot and howled, "What the hell do you mean? You can't quit. I can fire you, but you don't quit Cook's store."

"But Mr. Cook, I..." Tony got no farther. Mr. Cook was furious and stomped into the stock room and slammed the door, leaving Tony standing there with his mouth open and nothing coming out.

Before he could decide to follow Mr. Cook to try again to explain why he is leaving, Elsie, the clerk arrived. Tony quickly sought her advice.

"Elsie, I just tried to tell Mr. Cook I'm quitting this job, and I'll be working for the railroad. I only got as far as quit. He yelled like crazy and left. What do I do now?"

Elsie looking almost as upset as Cook had been, replied, "Tony, right now we better get busy with today's orders. No one can talk to Mr. Cook when he's mad, I know. Wait till you come back this afternoon. Maybe he'll have calmed down so you can talk."

Taking her advice, Tony got the orders ready and loaded on the truck for the morning deliveries. Getting back to the store around 1:00 PM, he found Mr. Cook was not back from his lunch at home. Elsie said Mr. Cook was still plenty mad about Tony's wanting to leave and it would be a better to try talking it over when he came back from his afternoon run.

Once again Elsie's advice seemed sensible, so Tony loaded the truck and took off. Returning about 4:30 PM, he found Mr. Cook and Elsie discussing his leaving. Mr. Cook had calmed down and even managed a bit of a smile when Tony turned over the day's receipts.

Tony was still uncertain, waiting for the right moment to bring up the subject, when Mr. Cook came right to the point: "Tony, your aunt called me this afternoon and explained you've been offered a job in Mr. Proctor's office, and you have decided to accept it. I'll have to admit that in time you will go a lot further with the railroad than here in the store. I'm sorry I blew up, but you've done a damn good job, and I hate to lose you. If you want to reconsider, I'm willing to raise your salary to $20 a week."

Tony was tempted for a moment, but replied, "Mr. Cook, I've accepted Mr. Proctor's offer and I'll stick to it. I've really learned a lot here and I'll miss you and Elsie. I'll be glad to help you train a new man before I leave on Saturday."

On the way home that night, Tony felt relieved Mr. Cook had been reasonable and realized he had to thank Amy, as her phone call to Mr. Cook had helped him out of a tough situation.

Wednesday morning Tony entered the store to find Mr. Cook talking with a young man about twenty-one who somewhat resembled Mr. Cook. Tony got busy with the day's orders. In a few minutes, Mr. Cook came over to inform Tony the young fellow was his nephew and he was going to try him out on the delivery job. He would start that day. After heavy instructions from Mr.

Cook, Bill Cook and with the new man helping where he could, the truck was loaded. As they were ready to leave, Mr. Cook spoke to his nephew, "Bill, you pay attention to Tony, learn about the routes, and how he sells all those customers on the Cook store. Now get going."

In reply, Bill managed a "Yes Sir, Uncle," and they left. Tony could easily see Bill was burning a bit about the sendoff he received. After all, it wasn't hard to see Bill resented being instructed in the job by a guy four years younger than he.

The first few deliveries were made in virtual silence. Finally Bill, with a sheepish grin, said, "Tony how in the hell have you put up with the grouchy uncle of mine all summer? His whole family stays clear of him if they can."

Tony thought for a minute, and then said, "Billy your uncle ain't easy to get along with, but sometimes he's fair even though he expects perfection. He works hard and he expects his help to work hard too. Just keep this lake business going and you'll be okay."

"Yeah," Bill replied, "I better get used to him, and the job, and try to keep the lake people happy"

By the end of the week, Bill seemed to have the routine deliveries and store clerking well in hand, and Mr. Cook appeared satisfied. Saturday night he handed Tony his final check with a five dollar bonus included. After goodbyes all around, Tony headed home. Monday morning would see him starting his new job with Mr. Proctor at the railroad.

CHAPTER 3

FIRST LOVE AND FIRST CAR

By 6:30 AM on Monday, Tony was dressed and ready to join his uncle Oscar and Mr. Proctor for the 50-minute trip to Chicago and his new job. After a hasty breakfast, his aunt had the car out and ready for the 1-mile trip to Grayslake station. As he boarded the 7:15 AM commuter express, Tony was surprised to see how many Grayslake people worked in Chicago. It seemed like half the town was getting on board. The conductor greeted Mr. Proctor and Uncle Oscar with a cheery, "Good morning gentlemen, your seats are reserved as usual."

Making their way to about the center of the car, seat for four was marked with a reserved sign. Mr. Proctor and Oscar Olsen took those facing forward, while Tony slipped into the opposite seat beside Doug Mitchell, a friend of the Olsen's who lived in Round Lake. These three men did and would have a great deal of influence on Tony's life, and while at 16 he was mainly interested in girls, dancing, and show business in that order, he was smart enough to learn from people he respected. Uncle Oscar was always well-dressed, well mannered, and taught Tony how to dress, even providing some used, but well-kept expensive suits until Tony could really afford good clothes.

Having known Mr. Proctor for a couple of years before and having done odd jobs at his home, Tony chose him as a man to emulate, along with his uncle. An impeccable dresser, handsome, stern, but with a sense of humor, Mr. Proctor presented a perfect picture of the confident, well-respected executive.

Almost exact opposites, neither Oscar nor Mr. Proctor were particularly humorous, but Doug Mitchell would have made a great standup comedian. He was a great storyteller. His dialects, especially Swedish, were hilarious. Standing about 5'-11", slightly heavyset, with a round face always ready to grin, and laugh, Doug was liked by all who knew him, and especially by Tony and his uncle.

Tony's thoughts were interrupted by Mr. Proctor: "Here's your monthly railroad pass Tony. This allows you to ride any train on this division. Later on, you will receive a yearly system pass good for the entire line."

"Thanks Mr. Proctor." Tony took the offered pass with the realization he was actually one of several thousand employees of a great railroad, the Chicago, Milwaukee, St. Paul and Pacific. The Milwaukee Road ran from Chicago through Milwaukee and all the way to the Puget Sound in Washington.

The train made one stop in Glenview, then thundered on toward Chicago's Union Station. Upon arrival, the four parted company. Oscar Olsen went to the steel plant and Doug Mitchell to his fabric business on Jackson Boulevard. With Tony in tow, Mr. Proctor headed for the freight department offices which took up the entire fourth floor of the Union Station building.

As they walked toward the elevators, thousands of people who commuted to Chicago via the three railroads used this terminal, entering and leaving in all directions. Noting the many shops and snack counters in the Harvey restaurant, it occurred to Tony the Union Station was really a small city within a city.

Arriving at the bank of elevators on the Westside station, several people, including the operator, offered Mr. Proctor their pleasant, "good morning". Getting off on the fourth floor with his new boss leading the way, Tony found himself in the outer office of the assistant freight traffic manager, next to the office of the freight traffic manager, Mr. Sheldon, who was Mr. Proctor's immediate supervisor.

Mr. Proctor proceeded to introduce Tony to his office personnel, starting with Bill Murphy, the cheerful and balding chief clerk, then Miss Rafferty, his personal secretary, a tall rawboned redhead of 40 years or better, with flashing green eyes. Her face hardly resembled that of an Irish colleen, but rather had the rugged countenance of a plowed field. Tony caught himself staring. Could this be the secretary of his idol? He later learned someone in the office was sure Mrs. Proctor must've hired this gal for him. He also later learned Miss Rafferty was a most efficient secretary. No small detail of executive intrigue or backstabbing prevalent in the higher echelons of the railroad escaped her attention. She always managed to know what or who was trying to do what to whom and kept Mr. Proctor alerted to all nefarious schemes.

Mrs. Dorothy Johnson, next be introduced, was the stenographer who worked for Bill Murphy, the chief clerk. Dorothy was a rather pretty girl of about 25 and would prove most helpful to Tony in learning the office routine.

Introductions accomplished, Mr. Proctor advised Tony he was now in the tender care of Bill Murphy and Miss Rafferty. Miss Rafferty followed with the morning mail, and Mr. Proctor entered his private office.

Taking his seat opposite Bill Murphy at the large double desk, Tony began his first day as Mr. Proctor's office boy. Bill Murphy proceeded to outline his duties such as opening the mail, deliveries to other offices, filing, and running errands for Mr. Proctor. Tony decided this job would be much less strenuous than delivering groceries for Mr. Cook's store.

The months of October and November passed quickly. The first excitement of the new job as an office boy had evolved into a routine of working and commuting. There still remained the excitement of meeting for lunch with coworkers. This included an occasional lunch with Mr. Proctor at the Illinois Athletic Club of which he was president. Johnny Weissmuller, a swimming champion and eventually Tarzan of movie fame, was sponsored by the IAC and worked out in the club pool. He proved to be one of the first celebrities Tony would meet through Mr. Proctor.

Tony had heard Mr. Proctor mention his oldest son., Ralph, who was in Hollywood and involved as a manager for both Charlie Chaplin and Rudolph Valentino, the great screen lover and one of Tony's favorite stars.

Returning to the office from an errand one day in early October, Tony found the girls chatting excitedly, while keeping a close watch on the door to Mr. Proctor's office. Before he learned what the excitement was all about, his desk buzzer sounded, signaling him to report to Mr. Proctor. Rising rapidly, he knocked, and then proceeded into the spacious private office. Two men occupied the guest chairs facing Mr. Proctor's desk. Rising and signaling Tony to his side, Mr. Proctor grinned saying, "Tony, I'd like you to meet my son, Ralph, and his friend Mr. Valentino."

Hardly believing his eyes, Tony stammered, "Pleased to meet you gentlemen."

Taking the extended hand of the great Valentino, a hand millions of women would die to hold, Tony was surprised at the firm grip and friendly smile of Valentino as he replied in his Italian accent, "Thank you, maybe you come to Hollywood someday, and we meet again."

Turning to shake hands with Ralph Proctor, Tony left the office on cloud nine, not even remembering to ask for Valentino's autograph.

A few minutes later, Ralph Proctor and Valentino were escorted by the Union Station police to the New York Central station to board the 20th Century Limited to New York. Unknown at the time, the end of Valentino's movie career was only a few weeks away. He would be dead of peritonitis and mourned by millions of his fans.

The summer of 1927 found Tony enjoying life as only a 17 year-old can. After several months of working for Mr. Proctor, he was offered a new job with the supervisor of the Heating and Icing Division of the Milwaukee Road's Freight Department. He took the job at the starting salary of $22.50 per week.

Before graduation, Tony and Rhoda had corresponded faithfully, still pledging undying love and hoping to be together again when Rhoda finished boarding school and returned home in the summer. However, the letters from Rhoda had become fewer and fewer until they stopped in the spring. Finally, in late June, Tony assumed Rhoda would have returned to Avondale, but he had not heard from her. Deciding to find out what had happened, he drove over to Avondale, going directly to the cottage Mrs. Prost supervised.

He received a decidedly cool reception when Rhoda's mother answered the door. Before he could utter a word, she snapped' "Good Lord, are you still around? I hoped Rhoda had written you about her upcoming marriage and that you'd forgotten all about your kid romance!"

Tony was stunned. No wonder he hadn't heard from her for the past of couple months. Apparently, she didn't have the heart to tell him what was going on.

"Mrs. Prost," he stammered, "Where is Rhoda? I thought she'd be here. I'm still in love with her. How can she be getting married to someone else?"

Relenting somewhat, Mrs. Prost answered his question, "Yes Tony, Rhoda's home. I'm sorry to see you're taking this so hard, but she will be married to a teacher from Iowa in a few weeks. You'd best forget about her."

Not ready to accept his apparent dismissal by Mrs. Prost, he said defiantly, "Mrs. Prost, I've got to hear this from Rhoda. I'm not leaving until I talk to her!"

"Very well," Mrs. Prost replied, "Go into the living room and I'll send her down. You can have an hour together, but it won't change anything."

A few minutes later Rhoda appeared in the doorway as pretty as ever. But her lovely dark eyes were filled with tears as Tony ran to hold her close once more. "Oh Tony," she sobbed, "I hoped you would come. I couldn't tell you about this in a letter. I'm not in love with the man I'm to marry."

She paused, searching for the words to continue, "Aunt Maude and my mother arranged the whole thing while I was at school. I only went out with him a few times. He's a nice guy but I don't want to get married. What can I do?"

Tony, at a loss for words which would solve anything, was still in shock. "Perhaps," he suggested, "We could go to Cap' Bagley's. Maybe we could get him to talk Aunt Maude and your mother out of this idea."

"It's no use," Rhoda managed with a wan smile, "Cap' hasn't a chance of bucking his wife or my mother. They've made up their minds to marry me off."

Tony thought a moment, "Honey," he said, "Why can't we run off and get married? I make almost twenty-five dollars a week and I'm sure we could stay with my aunt and uncle in Grayslake for awhile. How about that?"

Sadly, Rhoda shook her head, "That wouldn't work. We're both underage and mother would never give her consent. If we went ahead, she'd stop us, or have the marriage annulled. It's no use dear. Every time I try to get out of the marriage, mother threatens to have a heart attack."

Tony could almost believe the heart attack bit, for between Mrs. Prost's excessive weight and violent temper, it could happen. Not knowing what to say, he held Rhoda close, and kissed her tear-stained checks when Mrs. Prost called down the stairs, "You will have to go now, Tony. Rhoda is upset enough. Under no circumstances will you see her again. She's getting married and that's that. Goodbye!"

Rhoda broke the embrace. Looking up at Tony, she said, "You can see it's no use talking any more. We have to say goodbye now.

I'll go through with this marriage, but if it doesn't work out, I'll never forgive my mother, or see her again."

Tony held Rhoda for the last time. kissing her goodbye, he said, "Rhoda darling, I'll always love you, but we don't have a chance at happiness now. Please try to be happy in the future. Let's hope your marriage will work out."

Turning away, he walked out the door, not looking back as he drove away.

A few weeks later, Tony received an invitation to Rhoda's wedding. He did not attend and was sure Rhoda didn't expect him to.

The pining for Rhoda got less painful with time and there were a few local girls who helped soothe his suffering. However, going on dates presented problems at times, as Tony was reluctant to use his uncle's car. Doug Mitchell allowed him to use his model T pickup frequently, but Tony longed to have his own wheels. The answer came one evening as the Mitchells were having dinner at the Olsens. All through dinner, his uncle seemed to be enjoying a private secret. This was unusual as the two played golf and made bathtub gin together. Tony simply figured they had some new activity in mind.

Finishing his coffee, Doug said, "Tony, how would you like to own a practically brand-new Model T Ford?" Tony jumped and rattled his dishes. "Mr. Mitchell, how the heck could I afford a car like that?"

His uncle broke into the conversation. "Sit down Tony and Doug will tell you all about it."

Tony was all ears as Doug explained, "I have a friend who is, or was, a dining car chef for the C.B. & Q. railroad. He bought this car about six months ago." Pausing to get more coffee, Tony continued, "We call this guy the Boomer. He never keeps a job very long, has a habit of getting off trains, getting drunk, and forgetting to get back on board. This seems to annoy the dining car steward no end. Anyway, he doesn't have a job now and can't meet his car payments of $20 a month. He would give you title to the car if your uncle and I guarantee you can finish the payments. He still owes $270 on the car."

"Wow! My own car!" Tony yelled, waking the cat, "I'm sure I can pay for it. I'll work weekends, anything to get that car."

Calming down long enough to thank Mitchell and his uncle for the surprise of a lifetime, Tony managed to sit quietly as they discuss the legal details involved. If all went well, the finance company, and if the Boomer doesn't change his mind, they figured Doug would bring the car from Chicago the following Friday night.

The next couple of days seemed like a lifetime. Tony had trouble paying attention to his job. On Thursday night, his uncle Oscar caught up with him as he was boarding the train for Grayslake. Once seated, his uncle picked up the newspaper and casually announced, "Doug called me today at noon. Looks like you'll have a car tomorrow evening. Okay?"

It took a moment for his uncle's statements to sink in. Then letting out a whoop which scared the hell out of the nearby passengers, Tony managed to say, "Unc, you're not kidding me are you? Boomer will let me have the car. Why, I can't believe it, my own car, and I've got you and Mr. Mitchell to thank."

Assured he wasn't being kidded, Tony was silent, letting his uncle get back to the paper. For the rest of the trip home so many thoughts raced through Tony's head. There were two or three girls to be notified, especially for Saturday night. Then he thought about all the special places a car could take him and his friends like the lakes, dance halls, and movies. He just hoped there was some way to earn enough money. After all, a car meant expenses he hadn't considered before.

Up until this time, Friday proved to be the longest day of his life. Having told his coworkers about his good fortune, the rest of the day dragged by. Five o'clock finally came, but the trip back to Grayslake seemed endless. His aunt was waiting at the station, as usual, for Tony and his uncle. Kissing his aunt, he asked hopefully, "Amy, any sign of Mr. Mitchell yet?"

His aunt replied "Tony, Doug can't possibly make it from Chicago before 7:00 PM. It's 50 miles out here so you have plenty of time for dinner."

His uncle chimed in, "It's only a model T, not a race car or a Cadillac. Keep your shirt on."

They both laughed as Tony replied, "Mr. Mitchell got his old Ford up to 50, so mine ought to do at least 55."

When they turned onto their street a few minutes later and passed a clump of trees, Tony's heart jumped. In the driveway stood a beautiful model T Ford and a grinning Doug Mitchell leaning on the front fender.

Tony almost fell out of his uncle's car on his face. He, give Doug a big hug and exclaimed, "Mr. Mitchell, it's beautiful. Wow! What a car! How did you get here so early?"

Not waiting for an answer, Tony got busy inspecting his car. It was a beauty, with dark green body, black fenders, a winged radiator ornament, and a chrome spotlight on the driver's side. It even had a special large steering wheel which locked. The Boomer had done a great job of dressing up the 1927, which would be the last of this model Ford would build. In 1928, the new Model A came out.

Tony's inspection was interrupted by his aunt calling them all to dinner. Hardly able to eat, Tony insisted his aunt and uncle go for trial spin right after dinner. The car performed beautifully and with great reluctance after carefully locking it up, Tony headed for bed. Saturday there would be time to wash and polish the car and arrange a date for the evening after he got back from his railroad job at about 2:00 PM.

During the several months he had lived with the Olsen's in Grayslake, Tony had dated several local girls, imagined himself involved with one or two, but never allowed romance to go beyond the petting stage.

His favorite recent date was Doreen Sweet, a very pretty brown-haired girl with gorgeous blue eyes and a temperament to match her last name. Doreen thus became his first choice to try out the new car.

Doreen had a job in Chicago involving commuting as did Tony. On the return trip Saturday, he lost no time locating Doreen on the train. Fortunately, she was free for the evening, so he suggested they go dancing at Channel Lake. Usually there was a well-known name band there on Saturday night. The Channel Lake dance pavilion had a large open-air floor located on the edge of the lake and was a favorite spot for young people from the surrounding area.

After an evening of dancing, they stopped in Antioch for hamburgers, cokes, and a couple of hours of serious necking in the soft light of Doreen's living room, Tony decided the car would surely enable him and his friends to enjoy life.

He thought how lucky he was. Mr. Proctor had helped him get a new job in Mr. Bennett's department and now his uncle and Mr. Mitchell helped him get a car.

A couple of weeks later at the end of another Saturday night date, Doreen announced she was going to visit her cousins in Milwaukee for the rest of the summer. With Doreen's departure, Tony was back in the hunt. He soon found many of his female acquaintances had new boyfriends and were therefore unavailable. It seemed it may take more than a nice to car to make him the 'man about town'.

On the Saturday after Doreen's departure and the morning of Rhoda's wedding, a glum faced Tony searched for a vacant seat on a rather full car. The fates which guide our lives and the sharp eye of youth for a pretty face placed Tony beside a young lady who might make him forget his sadness. She had auburn hair, big brown eyes, and a pert red mouth which laughed at the world. Just an extremely pretty girl. There was, as he perceived, nothing wrong with her figure either!

He was silent for awhile, but managed to steal sidelong glances at her while she was reading a novel. As the train gained speed, he realized he only had about forty-five minutes before they arrived at Union Station. If he wanted to get to know this young lady, he'd better get busy before it was too late.

Pretending to be interested in the book, he asked, "Is your book really good?"

Brown eyes looked up, smiled and answered, "Not that good. I'd rather talk. Who are you?"

He introduced himself, and after learning her name was Ellie Hanson, said, "How come we've never met before? I take this train every day and I'd sure remember you"

She laughed, "You're kind of fresh, but if you must know, I live in Fox Lake. This is my first week working for the phone company in Chicago."

"Good," he replied, "I work for the railroad at Union Station. Maybe we could ride together every day."

Ellie thought about that idea for a moment, then finally said, "Look, we've just met, but just to see how we get along, we can ride back together at noon, fair enough?"

Taking advantage of this opening chance for what could be an interesting new romance, and remembering most girls love sad stories, he answered, "Ellie, thanks, but I may not be good company today, you see, the girl I was engaged to is getting married this afternoon."

Ellie's sympathy was aroused, "Tony! That's terrible. No wonder I thought you looked sad. I'm so sorry for you. If you want to talk about it, maybe it would help"

The ham actor in Tony's personality couldn't resist this golden opportunity. Managing to look even sadder and heartbroken, he poured out the story of his unrequited love, climaxing in the wedding which was taking place that very afternoon.

Ellie sat wide eyed as he told the story. He really must have done a good job, for by the time he finished, Ellie's brown eyes were filled with tears. She said, "Meet me at the doughnut shop in the station so we can ride back together this afternoon and talk again"

As the train entered Union Station, Tony had little time to say more than, "OK, I'll meet you at 1:15 PM at the doughnut shop."

The morning hours passed as Tony busied himself with filing and mimeograph jobs which had to be finished by noon. One o'clock finally came. Clearing his desk quickly, he grabbed his jacket and raced to the doughnut shop on the station concourse. A quick glance in the small shop reveled Ellie hadn't arrived yet. Seating himself, he placed his hat on the stool next to him and ordered coffee and doughnuts for two. A few minutes later he spotted Ellie making her way across the concourse. She was even better looking than when he'd first seen her.

Greeting him with a smile, she asked, "Feeling better now?'

As she seated herself, he replied gallantly, "Being with someone like you for a while has sure helped a lot Ellie, but when we say good-bye at the Grayslake stop, I'll be all alone again. Looks like this will be a long lonesome Saturday night."

Taking a sip of her coffee, she said, "We'd better get moving or we'll miss our train," then grinning mischievously added, "I'm beginning to wonder just how heartbroken you really are!" She slid off the stool and waited for Tony to pay the check.

Her remark left him wondering if maybe he was pushing too hard. It also occurred to him that Ellie might not be interested in him, just sympathetic. Besides, a girl like this would surely have a date on a Saturday night. In spite of his fears, he intended to find out before he left the train at Grayslake.

A few minutes later, they were seated together on the train. Tony decided to find out a little about Ellie before continuing his pursuit. He opened the conversation, "How long have you lived in Fox Lake?"

"Oh," she replied, "We're only there during the summer months. My folks have a small cottage. The rest of the time we live in an apartment on the north side of Chicago."

Tony continued the questioning, "Any brothers or sisters?"

"No, just me," she answered, "Sometimes it's a bit lonesome, unless my cousin comes to visit on the weekends."

Tony felt relieved. Maybe she didn't have a boyfriend in Fox Lake, but now was the time to find out. He blurted out, "Ellie, do you have a boyfriend in Fox Lake"?

Ellie looked at him and laughingly answered, "No steady boyfriend. We just moved to the lake last month. I haven't met anyone I particularly liked yet, why?"

"Why!" raising his voice enough for other passengers to look their way. Tony lowered his voice, "Because I'd like to take you dancing or to a movie tonight. Will you go?

Teasingly, Ellie responded, "I thought you were through with girls after what happened today? What's happened to your broken heart?"

Tony grinned sheepishly, "I guess it ain't as broken as I thought. Anyway, you're sure helping it to mend it fast."

Laughing, Ellie answered, "OK, I'd love to go dancing. Could we try the new dance hall near Antioch?"

"Sure could," replied Tony, "Give me your address and I'll pick you up about eight."

Tony looked at his situation and was pleased. He now had a good car and the potential of a romance with a singularly pretty girl. What else could be more important?

Tony quickly made friends with the young people in the Car Heating and Icing division. Mr. Ennis, the Superintendent, was a handsome slightly gray-haired man about forty, with piercing dark eyes. His secretary and all the stenographers secretly had a crush on him. If he knew it, he never let on, as he treated all the ladies with kindness and respect.

Tony had gotten his job in Mr. Ennis' department with the help of his former boss, Mr. Proctor. His title was File Clerk, but this encompassed many other duties, such as handling the interdepartmental mail, running the mimeograph machine and doing occasional errands for Mr. Ennis. It was quite easy work once he got it down to a routine.

Office rules were strict: no smoking or unnecessary talking. A ten-minute break was allowed at 10:30 AM and 3:00 PM. Employees were allowed to smoke in the restrooms. If one was fast on his feet, it was possible to make it to the station concourse for coffee. But if you were not back at your desk on time, you could be docked a half hour's pay. Getting docked three times in a month usually meant dismissal. Tardiness was not tolerated. If you were ill for a day or more, it was advisable to obtain a note from your doctor when returning to work. Otherwise, you could be docked for the time off. The company expected a full day's work for a full day's pay, and they got it. Even in 1927 there were a lot of people looking for jobs, and railroads were considered good places to work with reasonable security. Therefore, if you liked your job and wanted to keep it, you obeyed the rules.

By late August 1927, Tony had become quite involved with Ellie Janson, to the extent he spent every weekend at her house. Between dances, parties, boating, swimming at Fox Lake, and paying for board and his car, his once ample salary was taking a beating. While money problems didn't bother him too much, he was afraid he was getting in pretty deep with Ellie. Their romance had not progressed beyond simple petting and fondling. Although they had not committed the sexual act as yet, it was just a matter of time. Tony found her simply irresistible.

About this time, Tony noticed several ads in the Chicago Tribune for full or part time ushers at the Balaban and Katz chain of theatres. All of the larger shows featured name bands, the current great stars, plus first run movies. Tony was a ham actor at heart, so when he wasn't thinking about girls, he was trying to figure out some way of getting into show business. He decided ushering at a big theatre might be a start. At least he would see some of the great acts of the day with little or no cost. Besides, this was a chance to make some extra money and pay off the car.

Impulsively, Tony acted upon his idea. Saturday after work, with the ad in his pocket, he presented himself to the Chief of Service at the Oriental Theatre on Randolph Street in Chicago's Loop. He hadn't told anyone of his intention to apply for an usher's job. If he didn't get it, no one would know he failed. Along with several other applicants, Tony filled out the forms for part time work, seven nights a week, plus Saturday and Sunday swing shifts.

After a few minutes, the would-be ushers were directed to the lower level of the theatre where the usher's locker room was located. There they were interviewed by Mr. Pazzaloni, a captain of ushers. Being on duty, the captain was wearing the distinctive uniform of the Oriental Theatre. His head piece was a white silk turban; a collarless maroon bolero jacket trimmed in gold braid was worn over a winged collar and dickie with a black bow tie. Fawn colored slacks and patent leather shoes completed the uniform. He looked like an Oriental potentate.

Mr. Pazzaloni's first question was, "How many of you men have had any military training?"

Tony and two other men raised their hands. Looking at Tony, the captain said, "Please explain Mr. Harte."

Tony answered, "Well, I know the manual of arms and close order drill, captain. I went to a semi-military school."

Questioning the other two, Mr. Pazzaloni learned they had belonged to the Illinois National Guard. To further satisfy himself, the captain had them line up and proceeded to give close order drill commands. The three performed well.

After a few more questions, and a short lecture regarding what was expected of an usher at the Oriental, Mr. Pazzaloni told them to sit down and said he would return in a few minutes. With that he went up the stairs. Shortly, he reappeared, accompanied by Mr. Kenny, the Chief of Service. Without more ado, Mr. Kenny announced Tony and the other two had been accepted for the part-time jobs. They would be expected to start in two weeks from

Saturday. The pay was $12.00 per week. They were invited to see the current show for free.

Tony declined the invitation; instead, he went across the street to De Met's Restaurant for a sandwich, and to think. It suddenly dawned on him if he took the job, he'd have to move to Chicago. But where would he live? What would his relatives, the Olsen's, think of the idea? Ellie would surely take a dim view of the situation. She was probably already wondering why he hadn't joined her on the 1:30 PM train today.

It was 3:00 PM. If he hurried, he could catch the 3:30 PM train to Grayslake. He'd call Ellie as soon as he got home

Arriving home about 4:45 PM, Tony found his aunt worrying about what may have happened to him. Tony apologized, and only told her he had seen someone in town and would explain after his uncle got home. He then called Ellie and apologized but assured her he'd tell her what had happened when he saw her later.

By dinner time, Tony was dressed for his date with Ellie. His uncle came in shortly, and as they sat down for dinner, Oscar asked Tony, "What happened to you? Did you have a date in town?"

Tony laughed as he answered, "No sir, I had a business appointment. I applied for an usher job at the Oriental Theatre and got it. I'll have to work nights and weekends and means I'll have to move to Chicago soon."

His aunt and uncle stared at him in amazement. "Claudie, that's impossible! You can't live in Chicago alone at your age." Stamping her foot, Aunt Amy continued, "We're responsible for you. Your dad would never forgive us if anything happened to you."

Oscar broke in, "Now Amy, don't get so upset. I'm really proud of Tony for going after the job on his own. Besides, he's almost eighteen and can certainly take care of himself."

He turned to Tony and said, "Tell us all about the job son, and when you're expected to start.

Tony related the events of the afternoon and told them he was expected to start in two weeks if he took the usher job. He also said he had been thinking he might be able to room with George Anderson. He intended to call George on Monday to learn if this was possible.

Oscar thought it might be a good idea. With his uncle on his side, he was sure he could win his aunt over. He was also sure explaining it to Ellie and her parents wouldn't be so easy. They would probably think he was running out on Ellie.

On the drive to Fox Lake, Tony was thinking about possibly living with George Anderson. George often referred to him as his kid brother. George had been at Avondale along with Oscar back in 1907 when both of Tony's parents worked at the school. George, an orphan, lived in their cottage. George and Tony were close friends, and Tony did look upon George as an older brother.

George was the night manager in the photo department of the Hearst Newspaper Offices in Chicago. He lived in a small hotel, the Foswyn Arms on the North side. Tony was sure he could get a room there.

Ellie was waiting for him on the porch, and Tony assumed also waiting for an explanation as to why she hadn't seen him on the train that afternoon.

"Hi Ellie," Tony called getting out of the car. "How about a movie tonight? There's a good picture in Waukegan."

"OK," Ellie laughed as she ran to meet him with a welcoming kiss. "But first you can tell me why I got stood up today!"

There was no use putting off the inevitable, so Tony's answer went directly to the point. "Well Ellie, I got an extra job today. If I take it, I'll have to move to Chicago in a couple weeks."

Ellie's reaction was not totally unexpected. Her smile disappeared as she wailed, "Oh no! Tony, why would you do a thing like that?" Her brown eyes filled with tears, "Are you tired of me, do you want to break up, is that it?" she asked.

Tony held her close, "Hell no, Ellie, it isn't that at all. "It's just I want to pay off the car and make some extra money, so I applied for a part time usher job today and they accepted me." He continued, "Look Honey, we've got two weeks until I start. By the end of September, you will have moved back to Chicago for the winter. I'll see a lot more of you there than if I stayed in Grayslake for the winter, right?"

Ellie's smile reappeared as she dried her eyes. "Gee, that's right. But where will you live in Chicago?" Not waiting for an answer, she chatted on, "Just think, I can visit you at the theatre, then we can go out when you're off duty. Boy, we can have loads of fun! Let's go tell my folks about your new job."

Knowing what his hours at the theatre would be, Tony doubted they'd have much time together as Ellie seemed to think, but he was relieved to see her smiling again. Crying girls always scared the hell out of him. He doubted if he'd ever learn to cope with a woman's tears.

Over cake and coffee, Tony and Ellie told her parents all about his new job. Both congratulated him and Mr. Janson said, "Well, it's sure good to know you've got some ambition. Ellie better hang on to you."

Disturbed a bit by the implication in Mr. Janson's remark, Tony suggested they'd better head to Waukegan and the movie.

The Janet Gaynor movie was a typical tearjerker of the era, and to Ellie's disgust, Tony laughed in all the wrong places.

It was prohibition, and Tony's budget didn't allow for bootleg booze. Occasionally for special events, he managed to swipe enough from his uncle's homemade gin to fill his half pint flask. This was one of those events. On leaving the movie, Tony stopped to pick up a couple of cold Cokes. Thus fortified, they headed back to Fox Lake and a secluded spot where they were unlikely to be disturbed. Parking, he uncapped the Cokes and after drinking a fourth of each bottle, he spiked the balance with gin. They sipped their drinks slowly as they chatted. A few minutes later, both had finished their Cokes. Taking the empty bottles, he smashed them against a tree and hid the flask under his seat cushion. No sense having available evidence of drinking in case some local police were prowling about.

The gin spiked colas and the summer night combined to warm their bodies as they kissed passionately. Within seconds Tony's hand was inside Ellie's low-cut blouse. Then shifting about in the small space, they found a comfortable position which allowed each to explore the other's erotic zones. A couple of kisses later, they managed a position for the final act of passion, an extremely difficult feat in a Model "T" coupe.

Both were exhausted as they rearranged their clothing, then headed for Ellie's home. As usual, Tony was invited back for a day of swimming and Sunday dinner.

On the Tuesday following his interview at the theatre, Tony arranged to stay in town and have dinner with George Anderson before his night shift at the Hearst Building.

George Anderson was one of those characters you meet in your life who, due to their force of personality or escapades, become legendary in your mind. At the time Tony moved in with George, he was 38 years old. He was almost as broad as he was tall, standing five foot four and weighing in at three hundred ten pounds. He sort of looked like an overgrown elf and his clothes always looked like he'd slept in them. From his food spotted tie you could usually determine what he had for dinner. His round face always wreathed in smiles, George was one lovely guy. He had two loves in his life, people and music. He was always broke, since he spent his money on helping friends or buying the latest great classical or opera records. Several George stories were told when his friends were together and the gin was flowing. Many of the stories centered around his rotundity.

George could have been a great musician himself had not an accident destroyed his lip on one side of his face. This made playing the trumpet difficult, but it didn't stop him from trying. When he was about 32, he worked for short time in a food processing handling shipment. Waiting for a heavily loaded freight elevator which seemed to be stuck between floors, George looked up the shaft to see what was wrong. Suddenly the elevator arrived, pinning George to the floor. His face was laid open from his ear to his mouth. His body had stopped the elevator, but George had at least eight fractured ribs. He spent the next month in the hospital. Later he would say, "If I hadn't been such a fat bastard, the elevator would've cut me in half!"

On an earlier occasion, George was working as a mechanic for Mogul Tractor Company. The Mogul was a two-cylinder job with five-foot-high front wheels. The huge crankcase was essentially located between the front wheels. George had removed the piston and crankshaft, which left a tank full of oil. Standing on the wheel, when George bent over to retrieve a wrench, his foot slipped, and he went headfirst into the oil spill crankcase. Two other mechanics saw the accident and ran over to help get George out. But there was no way to lift 300-pound George out. Seconds later, the two mechanics got a hydraulic chain lift, wrapped a chain around his feet and hauled George up and out. His classic remark, when he could speak again, "The next time I get oiled, it will be with gin!" He then quit the job and went home to scrub the oil out of his mouth.

One more George story before we get back to business. It seemed George was destined for trouble with all things mechanical. Some years after the tractor incident, he bought a 1923 model T roadster. George, in a model T, was a sight to behold since he could barely squeeze under the steering wheel. It looked as though George had gone through the assembly line and Ford built the car around him.

Cruising down Irving Park Boulevard one day, George stopped to pick up a young boy who was hitching a ride to the beach. Getting more involved in a conversation with the youngster than his driving, George suddenly met the rear end of a Mack truck loaded with coal. His young passenger flew out of the car, landed on his feet, and according to George, he started running and never looked back! George, however, had no chance to run; he was sitting tight in a car full of coal with the engine steaming in his lap. His front end looked like a closed accordion. He was forced to remain in his uncomfortable position until two wreckers arrived. With one hooked to the rear and one in front, they pulled the car apart enough to get George out, shaken and bruised, but with no broken bones. The Mack truck lost a ton of coal but had no damage other than a small dent in the bumper.

George, never at a loss for words, informed the bystanders "I damn near got castrated this time. I thought the family jewels were gone for sure!"

George finally concluded he was accident-prone. He gave up the world of freight elevators, tractors, and Mack trucks for the relative safety of a job as a photographer with the Hearst international news service.

Tony and George settled in on the Pixley and Ehlers Restaurant across from the Hearst Building. Pixley's had the best, flakiest pies in Chicago. Taking their trays to a corner table, they sat down.

George's tie promptly dipped into his soup. Mopping his tie with a napkin, George said, "Well kid brother, I haven't seen you in months. Still living with Oscar and Amy?"

"Yes, but not for long," Tony replied. I've got to move to town and thought maybe I could get a room at your hotel."

George appeared delighted with the idea; then frowned, "Damn it Tony there's no rooms available at the Foswyn right now and won't be for at least three weeks. He continued, "Right now I've got Cliff Birdwell sharing my rooms. He works days at the Herald Examiner. You know Cliff, right?"

Tony replied, "Yeah, I know Cliff, we had a couple of misadventures together at Avondale."

George went on, "Cliff's mother died recently leaving him an orphan. As he is only seventeen, the court appointed me as his guardian. He ain't a bad kid, but he sure can be a pain in the ass sometimes." Tony nodded his agreement.

Getting back to his reason for moving to Chicago, Tony explained about his extra job, then asked, "You got any idea of what I could do until there's a vacancy at your hotel?"

"Yeah," George replied, "Take a room at the Wabash Avenue YMCA for a few weeks. It's reasonable and close to the theatre. I'll call you when I can get you into my hotel."

Tony agreed. "That sounds OK, I sure can't afford a real hotel downtown."

CHAPTER 4

THE ORIENTAL THEATRE

On the second Friday following his visit with George, Tony's bag was packed. He would check into the YMCA. that evening after work and start his job at the theatre on Saturday afternoon.

Tearfully Aunt Amy bade him goodbye on Friday morning while warning him of all the evils of the big city he would likely encounter. He hoped she was right about several she mentioned.

"Oh, I'll be all right," he assured her, "I'll call Unc' if I have any problems."

Oscar laughed, "Cut out the tears, Amy, He's only going to Chicago. Boy, you'd cry at a grocery store opening."

Boarding the train, he went in search of Ellie who would be saving a seat for him. He suspected he may have to deal with more tears, but was relieved to find her all smiles as she handed him a box of her mother's Danish pastries.

Tony decided not to say anything to his friends at the office about his extra job. His boss might not like it either, so no sense asking for problems. He'd simply tell them he decided to move to town.

By 5:30 PM Tony had checked into the YMCA., located on South Wabash Avenue at Harrison Street. It was an unattractive seven story brick building. There was a large bare lobby, a gymnasium, and meeting rooms. He paid for two weeks in advance and was given a printed copy of the house rules.

He opened the door to his new home. The room measured about five by eight feet and was tastefully furnished with an army type bed, a straight-back chair and a small three drawer dresser. A flimsy once white curtain hung dejectedly on the only window. A hot night was ahead, as the temperature in the tiny room must have been about ninety degrees. Tony put down his suitcase and hurried to open the window which only revealed an uninspiring view of a brick wall four feet away. He was sure the county jail couldn't be much worse than this.

Deciding to wash up and have some dinner in the YMCA. cafeteria, Tony headed for the nearest bathroom about four doors down the hall. It was equipped with two wash basins, two showers and two uninviting commodes. Only two such bathrooms served the whole fourth floor.

The cafeteria on the main floor certainly didn't offer candlelight and quiet dining. As Tony entered, the rattling of trays and dishes, the pushing of men through the line, and the rush for tables didn't improve his appetite. Getting in line, he pushed his tray along the counter and chose the Salisbury steak, mashed potatoes, peas, apple pie and coffee. Finding a vacant table, he sat down to eat and survey his dinner companions. The food wasn't at all bad and had only cost him $0.75 so he felt better.

Looking about him, he noted most of the men were young. Evidently they didn't make much money and lived at the Y for economic reasons. Certainly no one would live in these cells if they could help it.

After Tony finished eating, he went back to his room. Without a radio, there wasn't much to do except read. He looked over the house rules and learned he had to be out of his room by 8:00 AM every morning and not allowed back in before 11:00 AM. These three hours were set aside for the maids to clean, and no men were allowed in the rooms during this time. After seeing a couple of the maids, Tony decided the YMCA had nothing to worry about.

Remembering he had received a theatre pass when he accepted the usher job, Tony decided to go to the show at the Oriental. He was bored and the small room was hot as hell. As he turned in his key, the night clerk warned him he had to be in by midnight unless he worked nights.

State Street was blazing with lights and crowded with shoppers, and theatre goers. Reaching Randolph Street, Tony noted the long lines of people waiting to get into the Chicago and the State Lake Theatres. Turning west on Randolph, he found the line even longer for the Oriental Theatre. Paul Ash and his great stage shows always drew the larger crowds. Showing his pass to a resplendently dressed doorman, Tony was waived in by Mr. Pazzaloni who stood near the ticket taker and recognized Tony as one of his new men. "Ready to go to work tomorrow?" he asked.

"Yes sir," Tony assured him.

"Then you'd better enjoy the show tonight because you won't have time to see it tomorrow. You're to be on the floor by 2:00 PM so be sure you're on time," he said, then turned to help a lady with a package she wanted to check.

The stage show was great, as was the movie. Between the stage show and the movie, a mighty Wurlitzer organ led the audience in songs as the words appeared on the movie screen. Tony kept a watchful eye on the usher, hoping to learn about the routine. They sure kept busy and seldom glanced at the stage or the screen. Tomorrow, I'll be one of them, he thought.

Leaving the theatre, Tony joined the crowd at De Mets for a milkshake, then headed back to the Y. Setting his alarm clock for 6:00 AM so as to be the first in the bathroom if possible, Tony undressed and climbed into the squeaky bed. It was still hot in the room, but he soon fell asleep.

By 7:00 AM, Tony had showered, shaved, dressed and was headed for a coffee shop on State Street. He had to work at the railroad until noon and be in uniform by 1:30 PM. If he worked fast, he could possibly squeeze in a quick lunch.

Mr. Pazzaloni was waiting in the locker room when Tony arrived. It was his business to see the ushers were properly uniformed and then he would supervise their training on the floor. The uniforms didn't present a problem except for the seven-foot-long silk scarf which became a turban. It had to be wound around the head, leaving about 6 inches of material which was neatly tucked into the back. After several tries, Tony managed to make a fairly decent turban. The uniform fit perfectly since his measurements had been taken the day he applied for the job. Surveying himself in a full-length mirror, Tony decided he cut a rather dashing figure in the Oriental uniform.

The ushers moved with military precision with two men for each aisle. The inside man seated the patrons, kept count of vacant seats by continually checking the aisles and informing the outside man which seats were available. It was the outside man's job to keep track of patrons waiting for seats and, if possible, admit them in their proper turn. As patrons were about to enter, the outside usher would hold the door and with his left hand and elbow across the body at the beltline, direct the patrons inside. The inside usher was equipped with a flashlight to escort the patrons to vacant seats. The flashlight was directed to the floor, then slightly elevated to enable the patrons see their seats. God help the usher who inadvertently allowed his light to hit the stage or the screen!

The Oriental seated about 3,000 patrons between the main lodges and two balconies. Beautifully decorated in an oriental motif with wide foyers and comfortable sofas and chairs, it was downtown Chicago's favorite theatre.

The stream of people seemed to have no end. The lobby was full, and lines extended for a block or more on Randolph Street while waiting for the first show to break. After the break, things quieted down a bit and Tony was allowed to replace an outside usher under the watchful eye of Mr. Pazzaloni. After his supper break, Tony worked the inside aisle for two hours. It was still the silent movie era, but snatches of the stage show could be heard. He was too busy to think of looking at the screen. Besides, he had seen the show the night before.

By the end of the first week, Tony was assigned to a number two aisle where he and his partner alternated positions every two hours.

Tony was fascinated with his new job. The exciting stage shows, the thousands of people, and being a part of a great theatre operation kept his new job from being boring. There was little time for dates with the new tight schedule. He was lucky to eat three times a day. Getting the hell out of the Y was his next priority.

By the fourth week of his enforced sojourn at the YMCA, Tony received a most welcome phone call from George. "Hey Kid," he announced, "I've got you a room and you can move in on Sunday morning. Actually, you'll be rooming with me I found another roommate for Cliff. How does that sound?"

Gratefully, Tony answered, "George, that's great Boy will I be glad to get out of here. I'll stop by your office tonight after the show closes."

At 11 o'clock on Sunday morning, Tony entered the lobby of the Forswyn Arms. The hotel was located on Chicago's North Side, a 20-minute ride on the L express from downtown.

Tony asked the desk clerk to call George's room. George was down the stairs in a matter of minutes and introduced Tony to Mrs. Morrison, the hotel manager, a well-preserved gray-haired lady of 45.

"George," she exclaimed, "you've brought me another fine looking young man to take care of. Good"!

Tony decided he was going to like Mrs. Morrison. Before he could get a word in, George answered her, "Yeah, although he don't look like much to me, I consider him my kid brother, and it'll take both of us to keep him out of trouble."

Tony said, "Wait a minute, I workdays and nights. How much trouble can I get into?

They both laughed as Tony picked up his bag and headed for the elevator. George
followed.

The room, large enough for two people, had a comfortable double bed, two easy chairs, a large bureau and a fair-sized clothes closet. The room was on the third floor with a front window allowing for a reasonable view of Winthrop Avenue. This was not the ultimate luxury, but a far cry from Tony's quarters at the Y. Cliff Birdwell and his buddy occupied the room next door. The connecting bathroom served both rooms.

"Well Kid," George said grinning, "welcome to the famous Foreskin Arms Hotel!"

Laughing at George's uncouth reference to his new home, Tony unpacked. This chore done, he glanced at his watch. He'd just about have time for lunch with George, then back to the theatre.

Before he left, George reminded him, "Look Kid, I don't usually get home before two or three in the morning, so you'll be asleep by the time I get in."

"Don't worry," Tony answered, "I'll be okay."

An hour later, Tony was on his way to the theater.

After a month of ushering at the Oriental, Tony was used to the routine. Except for the rushing about and trying to do two jobs well, he enjoyed the theater work.

Only the really great acts of the Keith and Orpheum Circuits played at the Oriental. He had already seen such greats as Sophie Tucker, Al Olsen, Eddie Cantor, and Jimmy Durante plus innumerable famous vaudeville acts.

Within the next two weeks, Tony settled into a new way of life at the Forswyn Arms. The manager, Mrs. Morrison, did all possible to make him comfortable. Most of the guests were young people between 18 and 30 and included some very pretty girls. Mrs. Morrison mothered one and all. She was interested in their jobs, personal problems, and gently admonished those who occasionally flaunted the rules of the hotel, which were not at all strict to begin with.

Since starting the theatre job, Tony had seen Ellie only once. She came in one Saturday night for the last show. By the time Tony got out of uniform and dressed for the street, it was almost midnight. After a late supper, Tony took Ellie home on the L, not having his car in town. The pair had a privacy problem, as Ellie's parents' two-bedroom apartment didn't offer the freedom they enjoyed at the lake. There was no way to get very physical without disturbing her parents, which didn't sound like a good idea. So far, Tony hadn't had a chance to meet any of the other hotel guests except for the two or three characters which attended George's Sunday morning coffee hour.

Awa Anderson was the Chicago representative for his father's brush factory in Massachusetts. His nickname consisted of the initials of the Aloyous Wellington Anderson. His friends readily understood why he preferred to be called Awa. A man's man, and a woman's dream, he was a good-looking, fun-loving character.

Bill Lamont, a quiet dapper young man with a thin, carefully trimmed mustache, was a linotype operator and part-time college student. Never boisterous, but always ready to have a good time, Bill was respected and liked by all his friends.

For several days, Tony had noticed an attractive girl riding in his car on the way to work. She was only about 5'-1" but well-proportioned with striking eyes, dark hair, and a pretty elfin face. He soon found himself looking for her when he boarded the train, and several times she caught him staring at her. Though neither one had spoken, Tony was sure there was an invitation in her eyes when she returned glances.

The next time he saw her, he worked his way through the car to stand next to her and blurted out, "Good Morning!"

She smiled and replied, "And good morning to you! I wondered if you were ever going to speak to me."

"Well," Tony laughed, "I'm usually not so bashful, but I wasn't sure you wanted to get acquainted. My name is Tony Harte."

"And I'm Gladys Champange," she replied, then asked, "Where do you work?"

Tony told her a bit about his job with the railroad, and learned Gladys worked at the Fair Department Store downtown. He also learned she lived at a girl's club on Winthrop Avenue, about four blocks north of his hotel.

Chatting until they arrived at her stop, Tony said, "I'll look for you tomorrow morning, okay?"

"I hope so," she smiled. "This has been fun. See you!"

Tony decided she was a girl he wanted to see again. Besides, Ellie would be moving back to Fox Lake this summer so he wouldn't see much of her.

The next day was Friday, and Tony located Gladys easily. He suggested they see a show at the Uptown Theater on Saturday night.

Gladys readily agreed saying, "I'd love it, Tony. Only thing is I have to be back in the damn club by midnight or I'll get locked out. If a girl has to ring the night bell to get in, she is fined."

"Oh," Tony replied, "I'll get you back in time." Secretly he thought it might be nice if she got locked out and had to stay with him.

They enjoy the show, sat close and held hands. Tony made no rash moves on their first date. After the show and a snack, they decided to walk to her club on this mild May evening. It was only 11:30 PM when they got to her club; Tony could sit with her in the small lobby until midnight.

The lobby didn't offer much privacy, as girls and their dates kept coming in, but he did manage a few very warm good night kisses in the dark hall. Before he left, he made a date for the following Saturday night.

Slightly suggesting, "Gladys, let's go to an early movie, then go back to my hotel for a couple of hours. I want you to meet my brother."

"I guess it would be okay," she grinned; You mean you aren't going to show me your etchings?"

Kissing her at the door, Tony hoped for more than etchings.

When Tony arrived at the office on Monday morning, Mr. Buchanan wasn't at his desk. Surprised, Tony asked, "Where is the old man this morning, is he sick?"

"No," his officemate answered, "He just went up to Personnel to get a new typist. She's going to work with Bill."

A few minutes later, Tony nearly fell off his chair when Mr. Buchanan walked in followed by Ellie Jensen. She grinned at him as she passed his desk but didn't say anything.

After settling Ellie at her desk, and introducing her to Bill, Mr. Buchanan came back to Tony's desk. Evidently he hadn't missed Tony's startled look or Ellie's blush. He asked Tony, "You know that young lady?"

"Uh, yes sir," Tony stammered "We used to commute together." He could have kicked himself for adding, "And we went out a few times."

Mr. Buchanan frowned at this bit of information as he warned, "Well, just remember, I don't tolerate any office romances. So, keep your distance in the office."

With this he strode back to his desk, leaving a red-faced Tony telling his laughing desk mate to shut up.

At noon, Tony found Ellie in the station cafeteria with the other girls and took her aside for a short chat. "Damned if you aren't full of surprises. How did you get a job in my office?"

"Well," Ellie giggled, "I planned it that way. Now I can keep an eye on you, Buster."

"Yeah, fine" Tony answered, "Just remember to keep your eyes off me in the office. Buchanan's already given me the word on that!"

Ellie agreed they had better keep things cool while in the office.

Tony felt a bit guilty he couldn't ask Ellie for a date on Saturday but was relieved when she said she was going to the lake for the weekend. It was time to get their cottage ready for summer.

Saturday night, Tony picked up Gladys at six. They had a hamburger, caught the 7:00 PM show at the Uptown and were out by 9:30. Arriving at the Foswyn Arms, they ran into Awa and his favorite redhead, Georgia. Tony introduced them to Gladys.

"Are you going to show Gladys some movies?" Awa asked with an evil grin.

"Nope," answered Tony, guiding Gladys toward the elevators. "I'm going to introduce her to George."

"Oh, sure you are!" Awa laughed, "George won't be home from work until 2:30."

Tony could have killed Awa in cold blood! Gladys gave Tony a surprised look when they got on the elevator. "I guess it'll be etchings after all," she said.

Tony escorted Gladys to his room, took off her light coat and busied himself with records on the victrola. He turned off all the lights except for one on the table. Turning back, he found Gladys curled up in an easy chair, but had left enough room for him.

"How would you like some coffee?" Tony asked, as he bent over to give her a warm kiss.

"Sounds good, but first let's try that kiss again," she said, putting her arms around Tony's neck to pull him closer.

"Damn the coffee," he thought, as he maneuvered himself into the chair with Gladys. Her warm body and perfume would do things to him that coffee would neither hinder or help.

Coming up for air, Gladys whispered, "I'd really like to meet your brother sometime, but not tonight. I bet you forgot he had to work, right?"

"Yeah," Tony grinned, trying to ease his cramped position. "This damn chair wasn't made for two. I've got a problem."

"I think you're right," agreed Gladys, following Tony's longing look at the bed. "I just got stabbed by one of your problems!"

"Let's solve our problem right now," Tony answered, as he picked Gladys up and put her on the bed.

Feverish hands shortly had another problem to solve clothes. For the next few minutes neither of them spoke. They were too busy doing other things to waste their breath. After the flames of passion died down somewhat, Gladys looked up at Tony and said smiling, "If you hadn't been such a slow poke at getting acquainted, we could have been right here weeks ago!"

"Sure, I know", was Tony's answer, "But brother George may have been home."

The final days of summer of 1928 were drawing to a close. Tony had spent a couple of weekends at Fox Lake with Ellie and fortunately he remembered not the call her Gladys. Ellie's dad was retiring in September, so they planned to give up their Chicago apartment and live year-round at the lake.

Deciding she didn't want to commute all winter; Ellie talked a girlfriend into sharing a small apartment. To Tony's surprise, she was considering moving into his apartment hotel. Tony could see future problems with his love life if favorite girlfriends were living too close for comfort. He would have to arrange future dates with Ellie and Gladys very carefully in order to avoid any conflicts.

For the time being, he was more concerned about doing something to get a show business career started. He felt he was now ready to try out for tap dancing engagements in some smaller clubs. He had also worked on a couple of short monologues in Swedish and Jewish dialects. His friends who had seen them thought they were pretty good.

To Tony's surprise, an unexpected chance came along. One of his friends in the hotel worked as a radio engineer for the WLS station. He told Tony there was to be an audition for someone to play a Swedish farmhand in the Saturday night barn dance program. Tony lost no time contacting the producer and got an appointment to addition for the part.

A few days later, nervous Tony Harte auditioned. His auditioners consisted of the producer and several other officials and radio announcers. His Swedish monologue went well, judging from the laughter of the decisive audience. The producer said he was pleased and that while the part, when used, was small, could lead to other things. Tony immediately pictured himself as a highly paid radio comic, but was brought back to earth when the producer continued. Tony would not be given a contract or be paid for the first six months, since this was strictly to tryout a new character on the show. If the radio audience liked it, and the studio received enough mail to justify keeping the Swedish farmhand aboard, then they would discuss a contract and a salary. In the meantime, Tony was to be on call for rehearsals and the Saturday night performances in case they used the character. He was also advised it would be smart for him to attend the show for the next few weeks where he could learn a lot about radio shows and broadcasting. He was given a studio pass and invited to visit the studio anytime he wished.

Tony saw his Saturday night dates would be a problem. The Barn Dance went on the air from 8:00 to 10:00 PM at the W LS studio located on the top floor of the Sherman Hotel, usually referred to as the Old Hayloft. Because Tony decided this would give him an opportunity to learn the business and to meet some radio stars, he readily agreed to the conditions.

In 1928, country and western music was just gaining some popularity on the radio. WLS in Chicago was known as the farm station. It was powerful enough to reach into the southern states where barn dances were looked forward to on Saturday nights. The WLS Barn Dance was somewhat in competition with the Grand Old Opry which originated in Nashville, Tennessee.

On the first Saturday Tony stood by on the show, he got to meet country greats Tex Ritter, Bagley Kincaid, and Red Foley.

Most of the show was made up of country and western singers, quartets, instrumentalists, and hillbilly bands. Usually, there were also a couple of skits featuring famous personalities. Tony's first performance came in late September when the Swedish farmhand was used in a skit with ten lines of dialogue in the script. The small studio audience seemed to like the character, and the producer said he had done a good job with his lines.

Tony stayed close to the W LS studio, learning a lot, and becoming much more confident each time his Swedish character was used.

He still wanted to get an entertainment job before a live audience where he could use his tap and soft shoe routines as well as monologues. To this end, he found observing people, and listening to entertainers on the radio and on stage to be helpful.

The times when George and Tony could get together for dinner were few and far between. George worked nights for the new service and Tony was working days and nights whenever he got a job. However, on the Saturday following Tony's romantic interlude with Gladys, George told Tony they were invited to have a steak dinner at a rather notorious Italian restaurant on the near North Side. The owner was an old friend of George, as they had attended Avondale together years before.

The restaurant had a reputation as a hangout for some of Chicago's lower echelon gangsters. George and Tony were supposed to be at the restaurant about 11:00 PM since it would not be too busy and the owner, Paulie, could sit and chat with them while they ate.

They found the restaurant to be something less than posh, and only a few people were eating at this hour. Paulie greeted them at the door, led the way past several high-back booths along one wall, and seated them in a rear booth fairly close to the kitchen.

As they followed their host, Tony noted two burley olive complexion characters seated two booths toward the front from the one they would occupy. A quick glance at the two devouring their steaks convinced him they certainly looked like the gangster type.

Once he and George were seated, Paulie said, "You guys have some wine. I'm gonna get some prime steaks I fix just for you." A few minutes later he was back with two huge sirloin steaks, baked potatoes, and Italian salad. George and Tony lost no time diving into the sizzling steaks. Paulie refilled their wine glasses, then sat down to chat with them.

Paulie and George talked about old times at Avondale for a while. But Paulie didn't want to leave Tony out of the discussion. He started by asking about his years at Avondale and then about his current endeavors.

Tony told him of his efforts to become an actor and his dialect stories which were a big part of his comedy routine. Paulie said, "Great, tell me a joke."

Considering his audience, Tony picked a story in an Italian accent. "This old Italian guy goes into a local drug store for some help. He says, "Itsa drivin' me nuts, mi wifea, she hasa the bugs in the bush. I needa something to get rid ofa the bugs." The druggist, not understanding the customer, found some powder for killing bugs on flowers and bushes. A couple of weeks later the old Italian is back in the drugstore. The druggist recognizes him and asks if the bug powder had worked. The old guy responds, "Worksa fine, worksa fine. The bugsa gone, the bush a gone and the dirty Greek next door, he'sa dead too."

Paulie and George both laughed at the joke, then Paulie, responded "That was good kid. Do you really have a whole routine?" Tony, responded, "Do you want to hear more?"

"No, that's OK for now." said Paulie, "But I may be able to help you get some gigs. I have a friend who runs a club not far from here."

Tony, "You mean a Speakeasy?"

Paulie, "Yea, is that a problem with you?"

Tony, "Not at all."

Tony sat facing the kitchen service door and was about half finished with his steak when the door suddenly burst open and two swarthy, mean looking men strode in. They passed the booth, and almost knocked Paulie over. Paulie cursed, but after seeing the two hoods, said nothing more. They surveyed the row of booths. Tony froze as the one with the scar on the right side of his neck pulled a.45 automatic from his belt while the other leveled a Thompson submachine gun waist high. Without a word and barely glancing at the booth Tony and his friend occupied, they moved quietly to the rear of the booths of the two men Tony had noticed on the way in. Still without saying anything, they opened fire on the two in the booth. The gunmen sure knew their business. Shots from the.45 and two short bursts from the 45-caliber machine gun injured no one but the intended victims thought they were dead. Tony never had time to warn George or Paulie but all three of them dove for the floor when the shots rang out.

The two gunmen, their job finished, simply walked out of the front door. Acrid smoke from their weapons drifted over the booth as the few late diners beat a hasty retreat, leaving only Paulie and his two guests in the restaurant. It had all happened in seconds. Tony recovered his voice, "Good God, what do we do now?"

With reasonable calm Paulie answered, "Finish your steaks while I call the cops."

Looking at the floor where a thin river of blood made its way towards their booth, Tony lost all interest in his steak. He was having enough trouble controlling his heaving gut.

Getting up, his face a bit pale, George said "I'm going to call the news service and get a photographer and reporter down here."

Tony followed George as he headed to a phone booth near the cashier's desk. Both paused to take in the carnage in the hoodlum's booth. One was slumped over the table, his face in the steak platter. The other sat straight up plastered against the back of the booth as if nailed there. He still clasped a wineglass, his dead eyes seeing nothing. Blood seeped from the several wounds each had received. It was doubtful they ever knew what had happened, and now they could care less.

The police, a reporter, and a photographer arrived within twenty minutes. Tony had been cautioned by both George and Paulie to say as little as possible to the police.

The Police lieutenant glanced at the two victims. "Looks like a couple of Capone's muscle men to me. He must've caught them helping themselves to the take. Somebody done a real job on these bums," he grinned, "I bet they never even had time to fart."

A new photographer was busy getting shots from all angles, and the area was covered with smoke from the flash gun.

Cornering George and Tony, a reporter peppered them with questions. Pulling out his press card and showing it to the reporter, George said, "and no pictures. It happened too fast for any of us to see anything from our booth, okay?"

"Okay buddy" the reporter answered "if that's the way you want it. I'll go talk to the owner"

Tony was relieved. If Mr. Buchanan saw his picture in the paper along with a couple of dead guys, he would get fired for sure.

A few minutes later, the Lieutenant came over to question the alleged witnesses. Tony let George do the talking as much as possible. To the officers' obvious questions, George answered, "Hell we didn't see anything. We were two booths back so all we heard was the shots."

As the Lieutenant looked at him, Tony nodded in agreement to George's statement.

Though he still pictured the ugly face with the scarred neck, he said "That's right officer, we didn't realize what happened till it was over."

Turning to Paulie, he continued the interrogation "How about you Mr. Paulie,

Did you know the dead men?""

"No," he answered. "They've been in here a couple times, but I never knew their names. I didn't see or hear any more than my friends here."

The Lieutenant turned away and walked back to the gangster's booth. Either he was satisfied with their answers or he couldn't care less about the hoodlums. Another siren announced the arrival of the meat wagon.

"Okay" barked the Lieutenant "Get their bodies out of here and down to the morgue!"

A few minutes later the restaurant was practically empty as a bug-eyed dishwasher gingerly stepped around the riddled booth to mop up the blood of the two hoodlums sent to glory by their peers.

Shortly, George and Tony left. "George old buddy," Tony said, "the next time we go out for steaks, for Christ's sake make it to old aunt Minnie's café. They don't kill off the customers there."

"Yeah" George replied, "I don't want to think about this steak for a while."

The next morning, Tony found a one column story on Page 24 of the Sunday paper, and a picture of the recently deceased gangsters which certainly reflected their importance in the annals of Chicago's history of paid murders. "Slain by person, or persons unknown," became the epitaph of the two toe-tagged occupants of the Cook County morgue.

Tony put down the newspaper, "George, Paulie was about to find me a job actually doing some comedy, then those goons came in and shot up the place, so I forgot all about it."

George, "yeah but those two guys that were shot may have been the keepers of the speakeasy. You saw what happened to them. Dealing with those guineas can be dangerous business."

Tony, "As we saw in Chicago, you can get your ass shot at just having dinner. I think I'd like to talk with Paulie to see if he really does know some people who can help me get on the stage."

George said, "If you want to, you may as well go see Paulie and see where it goes from there."

CHAPTER 5

CHRISTMAS 1928

Christmas was fast approaching, and Tony's financial situation was at a low ebb. Trying to keep up with parties, Sundays at the Aragon, and his share of the food bills, dates, and helping big Bill Foy occasionally with cash, left little of Tony's salary of $28.50 a week. There were presents to be bought for girlfriends, his buddies, and the folks in Alabama. While he had appeared on the WLS program, there was still no sign of a contract. He was about to consider it a lost cause.

Tony had two options after mulling over the situation. One, he would have to keep the cost of dates to a minimum and hope to land a couple of entertainment jobs during the month of December. Two, a future, but remote possibility. After the first of the year, he would talk to his boss about a raise or a promotion.

His resolutions made, he told Ellie and Gladys he would be out of circulation, except for apartment business, through December. There was one resolution, however, Bill Foy almost totally lost one Saturday night in December. Tony and Grover were spending the evening home alone, while Bill Foy had gone out somewhere after dinner to hang out for the evening.

Around 9:30 PM, Bill came barging in with three girls in tow.

"Look what I found!" he announced. "You guys ready for a little partying?"

Three girls were not bad looking, but they were the blind pig swinging singles of 1928. Bill introduced the three to girls to Grover who found them less than interesting, but not wanting to embarrass Bill, he put some records on the victrola, then started rummaging around for something he could use to make some drinks.

Excusing themselves, Tony and Grover joined Bill in the kitchen.

"Okay, wise guy," said Grover sarcastically, "what the hell can we do with these three bimbos, satisfy 'em all?"

"Hell no!" answered a grinning Bill. "I settle for cool homework, you guys."

"Thanks a bunch," butted in Tony. "We told you no outside dates this month, remember?" Besides, they think they have three patsies on the line."

"Aw, come on, all they want is a drink and a little fun. It won't cost us anything." With that Bill went into the living room with drinks for the girls who had had a little conference of their own.

After finishing their drinks, one of the three girls, a hard-eyed blonde said, "That's enough drinking for now. Let's get going!" The two brunettes nodded in agreement.

"Going where?" asked Tony hopefully. "Home?"

"Heck no" was Blondie's reply. "Bill promised us you guys would take us to the Colossus. Hal Castle and his band are playing there."

"What!" yelled Grover. "The only way you'll hear Hal Castle is on the radio. We can't afford that place."

"Sure, you can," said one of the brunettes. "We'll just have one drink, listen to the band and go."

Tony was all for throwing the three out, followed by Bill, but they might feel differently later. Wait a minute," Tony said, "Let me make a phone call. Maybe I can work this out, so it won't cost us anything." Tony then called Ben Hammond, the WLS radio engineer who had kicked him off on the barn dance job. He was also the engineer who set up for the 11 o'clock WLS broadcast from the Colossus club.

Getting on the phone he said, "Hey Ben, I've got a favor to ask. My friend, Bill Grover, and another guy and I have a date with three girls who want to see the broadcast tonight. Can you arrange for us to sit at your table as WLS?"

"Sure," answered Ben, "No problem. Come on down. I'll even remove the cover charge."

"Okay Ben. Thanks a lot. See you later."

Tony hung up the phone and faced the group. "Okay "we're going, but remember, we only get one set up. When the gin is gone, so are we."

"Wow," yelled the girls, as Blondie said, "Boy, you must really know somebody important."

While the girls adjusted their make-up and put on their coats, Tony got Grover and Bill in the kitchen, "Look, we're all set, but we only stay for one drink and the broadcast. Don't let those dames order any food or we'll be in trouble."

Checking their combined cash, they discovered they only had six dollars and some change for a night at the Colosseum.

Their timing was about right. After getting on the L, they had a three block walk to the Colosseumon on south Wabash. They would get to the club about 10:45 PM.

The Colosseum was a swanky supper club featuring name bands. Hal Castle and his Castles in the Air were one of the best dance bands of the era. It was rumored the club was owned or controlled by the mob. Certainly, you could see any number of gang members there most any night of the week.

A resplendently uniformed doorman ushered them into the club. The girls were so excited Tony was sure this was the first time they had been in a decent place. Looking about for Ben who should have been near the bandstand getting ready for the broadcast, Tony didn't see any sign of him. With the WLS broadcast about to go live, Ben had to be around somewhere.

An impatient maître d' was urging them to get seated before the broadcast. A reluctant and worried Tony, followed by the group, allowed the maître d' to seat them at a table for six. After the group was seated, a waiter hovered over them for an order. Tony ordered a Collins set up for the group. The waiter must have known he had snagged a cheap group for his table. "Is that all?" he sneered.

Before Tony could say yes, Blondie piped up, "And club sandwiches too."

The waiter almost smiled as he turned away to the kitchen. Tony and the boys glared at Blondie. She never really knew how close she came to getting choked in front of 200 people. Blondie simply glared back at them "You cheapskates don't think you're gonna get away with one lousy drink, did you? We're hungry too." Blondie informed them in a voice loud enough for nearby people to hear.

Blondie was about to get choked twice. Tony's heart sank, while Bill and Grover looked sick. Their six bucks wouldn't cover the setups, let alone club sandwiches. No telling what they would cost at the Colosseum.

Two minutes before the broadcast was to begin, the band was already back on stage. Tony had to find Ben, and fast. Making his way over to the bandstand, he asked the drummer if he knew Ben Haley, the WLS engineer.

"Sure," he replied, "Ben was here an hour ago, he set up for the broadcast, then got a call back to the station. I don't know if he's coming back here or not."

Tony thought "We're really in for it now." He could see the three of them going home with broken arms when the maître d' finds out they are broke and can't pay the tab. Going back to the table, Tony whispered to Bill and Grover to follow him to the men's room.

As they left the table, the brunette called after him, "Don't try to ditch us here 'cause we'll tell them where you live."

"Shut up!" answered Bill, as the people at the surrounding tables burst out laughing. Tony quickly told the boys Ben wasn't there, and it looked like they were not only stuck with three crazy broads but a healthy check as well.

Grover suggested, "Maybe they'll accept our watches as collateral until can pay the damn check."

"Tony answered, "I guess they will, or else."

"Well," said Bill with some logic, "Let's go back and eat the damn sandwiches. We may as well die on full stomachs."

"Yeah," growled Tony, "You better eat up. If those waiters don't kill you, Grover and I will!"

They had just gotten seated again when Art Castle announced they were on the air and would be broadcasting for the next hour. Tony figured he might as well enjoy the music; he sure as hell was going to pay the fiddler later. Tony was watching the band when he saw a familiar face at a table facing the stage. It was Hal Brooks, the Barn Dance producer. Tony's heart leaped; they might get out of this mess with their skins after all. Jumping up, and without a word to the others, Tony plowed through the dancers to Hal's table.

"Hi Tony!" Hal greeted, "Didn't expect to see you here."

Tony answered, "Yeah, I didn't expect to be here either and wish I wasn't."

Tony told Hal the whole sad story of the mess he and his friends were in, and how it had happened. Hal couldn't help but laugh at Tony's story, and then said, "Lord, no problem. Bring your group over to my table. Tell the waiter you're my guests, and to give your check to me. "Geez, thanks. Hell, I think you've just saved our lives," Tony replied. "I'll go get them right now."

Getting back to his table, Tony found their steely eyed waiter flipping a check toward Bill as he said, "I'm sure you big spenders will want to pay the check now because this table is reserved for late customers."

Grover took the check, looked at it and turned pale. Bill then handed the bad news to Tony. The check for $26.50, was practically a week's pay for Tony.

Turning to the hard-eyed waiter, Tony, with what he hoped would be a low shot, said, "Are you sure this check is correct, my good man?"

The waiter's leering face turned even redder, "Are you going to pay the check now, or do I call the maître d'?" he snarled.

Grover and Bill stared at Tony; pretty sure he'd lost his mind. "Oh my God," Grover whispered to Bill, "Tony's going to get us maimed for life."

Tony thoroughly enjoyed the role he was playing. Guests at the surrounding tables were watching with bated breath, absolutely sure blood was about to be spilled.

Handing the check back to the waiter, Tony said, "I have no intention of paying this check, but," Tony continued, "you may escort us to Mr. Hal Brooks' table over by the band as we are his guests. Please be quick about it."

Unbelieving, a great change came over his swarthy face as Tony nodded affirmatively. What passed for a smile creased the waiter's face as he said, 'Please ladies and gentlemen, right this way. I'll be right back with your drinks. Just tell Mr. Brooks there won't be any charge. They're on the house."

Grover had trouble believing his ears, as he and the girls followed Tony across the room.

"Oh goody," squealed Blondie, "now we can order again."

Bill glared at her as he said, "You order anything, and you'll be out of here like we almost were, with broken noses."

Hal Brooks greeted Tony's group graciously and ordered a round of drinks.

Looking at the girls, he said, "I don't suppose you know Tony here appears on the WLS Barn Dance? You're out with a near celebrity." The girl's ooh'd and ahh'd a bit and did their best to act like ladies for a change.

Turing back to Tony he asked, "Tony, are you still interested in trying out your routine in a night club?"

"Boy, am I," Tony replied, "I just haven't figured out how to get started."

"Well, maybe I can help you. Even hear of Coffee Dan's downtown on Clark Street?" was Hal's next question.

Tony replied, "I've heard of it, but didn't know they had a floor show."

"They do, in a way," Hal replied, "On Friday and Saturday nights they have tryouts for entertainers. I'll call the manager and tell him about you. I'm sure he'll give you a chance. Call me on Wednesday."

"You bet I will Hal, thanks. My friends and I sure thank you, too, for getting us out of a real mess."

Turning back to the group, Tony said, "We've got to be going, Mr. Brooks expects other guests."

Grover and Bill shook hands with Hal and also thanked him for his help. The girls were reluctant to leave, but they were firmly guided to the door by three angry men.

Once outside, Bill said, "I hope you ladies know your way home, or maybe you'd like to hang around here and try to nail three more good time Charlies?" "Anyway, we're going home and you ain't invited."

Arm in arm, the three big spenders headed to the L station, leaving three mad hussies on the street.

"I hope you cheap bastards all break a leg!" yelled the blond.

A phone call to Hal Brooks confirmed he'd kept his promise and spoken to the manager at Coffee Dan's. Tony was to come in on Friday for a tryout. Coffee Dan's was exactly what the name implied, a coffee house. Located on Clark Street near Randolph in the heart of Chicago, it provided coffee and good food, dancing to the five heats combo and some entertainment, all at reasonable prices.

The manager greeted Tony in a friendly manner and introduced him to the band. He said he was sure Tony had a good act, or else Brooks wouldn't have called him. He did warn Tony about the Coffee Dan's audience. Tony shortly found out what he meant. The first show started at 10:00 PM. Each patron was given a small wooden mallet, used to keep time with the music, wrap your table mate's knuckles, or at the end of a performance, take the place of clapping.

Should, however, the audience not like the act in progress, the din of those mallets on the bare tabletops could drown out the voice of Caruso. There were five acts scheduled for the first show, Tony was number four. The first and third acts saw the mistreatment, accompanied by some very uncouth remarks and catcalls.

A very nervous Tony was introduced and opened his act by saying, "I wish they'd use the hook instead of the damn hammers. I've got a headache already."

This remark got a reasonable laugh, so he quickly went into a Swedish dialect monologue. He figured if this audience really had to listen to know what an act was all about, they wouldn't be in a hurry to use the mallets. He was right. They liked the dialects. He did a couple of Jewish stories, then went into a tap dance routine. There had not been a chance to rehearse with the band, but they were great. The mallets beat out a steady hand of appreciation. Tony took two curtain calls and was held over for the second show at midnight. Nothing had been said about compensation, but as Tony sat down for a late supper on the house between shows, the manager came over and gave him $20 and asked him to appear again the following Friday. Tony was elated.

Christmas of 1928 was a quiet time for Tony, as most of his girlfriends had gone home for the holidays and George and Cliff had to work at the paper. Grover and Tony joined them downtown for Christmas dinner in the evening. Bill Foy had been invited to his mother's apartment for the day and hopefully to get to know his stepfather. Bill's report on the visit indicated he was far from impressed with his new father.

On occasion, Grover drank too much and was often belligerent. Tony's first experience with Grover in his cups occurred a couple weeks after a party. Two members of the Chicago Cubs ball team lived in the building, Woody English, a pitcher and Gabby Hartman, the famous Cubs catcher. Gabby had just gotten married and had an apartment on the seventh floor directly below Tony and the crew. The Cubs were out of town and Gabby's bride was home alone on a particular Saturday night. Grover was still out on a date and Tony, who got in about midnight, was shortly in bed asleep. Later he was awakened by loud voices, one mad, one slightly hysterical. The voices seemed to be coming from directly below him. This consciousness overcame sleep as he recognized Grover's voice hollering, "For Christ's sake, let me in. Tony shut that dame up and open the damn door!"

Struggling into a bathrobe, Tony headed downstairs, thinking if Grover was trying to get into Hartman's apartment, no wonder his wife was screaming. A moment later he found Raker still yelling and pounding on the wrong door. Grabbing the drunken Grover Raker by the arm, Tony hustled him upstairs to their apartment. Once inside, he breathed again, hoping Mrs. Hartnett hadn't had time to call the police. A befuddled Raker mumbled "Why da hell didn't you let me in? What was your girlfriend hollering about? She should've knowed me by now" With that, Grover collapsed on the bed.

By late morning Raker was able to understand as Tony explained the possible pickle they were in. "Look Grover," Tony said, "when Gabby Hartman comes back from this road trip, you better get your ass down there and apologize."

"Yeah" promised a hung over Raker," I'll take care of it Monday for sure."

Raker's promise wasn't kept, as Tony found out Monday evening. It was 7:30 PM and Grover hadn't shown up for dinner or phoned. An hour later, there was a loud knock at the door. Opening the door, Tony found himself confronting a very mad

Gabby Hartman. Easily twice the size of Tony, his greeting was to the point.

"So, you're the bastard who tried to get in my apartment and scared the hell out of my wife!" he barked.

A scared Tony couldn't miss seeing the two ham-like fists ready for action, as he stammered, "Hold it, Mr. Hartman, it wasn't me."

"My wife said she heard the name Tony. That's you, right?" asked Hartman.

"Come in and sit down, Mr. Hartman and I'll explain." Tony answered, while backing into the room."

This better be good. My wife was pretty upset," Hartman replied as he took a seat.

"I don't blame her. "My roommate, Grover Raker, was really raising cane outside your door Saturday night," Tony continued, "He was drunk, got off the elevator on seven instead of eight, then started yelling because he thought I had a girl in here and wouldn't let him in. When the racket woke me up, I went down and got him. Raker was supposed to apologize but I guess he hasn't done so yet."

"No, he hasn't, but he sure better be getting to it. I'm sorry I jumped on you." Hartman answered. As he left, he said, "Any time you want passes to Wrigley Field, just let me know." Minutes later, Raker came in, but before he could open his mouth, Tony led him back out saying "You damn near got me killed. Gabby Hartman was just here and he's expecting you down to his apartment to apologize, and right now."

A rather pale Raker took off on his mission. "Okay," he called from the hallway, "but if I don't come back in ten minutes, call an ambulance."

A couple of nights after the Gabby Hartnett incident, Tony waited for the evening dinner crowd to be done and stopped in at Paulie's restaurant. He ordered a cup of coffee and waited until Paulie was not too busy. Paulie recognized him, came over and sat down.

Tony, "The other night when George and I were here, you said you might be able to fix me up doing some comedy at a local club. Then the world turned to shit, and we never got to finish our conversation. Were you serious?"

Paulie, "Yeah, I know some guys who run some clubs around town. I'll talk to some of them to see if I can get you fixed up."

Paulie, "let me see what I can do. I'll talk to a couple guys I know about this really funny young lad named Tony Harte and see what I can come up with."

Tony stood up and shook Paulie's hand. "Thank you, Paulie. Anything you can do will be greatly appreciated."

Two weeks after meeting with Paulie, Tony received the news he was wanted for a gig at a real nightclub. The night of his first performance, Tony put on his best suit, trimmed his own hair as best he could, and showed up at the address Paulie had given him for the Stardust Club. What was in front of him was an empty storefront. Undaunted, he went to a side door and knocked.

A menacing-looking fellow opened the door halfway and asked what he wanted. Tony told him why he was there, used Paulie's name and was welcomed inside. The interior was as it should be low lights set the mood in a smoke-filled room which smelled of stale beer, cheap whiskey, and women's cheap perfume. The tables were full of patrons talking and laughing.

Somewhat comforting, Paulie was there. He introduced Tony to Sal, manager of The

Stardust. Tony was shown to a backstage room where he could prepare for his first show which would be at 10:00 PM.

At 10:00 PM on the noise, the Master of Ceremonies introduced a nervous Tony Harte. The crowd clapped and Tony started his dialect stories. For obvious reasons he stayed away from Italian jokes. At first the audience was cool to his routine. Then he did some Swedish, Irish, and Jewish jokes and the drunken audience warmed to his pitch. He finally decided, 'What the hell,' and told the joke about the Italian whose wife had bugs in the bush story which brought the house down. The audience cheered and called for more. Not having any more prepared jokes, Tony curled his lit cigarette into his mouth, chewed and pretended to swallow. The crowd gasped and went silent. When he then rolled the cigarette back onto his lips and took a puff, the crowd again clapped and cheered.

As Tony left the little stage, Sal patted him on the back and told him to be ready to do his routine again for the midnight show. Though drained from his first performance, Tony was exhilarated, "Yes, I'm in show business!"

Tony's first gig was on Friday and Saturday nights for the next three weeks. Since the club had a regular clientele, it was hard to come up with new jokes each week and not become stale. After the 10:00 PM show on the third Saturday night, Saul came up to him and said, "Kid it's been real good, but I got to keep getting new talent to keep the crowd coming back. After your 12-midnight show, I'll have your final pay ready for you."

Tony finished the midnight show, then went to the bar for a nightcap and motioned to the bartender, "Hey, Nick, how 'bout a whiskey and branch water?"

He lit a cigarette and sipped his drink. While contemplating the next move to continue his stage career, a lady sat down on the stool next to him. She ordered a drink and began a conversation. "You know, you're really funny. I have enjoyed the hell out of your acts. But will you do that swallow the cigarette thing again? I just don't know how you do it."

Tony took a long drag on the cigarette, got it down to the proper length, and as always, rolled the cigarette back onto his lips. But before he could roll the cigarette back onto his lips, the lady squealed, "My God, he's swallowed it!" She slapped him on the back, and he really had swallowed the lit cigarette. Grabbing his drink, he chugged it down which did put out the fire but caused him to cough and almost lose his cookies.

The lady apologized and offered to buy Tony another drink, but the thought of pouring alcohol on his freshly scorched throat was less than appealing. He quietly departed the club and took a streetcar for home.

One evening George called Tony from his office and asked, "You got any objection to having a guest for a couple weeks?" Without waiting for an answer, he continued, "Bill Foy is in my office and needs a little help. I'm sending him over to the apartment, okay?"

"Sure, it's okay," Tony answered, "Send him out. It'll be good to see ole Bill."

Tony hadn't seen Bill since the summer of 1927. Shortly after that, Bill had gone to Cleveland on some job. Bill hadn't changed much since their Avondale days when Bill helped Tony with his romance with Rota. Bill was the same age as Tony, about five foot ten, and had an exceptionally large head, brown eyes and hair. He was a good-looking young man with an outstanding personality. Bill was inclined to brag about his sexual prowess and was certain he was the answer to every woman's prayers.

About an hour after George called, Bill knocked on the door with all his worldly possessions stuffed in a beat-up Gladstone bag. Bill didn't look like a picture of success, with a dirty shirt and shoes which hadn't been polished for some time. His apparent bad luck didn't seem to bother Bill as he greeted Tony with the "Hi Ya, old buddy, got any hot coffee?"

"Sure, friend," Tony answered, "how about some bacon and eggs to go with it?"

"Yeah," replied Bill," I didn't have time to eat dinner, just had coffee and a doughnut with George."

In a few minutes, Bill was doing justice to the bacon and eggs. Tony let him finish before he asked, "Where did you come in from?" I thought you were working for some company in Cleveland."

"Yeah, that was Procter & Gamble; I've been working on a soap crew, selling to stores and door to door in Ohio and Indiana. I got my ass fired last week in Ohio and hitchhiked to Chicago," Bill answered.

Tony replied, "That's too bad Bill. Maybe you can find something here."

Bill grinned, "I'll find a job quick," he added, "it's just as well I got fired. That damn crew manager worked my tail off. We always ended up in some flea bag hotel every night, lousy meals, and damn little pay. In fact, I'm dead broke now."

"Well don't worry about it, Bill," replied a sympathetic Tony, "I guess George and I can help out a bit, and you won't have to pay rent here until you get a job."

Bill replied, "Thanks, I knew I could count on you guys."

The two old friends chatted until midnight. Tony had to get up the next day, so he finally got Bill settled down on the rollaway bed in the dinette.

True to his word, Bill was up and out the next morning looking for a job. After several days of job hunting and no luck, Bill sort of forgot about working for a while. According to him, there just didn't seem to be any jobs suited to his talents, and he wasn't about to pedal soap again. His lack of interest in an immediate job worried the boys a bit, but George advised them to give Bill more time to get adjusted. They agreed not to push him too hard.

The first Saturday after Bill moved in, he, Grover, and Tony were having a late lunch. Bill slyly brought up a subject dear to his heart, sex.

"Look guys," he announced, "it's been a while since I 've had a piece. I expect you know some gal dying to meet a real stud like me. So how about some introductions?"

Neither Tony nor George had any intention of letting Bill get within hollering distance of any of their girlfriends, at least not until he cooled off. But they did, after consultation, come with up with a solution to Bill's problem.

Tony suggested, "Look Bill, offhand we don't know any girl you can get in bed with the first time out. But we know of a place downtown where for two bucks you can get complete satisfaction. If you want to change your luck, it'll only be a couple of bucks, how about that?"

Bill's eyes lit up, "Boy, two bucks sounds okay, but I'm broke."

Grover spoke up, "Hell Bill, if you want to go downtown, we'll lend you the dough."

"Let's go then," said an excited Bill. "You guys sure know how to take care of a friend."

Within three quarters of an hour, they were downtown getting off the L at the Van Buren Street station. The house of ill repute Tony had in mind was just a few doors north opposite the Rialto Theatre. Located on the second floor of an old building, the "House" was reached by a long stairway. Grover handed Bill the two bucks, saying, "You go on up Bill. We'll wait for you here."

Bill started up the steps and disappeared into a gloomy upper room.

After 10 minutes or so Tony said," Grover, you think we really ought to do this to ol' Bill?"

"Hell yes," answered Grover. "Besides; we just might be saving him from getting a good dose!"

"Okay, here goes" Tony replied.

Waiting until Grover was hidden in a nearby doorway, Tony slipped up about four steps of the "House" entrance, cupped his hands and hollered, "Get the hell out. The cops are comin'!" Then he raced down the stairs to join Grover.

Within seconds, it sounded like a buffalo stampede as six guys, pants at half mast, with suspenders trailing, came flying down the stairs, followed by a white-faced Bill Foy!

The two-dollar Romeos headed in all directions, knocking down pedestrians in their flight. It took Grover and Tony 10 minutes to find Bill. He was huddled in a doorway two blocks from the scene, desperately trying to get his clothes in order.

Trying to keep a straight face, Tony asked, "What the hell happened, Bill? You sure came out of that joint in a hurry."

An angry Bill replied, "the damn place was raided, that's what happened." Then an evil smile spread over his face as he continued, "And I was about to jump the most beautiful babe in the 'House'."

Grover and Tony looked at each other. Even at a time like this, Bill just had to brag. With Bill in tow, the boys went back to their apartment.

Tony had to get ready go back downtown at 7:30 PM in case he might have to rehearse. He left Grover and a disappointed Bill listening to the radio.

On Sunday morning, they had breakfast with George and Cliff. Bill couldn't resist telling them how he almost got caught in a police raid at the "House" of ill repute. Finishing the story, George said, "For Christ's sake, that joint hasn't been raided in three years. The mob pays plenty to City Hall to keep it open." Looking at the grinning Tony and Grover, George said, "Bet I can tell you who yelled police."

A disbelieving Bill looked at his two friends and said, "You two bastards wouldn't pull a trick like that, or would you?"

It was no use. They broke up thinking about how Bill and the others looked when coming down those stairs.

Bill grinned as he said, "So I got took, but it was you two bucks, Grover. I can think of six other guys who would like to kick you both if they ever catch up with you."

Feeling they had been a bit rough on Bill, Tony said, "Bill, we're going to get you a date on Saturday night with a beautiful redhead who screws for the pure joy of it. We'll have a party here and from then on, it's up to you."

Bill's face lit up, "Is that a promise, no more tricks?" George looked at Tony, grinned and asked, "Are you talking about Awa's redhead? You think Bill can handle her?" Before Tony could answer, Bill chimed in, "I can handle any dame alive. Once I get her shoes up, she's all mine."

They both knew what Bill was in for. Tony said, "Okay Bill, I'll arrange it. You just have the save your strength."

Since Ellie had moved into the building with her friend, Tony invited them, and Ellie's roommate would be Grover's date. Both George and Cliff would be working late. Fortunately, Tony wasn't needed at W LS that Saturday. If things went as he expected, he certainly didn't want to miss the party.

About 10:00PM on Saturday night, the party was in full swing. Bill was at his best charming the girls. Bill found the redhead most attractive and couldn't keep his eyes off her. She was tall, 5'-7" in stocking feet, with dark red hair framing a very pretty face, flashing green eyes, and a beautiful body. She had Bill chomping at the bit. He couldn't get wait to get her alone.

Having done heavy damage to a fifth of gin, the six young people were in a relaxed mood listening to Wayne King's broadcast from the Aragon ballroom. Tony and Elsie were comfortable in George's easy chair, Grover and Elsie's roommate were making plan to visit her apartment shortly and Bill and the redhead were huddled on one end of the couch.

Suddenly strange sounds began coming from the rollaway bed in the dinette. So far, according to plan, the dinette had been reserved for Bill. He alerted Grover, and heard the girl saying, "In about five minutes you'll be hearing the fall of my lover Bill!" The noises grew even louder, and the rollaway bed seemed almost alive as it moved back and forth, banging against the dinette table and wall. No doubt about it, Bill was in the saddle riding hell bent for leather! Bill seemed to be holding his own when suddenly there was a loud crash when the bed hit the wall again, followed by a second bang. It knocked the dinette door open to reveal a bewildered Bill on the floor on all fours, wondering how he got there, while a pair of bashful green eyes stared down at him from the bed. Gales of laughter came from the spectator throng in the living room. Aggravated and embarrassed, Bill slammed the dinette door closed on the laughing faces. For sure, Bill had met his match. The green-eyed redhead had thrown him right out of the saddle!

Bill hardly spoke to his roommates the next day, except to say, "If I hadn't caught my foot on the damn sheets, I'd have been able to hang on."

George said with a grin, "Those guys should've warned you that you'd need stirrups and a whip to ride the redhead."

Bill didn't reply to that remark, he just stalked out of the apartment. His disastrous ride did, however, slow down his tendency to brag for at least two weeks.

CHAPTER 6

THE TROUBLE WITH WINE

Christmas and New Year's Eve of 1928 had come and gone. Tony hardly noticed the holidays since he had worked the whole time at the center theatre. Other than exchanging gifts with George and his girlfriend Ellie, it had not seemed much like the holidays.

On Thursday night after the Christmas show at the Oriental, Anthony Pazzaloni, Tony's captain, invited him to a birthday party for his sister. Anthony lived with his folks in an Italian neighborhood on W. Chicago Avenue. Arriving at Anthony's house about 8:30 PM, Tony found the party well underway. Introduced to Anthony's pretty 17-year-old sister, Tony presented her with a gift. He then met Anthony's parents who were presiding over a table groaning under the weight of a myriad of Italian food and wine.

Anthony's mother took charge. Filling a plate with antipasto, meatballs, pasta and dishes Tony had never heard of., Mrs. Pazzaloni kept saying "Mangiare, mangiare, you'a gonna lika this. You ushers never get a decent meal, so eat."

And eat he did, as Anthony introduced him to some other relatives and friends. Tony's wine glass was never empty, as Mr. Pazzaloni had him try at least three different wines. He announced,

"I maka all kinda them myself. No prohibition gonna keep a good Italian boy from having his wine!"

A couple of hours later, Tony decided he had to get out of there fast. Trying to stay on his feet and talk without slurring his words, Tony bid his hosts goodnight. Telling them he had to be at work at 8:30AM, he left.

Outside the cold air helped a bit. It had been stifling hot in the small house. Staggering to the corner, Tony waited for a streetcar to downtown, then he would have to take the L out to the North side. He hoped he would make it home. Finally, a streetcar showed up. Tony, struggling to board, missed the first step and banging his shin. If the conductor hadn't grabbed his arm, he would've fallen off. Tony was swaying more than the streetcar, only they weren't swaying in unison. Bouncing from one side of the vestibule to the other, he fished out the seven-cent carfare and made it to a seat, all under the watchful eye of the conductor.

The trip downtown was a nightmare. The car was hot, bumpy, and noisy which did not help Tony's swirling stomach and aching head. Arriving downtown, Tony wondered how he would make it up the L station stairs. It was a few minutes before he made a try. Knowing he was going to be sick, Tony clutched the station support pillar and got rid of about 8 pounds of antipasto and other Italian goodies. This helped somewhat. Negotiating the remaining L stairs, one step at a time, and desperately holding onto the rail, he finally reached the train platform. There were few express trains at that time of night. The first Northside train to show up was a local, leaving the train and his stomach to rumble all the way to his destination. It was close to 1:30PM when Tony painfully made his way off the L at his station, and erratically negotiated the two blocks to his hotel. Once safely back in his room, Tony's only thought was about getting in bed as fast as possible. Leaving his clothes in a heap on the floor, he crawled into bed. For the first few minutes, the room spun around and around as Tony's wine-soaked brain sought peace and quiet in blessed sleep.

Brought back to a still-swirling room by the jangle of a 6:30 AM wake-up call, Tony answered it, struggling to keep his bleary eyes open. A shower helped some, but didn't do much for his throbbing head and dry parched throat. At this point, Tony violated the first rule of wine drinkers: Never drink water the morning after. Coffee, juice or cyanide maybe, never water. But he did drink a tall glass of cold water, thinking it had never tasted so good. Little did he realize what he had done. Shortly he would know.

Surveying his pale face in the bathroom mirror, his eyes looked like two olives in a sea of catchup. He attempted to shave but gave up, for with shaking hands and a safety razor, there was nothing safe about it. Tony struggled into the same suit he'd worn one the night before, then headed for the L station and his office at Union Station. He was feeling almost human until he got on the train. Seldom getting a seat in the morning, Tony, hanging from a strap, suddenly felt ready to explode. His stomach churned again, his vision was blurred, and every passenger near him had two faces. Then it dawned on him: he was drunk all over again. Realizing he was going to be sick, he got off at the next station and headed to the men's room. Within a half hour, he decided to continue his trip downtown. Even so, he was going to be an hour late getting to work. The few minutes he waited in the cold for another train helped to clear his head a bit.

Twenty minutes later, he opened the outer door to the railroad office. According to the clock, he was, in fact, an hour late. Between the entrance and the inner door was a railing, with a gate which swung both ways to let people in or out. As nonchalant as possible in his condition, Tony swung the gate inward and stepped in, but not far enough. The gate swung back and caught his heel. Tripping, he landed in a heap on the floor. Amid the laughter of his coworkers, red faced Tony took hold of the corner of his desk, pulled himself up on unsteady feet. and made it to his chair. Mr. Buchanan, noting his lateness and unceremonious arrival, glared at him but said nothing.

Tony sat across the double desk from Don, who stopped laughing long enough to exclaim, "My God, you smell like you fell into a wine barrel. Just hope Mr. Buchanan doesn't recognize you're half drunk, or he just might fire your ass. He's dead set against drinking."

Tony moaned, "Right now I'm too sick to give a damn. Anyway, I may not live out the day."

Glancing around, when Tony noticed Mr. Buchanan's disapproving eyes closely watching his every move, he decided to get busy opening the pile of mail on his desk. But he couldn't get his hands to coordinate, as half the mail was going in the wastebasket. Bending over to retrieve the mail which had fallen into the wastebasket, Tony straightened up to find Mr. Buchanan at his side.

"Tony," he announced sternly, "you appear to be quite inebriated. If Mr. Ennis should find you in this condition, you'd be fired immediately. I want you to go down to the station and get a shave and plenty of coffee. Stay there until you sober up."

"Yes sir." Tony answered, as he left the office, thankful he had not been fired, at least not so far. With the shave, coffee, and an hour's snooze on a waiting room bench, he began to feel a lot better. For lunch he had soup. then reported back to work where he caught Mr. Buchanan in the hall. "Mr. Buchanan, I'm very sorry about this morning. Be sure it won't happen again, and thanks for letting me leave the office. I'm okay now."

Over his glasses, Mr. Buchanan looked at Tony and smiled slightly. "If you think you can get to your desk without falling down, go ahead, but remember, "Don't ever let this happen again." A contrite Tony went back to work vowing it would be a long time before he would mess with the nectar of the gods again.

While he was still enjoying his job as an usher, and needing the money, he had sense enough to realize the long hours with little time off were beginning to wear him down.

By the middle of January, Tony began having trouble staying awake during office hours and he felt exhausted most of the time.

One morning he even fell asleep at his desk. It took both his desk mate and Mr. Buchanan to rouse him. Mr. Buchanan was naturally suspicious after Tony's past drinking episode, so he took Tony into Mr. Ennis' office for a private chat.

"Tony," he said, "this is too much! If you can't stay awake on the job, you must be out all hours of the night. I'd like an explanation and it better be good or I'll have to let you go."

Realizing Mr. Buchanan was dead serious and suspicious about his activities, Tony hastened to explain. "Sir, I'm sorry about this morning, but I haven't been drinking. For the past five months I've been working nights and weekends as an usher at the Oriental Theatre. I'm afraid I just haven't been getting enough sleep. I took the extra job so I could get my car paid off."

"Well," Mr. Buchanan replied, "I'm relieved to hear that. Your ambition is commendable, but your extra job is going to ruin your job here. You will have to make up your mind as to which job you want to keep because it can't be both."

"Yes sir," answered Tony, "I sure don't want to leave the railroad. I'll quit the theater job on Saturday because I have to give them at least a couple of day's notice."

"That will be all right." Mr. Buchanan said, "You've got a lot more future with the railroad and we wouldn't want to lose you."

Tony returned his desk, relieved he still had his regular job and just as relieved he would shortly be through at the theatre.

Most of his extra money had been going toward the car payments but he still owed about $70 on it. One thing he didn't want to do was move back to Grayslake, although he was sure he would be welcome. Compared to the excitement of the big city and his new friends, Grayslake would be pretty dull.

That night Tony gave notice he would be leaving the theater on Saturday night. Mr. Balaban tried to get him to change his mind by offering Tony a full-time job and a captaincy to stay on, but Tony turned down the offer.

A few days later he phoned his Uncle Oscar. Explaining that he had to leave the theater job, he assured him he would somehow keep up with the car payments.

Oscar came up with a surprising suggestion. "Look son," he said "Your Aunt is crazy about your little car. Suppose I buy it from you, say for hundred and seventy-five dollars." He continued as Tony thought about the idea. "Trying to keep the car in Chicago on your salary will keep you broke, right?"

Tony hated the idea of giving up the car, but he definitely had use for the money the car would bring. He agreed his uncle's idea made sense and said, "Okay, sounds fair enough. Besides I can always get another car when I'm making more money."

For years Tony had been crazy about show business and the few months at the Oriental Theatre had only whetted his appetite. First of all, he wanted to learn soft shoe and tap dancing, figuring he could build a nightclub or vaudeville act around those talents.

Shortly after receiving the money for his car, he enrolled in private lessons with a theatrical agency at $5 an hour. For the first few lessons, both his instructor and Tony were sure he had two left feet. Gradually, however, as he became more confident, his feet began to obey instructions. With constant practice and lessons, he became fairly adept at a couple of standard routines, but it would be a while before he was good enough to try out for engagements.

Within a week after quitting the theater job, Tony began to feel like himself again. He caught up on lost sleep, ate regular meals, and gained some weight. He also had more time to enjoy dates with Ellie and the others.

After quitting his second job, Tony spent every Sunday afternoon and evening dancing at the Aragon ballroom, which Wayne King and his famous band opened in 1926 and would play there for the next ten years. The Aragon was one of Chicago's best-known spots to dance to the music of the most famous big bands of the era, alternating with Wayne King on Saturdays and

Sundays, and such greats as Kay Kaiser, Eddie Duchenne, Guy Lombardo, Freddie Martin, L'Kim and many others.

The Aragon had a Spanish motif with a starlit domed ceiling and small balconies built along two sides of the dance floor. A refreshment lounge on the second floor provided balconies for weary dancers to sit one out in comfort.

On Sundays, the Aragon opened at 1:00 PM. Alternating bands provided the music which was continuous until midnight. While the Aragon could accommodate several hundred people on the spacious dance floor at any one time, the Sunday crowd was usually a bit smaller. There were several groups of regulars who more or less hung together on Sundays. Most of the young people in the group belonged to the 400 Club. This club was made up of the best dancers and were the ones who taught newcomers on Thursday night. They were not paid a fee but were admitted free of charge on the class nights. Belonging to the 400 Club was a status symbol at the Aragon, and within a very short time, Tony became a member.

As was true with most in this group, Tony, except on a few special occasions, never took a date to the Aragon. This practice eliminated the dread of having to dance with one girl all evening and offered more freedom of choice. It was certainly less expensive, as both men and women paid their own admission of $2.00. It was, however, considered proper etiquette to invite your favorite partner to have a soda during the intermission.

Dressing your best for an evening at the Aragon was a must if you wished to impress the girls who always wore evening gowns and looked their prettiest. These were the days of Arrow and Boyed stiff collars. No one would think of wearing a soft collared shirt to the Aragon. During the colder months, the men in Tony's group dressed almost in uniform, usually wearing dark blue or Oxford gray double-breasted suits, and most certainly well-polished black shoes. Normally with this sort of outfit, one wore a pearl gray or light blue four-in-hand-tie. Proper dress was part of the fun and excitement of an evening at the Aragon.

Anyone's darling daughter was perfectly safe at the Aragon where the floor was continually patrolled by two polite, but stern gentlemen in tuxedos who watched for drunks, ear biters, outlandish dancing which interfered with others, or any guy trying to make out in a horizontal position. If spotted they would be quietly escorted to the front door. Fights were most uncommon, though on one occasion Tony was descending the balcony stairs when two irate Romeos on either side of the staircase swung at each other as Tony inadvertently stepped between them. Catching their punches on both sides of his head, it was a while before he did anymore dancing that night.

Awa Anderson had introduced Tony to a rather good-looking blond with blue eyes and a great figure. She seemed quite friendly, and Awa led Tony to understand that Jane could be more than just friendly if the right approach was used. Tony should have known Awa was up to something and he found out just what when he talked with George later about meeting Jane, the blonde.

"What!" yelled George. "That damn Awa is going to get you in trouble yet. The damn whore works the uptown area, and she don't do it for fun. She gets three bucks or better for every trick. You better stay the hell away from her, or you'll be seeing Doc' Zinn for a long time!"

"Boy!" Tony replied, "I sure don't need her. I'm doing okay for free. I'll let old Awa spend his money."

The discussion had taken place at the lobby desk with Mrs. Morrison nodding in agreement with everything which was said.

One Sunday, Tony had gone dancing at the Aragon ballroom, and arrived home about 12:30 AM. There was a no-name message at the desk asking him to call room 312 when he got in. Puzzled, Tony had no idea who lived in 312, or why he, or she, wanted to talk with him at this ungodly hour. Figuring it had to be one of George's friends, Tony stopped at 312 and knocked on the door. A very seductive voice said, "Come on in honey, the door's open."

Entering, Tony saw Jane propped up in a bed holding a water pitcher in one hand. As he turned to close the door, she screamed,

"So you're the lousy SOB who told the whole damn hotel I'm a whore!"

With this greeting, she threw the pitcher, missing Tony's head by inches and shattering on the door. Her face was purple with rage as she charged off the bed screaming choice epithets. Tony had seen some mad women in his day, but never one so ready to do him in. The accusation stunned him, and if she kept yelling, the whole hotel would be awake. She was not only furious, but she was also drunk. Struggling to hold her off, he already had a few claw marks.

He tried to calm her down as he said, "cut it out, Jane, I never said a word about you. Hell, I only met you yesterday!"

It was no use. Jane continued her tirade, "You punk bastard. When I get through with you, a fifty-cent hooker wouldn't want you!"

Up and down the hall Tony heard doors opening as the residents tried to find out what was going on. Jane was not about to quiet down as she continued to claw and slap. They fell on the bed with enough force to send it crashing against the wall and ended up rolling onto the floor, as Tony tried to pin her arms. Words of both encouragement and anger at having their sleep disrupted were heard from the folks in the hall. Tony was sure he heard Awa yelling, "Sock her one. That's all she understands!"

Tony had never hit a woman in his life, be she of the streets, or the 400, but it sure looked as though this was going to be the first time. Jane hadn't given up by a damn sight, as she continued to fight and yell obscenities at Tony. Pulling her to her feet, Tony had her arms at her side, but he'd forgotten how an irritated woman can use her knees. Just then Tony saw flashing lights and stars and almost went to the floor again. Hanging onto Jane and managing to avoid further slow blows, he gasped, "Sorry about this, lover" as he aimed her to a chair and let her have it on the chin! Jane collapsed in a heap on the chair and the fight was over. Even out cold, she looked mad as hell.

Gathering his hat, and what dignity he had left, a battered and embarrassed Tony pushed his way through the hallway crowded with residents waiting for details of the latest sex orientated brawl at the Foswyn Arms. Answering no questions, he got to his room fast. Luckily, no one thought to call the police.

Washing and patching his battered face, Tony reflected on the two thoughts uppermost in his mind. One, with Jane's energy, she must be one hell of a lay, drunk or sober! Two, how the hell would he explain to his boss on Monday why his face looked like to roadmap?

On Monday evening when he returned from the office, Tony found Awa and George discussing his midnight episode with Mrs. Morrison, who greeted Tony, "Well, if it's not lover boy himself. Look at that face. He managed a grin as he answered, "Yeah, and I don't feel so good in a couple of other places either. That damn broad nearly won the fight."

Awa chimed in, "If you hadn't taken my advice and smacked her one, you would've lost!"

"Look," Tony replied, "If you hadn't introduced me to that wildcat, I wouldn't have gotten into such a mess. And, who told her I said she was a whore? George should've had the fight, not me."

George shook with laughter, saying, "I think the hotel porter must've told her about our conversation, and gotten our names mixed up. It had to be him. I know he's been steering a few customers her way."

Mrs. Morrison cut in, "Forget about her. I gave her notice first thing this morning. She was packed and gone by noon." Turning to Awa she continued, "After this, introduce Tony to nice girls, if you know any! At least pick out girls who won't want to try to kill him"

"Never mind," answered Tony, "I'll pick them myself, and you can bet they'll be housebroken! I'm not about to go through another battle like that. I'd rather be a eunuch and I damn near became one!"

In late 1928, Tony was eligible for two weeks' vacation and full pass privileges on other railroads. He went south to Irvington, Alabama, for the two weeks. Upon his return to Chicago, he found George was mulling over the idea of getting a furnished apartment. During Tony's absence, another Avondale mate, Grover Raker, had checked in at the hotel. Within a week the four, George, Cliff, Grover, and Tony, agreed an apartment would provide more space and enable them to cook their own meals.

It was an ideal setup. George and Cliff worked nights; Tony and Grover worked days. Shortly they found an apartment on Kenmore Avenue, only four blocks from the Forswyn Arms. The apartment was on the top floor, nicely furnished and included maid service. There was a sofa bed and a wall bed in the large living room, a full bath, a kitchen and dinette. There was also room for a foldaway bed in the dinette. Split four ways, the rent of $80 a month was no more than the hotel rooms. On a bright Saturday afternoon, it took the boys only two hours to move in.

Upon leaving the Forswyn Arms, Mrs. Morrison saw them off. She shed a tear or two, and said, "God knows I should be relieved you characters are leaving. I'll probably live longer, but it sure won't be much fun with my favorite troublemakers gone!" They all kissed her goodbye and invited her to their housewarming party planned for the following Saturday night.

Fortunately, George was an excellent cook, and Tony was no slouch in the kitchen either, both having learned the finer points in the kitchen at Avondale. Otherwise, Grover and Cliff would have starved to death, as neither one could be trusted to boil water.

The housewarming party was attended by their favorite inmates from the Forswyn Arms, and their girlfriends. Grover and Cliff brought their loves of the moment, and Tony invited Gladys, his newest flame.

During their first week in the apartment, the boys learned bathtub gin and bootleg booze would be no problem as they had a live-in bootlegger on the fifth floor. His services were immediately solicited by the party.

By 10:30 PM the party was well underway. Up until this time there had only been two warnings from the night clerk to hold down the noise. Since they were new, Tony thought it was wise on the second call to go down and apologize.

It was an appropriate move, as the desk clerk was a pretty girl named Cookie. After apologizing and noting a wedding ring, Tony suggested she and her husband stop in for a drink later. His invitation was readily accepted.

By the time he got back upstairs, Dr. Zinn had just popped in. Introductions over, Tony offered the good doctor a high ball of booze and ginger ale. Taking a good gulp, the doctor promptly spit in the sink and gasping for breath, sputtered, "Good God, what was that? Horse piss?"

Tony hastened to assure the doctor, "That is the best money can buy. Ya just gotta acquire a taste for it."

"That will never happen!" growled the doc.

Sitting down at the table, the doctor pulled out his prescription pad and scribbled two unreadable prescriptions which he handed to George and said, "Go over to the drugstore and get these filled. Then we can all have a decent drink."

Within fifteen minutes a grinning George returned with two bottles of bonded Canadian whiskey. After a round of drinks, the three cheered for their friend, the doctor, and the fact he could write one hell of a prescription.

The party had gathered steam. By the time Cookie and her husband came in for a couple of drinks, no one was feeling any pain. Cookie had talked a friend into taking over the switchboard for a while. It wasn't long before the apartment phone was jumping again with other complaints about the noise.

Tony hollered, "For Christ's sake, pipe down or you guys will break our lease!"

Cookie stepped over and took for phone from Tony, "Look, she told her friend on the switchboard, "tell whoever is complaining that the managers are at the party and has everything under control, okay?" That ended the phone calls.

By 2:30 PM, everything was reasonably quiet. Most of the guests had gone home while they were still able..

Doc's good Canadian whiskey was gone so anybody wanting a nightcap was forced to go with the bootleg. George considered falling asleep on the living room couch. Cliff and his girlfriend had already left. Tony and Gladys were in the kitchen making coffee when they heard Grover easing down in the door bed. It was apparent he intended to waste no time getting better acquainted with his little blonde girlfriend.

Seated on the extra small bed in the dinette, Gladys and Don sipped their coffee. Suddenly Tony remembered the rules about Gladys' girl's club. It was close to 3 o'clock. "Holy cow, Gladys" he said, "you're sure as hell locked out tonight."

"Nothing to worry about," answered Gladys snuggling close, "unless, she continued, "you're going to throw me out. I told them at the club I was going home for the weekend."

"Good thinking, honey," answered Tony closing the dinette door. "This ain't exactly private, but maybe they'll at least knock before coming in."

Gladys laughed." Who cares," she said. They're too busy in there to worry about us. Now stop talking so darn much."

Tony did as requested, and both got busy with buttons and things. About half an hour later, the happy and biologically satisfied young people fell asleep.

The rattling of pots and pans and the delicious smell of coffee and fried bacon brought them awake. It was 11:00AM and George was busy doing what he did best. Opening her eyes, Gladys looked around and exclaimed, "Ooooh! It is day and I've been here all night."

"Right you are, Happy Bottom," answered George, pouring coffee. Gladys blinked at her new nickname. Nudging Tony she asked, "Did you hear what that great oaf your brother, called me?"

"Yeah," grunted Tony. Don't pay any attention to George. t's his idea of an enduring nickname. He loves you too."

Minutes later a bleary-eyed Grover and his girlfriend joined the group for breakfast. "Boy," George greeted them, "You two look like you've had at least an hour's sleep."

Raker raised his red rimmed eyes and looked at his blonde friend., "Yeah, every time I turned over, I got in trouble. I turned over a lot."

Blondie's blush matched Grover's eyeballs. "Baloney!" she answered. "You may have been sleeping, but your hands sure stayed awake!"

After breakfast, Tony and Grover took their girls home. No one knew what had happened to Cliff. It was assumed he ended up on his girl's sofa, since he was in no shape to do much else.

Grover Raker, the newest member of the group, took a little getting used to. Being three years older than Tony, they had not been close friends at Avondale, so Tony really knew little about him, other than he was 5'-10", rather thin, with brown hair and eyes. At some time or another, he had suffered a broken nose. He also walked with a slight limp having been injured as a child. He was very close mouthed about his affairs. In the two years he lived at the apartment, no one knew where he worked or how much income he had, and no one asked. He always paid his share of the rent and expenses on time. Grover was a likable person; he and Tony became good friends and double dated quite often.

PART II

CHAPTER 7

THE END OF
THE ROURING
TWENTIES

The old year was fast coming to an end, and the future was bright. The economy was in good shape, the gangsters were busy killing each other off, Herbert Hoover was elected president, and Bill Foy promised to get a job in 1929.

Even though Tony's economy had been beefed up a bit with three appearances at

Coffee Dan's, plus a couple of private engagements, there was no assurance of steady night club work. Then when Hal Brooks advised him the Swedish character on the Barn Dance was going to be dropped, his last hope of improving his financial situation would be a better job at the railroad. To that end, he sought an interview with Mr. Ennis to discuss his problem.

"Mr. Ennis, he began, "I would like to know if there is any chance of a promotion or a raise in our department?"

Mr. Ennis, "Tony, you know the jobs throughout the freight department are rated.

This simply means your job as a file clerk will never pay any more than it does now. The only way someone advances is if someone quits, retires, dies, or a new job is created. That's about all I can offer you at present. But if I hear of a job in another department that I think you can handle, I'll let you know."

"Thank you, sir," Tony replied, "I can wait, and I appreciate your help."

A couple of weeks after the interview, Mr. Ennis called Tony into his office where he was talking with a short, heavy-set man with a rugged, but pleasant face.

Mr. Ennis, "Tony, I'd like you to meet Mr. Brown, Chief of the Lost and Bad Order Car Department at the Fullerton Avenue offices."

Tony responded, "Pleased to meet you Sir."

Ennis continued, "Mr. Brown is starting a new type of customer service and needs two or three young men who know our rail system and connecting lines. The men he chooses must be able to handle customers on the phone, mainly advising them where their shipments are in route. Think you could handle a job like this?" Tony noted Mr. Brown was watching him carefully so he took his time answering the question.

"Yes sir," he responded, "I know the system well from working here and I enjoy talking with people. I'm sure I could handle the job if Mr. Brown would give me the opportunity."

Mr. Brown said, smiling, "Well, you certainly know how to speak up for yourself."

Turning to Ennis, he said, "Mind if I ask Tony a few questions?" Ennis replied, "Certainly not. I'll be in the outer office."

After Ennis left, Mr. Brown asked Tony what other departments he had worked for, where he lived, his hobbies and some questions about the Milwaukee Road system. Tony responded with the details, including his start in Mr. Proctor's department. Mind if I talk to Tom Proctor about you?"

"Certainly not, sir," replied Tony.

"This should be all the information I'll need from you," stated Mr. Brown as he got up from his chair. "Mr. Ennis seems to think you're a good man for me. I'll let you know what I decide. The new system won't start for a month. Thank you for your time."

Mr. Ennis came back in just as Tony was leaving. "Thank you for the interview Mr. Brown, and you, Mr. Ennis, for recommending me."

Back at his desk, Tony was elated about this chance. Mr. Proctor's recommendation would carry weight, as would Mr. Ennis'. He certainly had everything going for him. Just in case things didn't work out, he decided not to tell his co-workers about the interview, though he could see his desk mate, Don, was suspicious about the goings on.

A few days later, Mr. Ennis informed Tony Mr. Brown had decided he wanted him for the new job. The pay would be $32.50 per week, $24.00 a month more than his present salary. The job was to start the first of March, which would give him time to break in a new file clerk.

Later, Mr. Ennis announced to the office force that Tony would be leaving soon for the Fullerton Avenue freight offices, and a better job. Thanking Mr. Ennis and accepting the congratulations of his fellow employees, Tony then paid a visit to Mr. Proctor's office to also thank him.

At this time George was the night manager of the photo lab at the Hearst building. He was assisted by a crew which meant he and his crew did most of the work and put in long hours. It seemed most of the murders, rapes, gang killings, and other assorted crimes took place at night. Pictures of some of these events were taken with a graphic camera and a flash gun to light the scene, since flashbulbs had not yet been invented. Always eager for some excitement, there were times Tony would go with George to operate the flash gun. The flash gun had a narrow trough to hold the powder, and a handle centered on the trough which extended down about four inches. The flash powder was activated by a minute spark. The Flintlock mechanism wasn't much more sophisticated than the Revolutionary War musket and no more reliable. In any case, the flash gun was strictly loaded; if not enough powder you did not get enough flash, too much powder spelled real trouble for the photographer and the gun holder when it went off. There were also dangers if holding the gun too close to your head. You could lose a head of hair and/or a hat and could scare the hell out of the subject.

Having worked late the night before, Tony planned to sleep till noon and since it was Valentine's Day, he was going to see if he could find some romance. At about 11:30 AM George shook him awake. "Get your butt up, kid. I need some help. I need you to hold the flashing for a big story."

A bleary-eyed Tony mumbled, "What the hell is going on? I was having a good sleep."

George shook him again, "This is a big story, and we need to get going."

Tony got up, went into the bathroom threw some water in his face, jumped into his clothes and headed for the door. "Where the hell are we goin', George?"

"We're going to some warehouse on Clark Street near Lincoln Park." grumbled George, pushing Tony ahead of him. Outside of the warehouse at 2122 North Clark Street. the police were keeping people away from the entrance. George flashed his press card so the officers would let them inside. Up against a far blood-splattered wall where seven bodies lying on the floor.

George yelled, "Set up the flash Kid!" On my count 3, 2, 1, shoot." The flash powder went off and filled the area with smoke.

George, waving the smoke out of the way, yelled "Set up again!" "On my count 3, 2, 1, shoot." The flash powder went off again and added more smoke to the area.

George directed Tony "More reporters are showing up so let's get our asses out of here and develop this stuff."

Tony then accompanied George back to his dark room and instead of looking for love he helped George develop photographs for the rest of the day and part of the night. The photographs were of what was to become known as the St. Valentine's Day Massacre.

The February 1929 St. Valentine's Day Massacre ended the rivalry between the North Side Irish gang run by George "Bugs" Moran and the South Side Italian gang headed by Al Capone. Even though Moran was late for the meeting and therefore not assassinated, all of his major henchmen were killed. The Irish gang never recovered, and Capone then took over all of the Chicago gang's operations.

The Fullerton Avenue offices of the Chicago, Milwaukee, St. Paul and Pacific railroad were located in a building at the corner of Fullerton and Armitage Avenue. It was a long narrow four-story building made of dirty brown bricks and used for certain freight department activities and a warehouse for railroad records. It was certainly a far cry from the Union Station offices. Tony felt a little sick at the first sight of his new office building after the comparative elegance of Mr. Ennis' offices.

But he found the interior and Mr. Brown's offices to be reasonably decent. Reporting to

Mr. Brown on the first day of his new job, Tony was introduced to the chief clerk and his coworkers. He was assigned a desk alongside the other three members of the new customer service team. There was a phone with a headset and a dictation machine on each desk. The idea of the new service was simple: each morning the group would receive a series of manifest sheets. Each set covered a division of the Milwaukee Road with its connecting line for foreign roads. The manifest showed the location of freight cars of the Milwaukee Road and/or foreign cars which would have a final destination on the Milwaukee division or to be spotted to various Milwaukee yards.

Customers calling the service for information were quickly given their cars' present position, when it should arrive in a given yard, or if it might possibly be lost, or bad ordered. In some serious bad order situations, it would be necessary to transfer the shipment to another car. The most reliable information was required by shippers of perishable goods, such as fruit and vegetables.

Once accustomed to the job, Tony enjoyed the work. Over a period of time, he got to know customers by name, often recognizing their voices on the phone. Dictaphone records of the customer's calls were recorded throughout the day to protect the railroad as well as the customers in case of a claim.

Tony found the job most interesting. He also found several of the girls in the office

interesting. Tony had always believed there was safety in numbers as far as his girlfriends were concerned. The only problem he could foresee was how sad it would be if his steady girlfriends ever got together to compare notes.

Seems Cliff had not been fooling around last New Year's Eve when he announced Betty was pregnant. By the end of February there was no doubt about it, according to the good Dr. Zinn. George, as Cliff's guardian until he became of age, which would be in two years, blew a couple of short fuses when he heard the facts. George laid down the law: "You two are in a mess," he told the very scared young people. "As I see it," he continued, "Betty can tell her folks the truth. Cliff can marry you and have a baby. Or, and I don't like this idea, Betty can have an abortion. In any case, you two are going to get married, and fast. If you're going to play around in the future, you're going to play legal"

"Oh, George," Betty wailed, "I can't tell my folks. They will pull me out of school, and

send me away. They'll never let me marry Cliff, so I guess I'll have to have an abortion. Cliff can't take care of three on his salary!"

Cliff, to his credit, agreed reluctantly with Betty saying, "I guess that's the way it has to be, George."

In those days, pregnancy without benefit of clergy was a disgrace, abortion was even worse, and parents were not very understanding.

However, a couple of days later, Betty had the operation, so no one knew by who or where except George. Fortunately, there were no complications. Betty stayed in the apartment for three days to recuperate, then went back to her music studies. Within a month, they got a one room apartment of their own.

Between Cliff's salary and Betty's allowance, they managed quite well, though her folks took a very dim view of the hasty marriage and Cliff.

With Cliff leaving, Bill Foy became a permanent member of the Anderson entourage at the apartment. Bill still had his insurance sales job, but the drawing account was getting far ahead of the actual sales. Bill also found letting customers win the golf game was not the entire answer to successful selling. Tony and Grover were sure if Bill's performance didn't improve fast, he would shortly be unemployed.

It was the month of May, still a bit chilly at times but Spring was definitely at hand, and like most young men, Tony's thoughts returned to his second great love, cars. Tony had his heart set on a roadster. He started watching the ads, looking in dealers' windows for the right one, at the right price, figuring he could go as high as five hundred bucks and easily handle the payments on his increased salary.

Finally, he found just what he wanted at a local Cadillac dealer on Broadway. It was a beauty, an Oakland roadster, yellow body with dark green fenders, wire wheels, with spare wheels mounted in the front wells and a rumble seat. The price was $500.

Tony went to look the car over and talk to a salesman. The car was a 1928 model and only had 6,000 miles on it. The six-cylinder engine sounded like a purring cat to Tony's ear, and it shouldn't be too hard on gas, which was $0.15 a gallon at the time. Tony got into the car and settled back on the leather seat; this was his kind of car. The salesman, sure he had a live one said, "Well, young fella, shouldn't we be writing up a contract?"

"Maybe," answered Tony, "after I have a test run in it." The salesman readily agreed, and in a few minutes Tony was cruising up and down Broadway. She was fast and handled beautifully. This is it, Tony decided.

When they got back to the agency, the salesman was busy writing up the sales contract.

Looking up as Tony came in, he said, "I can see you've made up your mind about the car. Sit down here and we'll finish up this contract."

"Wait a minute," was Tony's best reply, "you haven't told me what I have put down, and what the payment will be." The salesman answered, "No problem, GM does its own financing. How about $50 down and $22.50 a month," he said. "Okay? Just give me your age, address, and phone number."

Tony gave him the information. The salesman looked a little sick, "You're only 19?" he asked. "Man, you can't sign a contract without a co-signer."

Tony felt a little sick himself, but said "my roommate, George Anderson, is home, I'm

pretty sure he'll co-sign for me. Hold everything until I get him over here. Be back in 20 minutes."

George readily agreed to sign the sales contract for Tony and an hour later they drove the new car back to the apartment.

By right of seniority, Tony decided Ellie should be his first date to break in the new car.

She was thrilled with the new wheels, and they took a long moonlight ride in the country.

Tony and his car were exceedingly popular, especially during the summer months. Trips to the country, the beach, wherever, Tony seldom went out alone anymore. There were more friends than he could handle, though they did help with the gas bill.

The balloon burst in the fall of 1929 when the stock market crashed. Every headline had a few more paper millionaires jumping out of windows. Small and even a few large banks were going down the tubes with disturbing regularity.

None of the occupants of the apartment on Kenmore Avenue where exactly tycoons to begin with, so the stock market had little effect on their everyday lifestyle. Even the bank scare didn't disturb them. Aside from possibly Grover, none of them had more than $20 in any bank.

The first casualty was Awa. His father's brush factory had to retrench so Awa's territory was dropped, and he had to return home to Massachusetts to work in the plant.

Bill Foy was the first to be unemployed. Bill just hadn't cut the mustard in the insurance

field. Bill himself said if all his active insureds dropped dead at once, the company would hardly notice. His golf game hadn't improved either. Bill stayed on at the apartment as no one wanted to lose his smiling good humor. And there was always the possibility he would find some kind of job.

George's job at the news service was the safest at the time, as husbands, wives, and gangsters were still busy killing one another. Sundry scandals in Hollywood, the political shenanigans of Big Bill Thompson, and the City Hall gang kept reporters and photographers busy supplying fodder for the yellow tabloids of Randolph Hearst.

No one knew where Grover worked, as he was very closed mouthed about his job, but he certainly, didn't seem worried about losing it.

Tony heard all sorts of rumors and one fact at the railroad office. The fact was the

Milwaukee Road was back in receivership which it had just gotten out of the year before. Rumors flew that unless the economy improved fast, many heads would roll. This behooved all employees to knuckle down to business and look as important as possible in their particular jobs, in case they should be among the chosen ones when the axe fell.

Quite possibly, each of the unmarried and carefree young men of Tony's group had some reservation about a rosy future, but the optimism of youth prevailed. About the only concessions they made to the uncertainty of the time was to cut down on the parties and liquor bills.

Throughout the remaining months of 1929 and the winter of 1930, life went on as usual for the group. The only slightly disturbing factor was Bill couldn't seem to get a job with any degree of permanency. But he managed to keep afloat with part time employment of various sorts.

By the spring of 1930, there was little doubt the cutbacks had begun in earnest as those with marginal jobs and those with little seniority in the railroad offices were being let go. Ellie and her roommate were among the people in Mr. Ennis' office who were terminated. The girls had to give up their apartment and move in with relatives.

Ellie moved to the Southside to live with an aunt, so Tony's dates with her would be lessened considerably.

July 1930 proved to be the month of the disaster. The dreaded pink slips with final checks were passed out to over five hundred employees of the railroad. Tony was among the unfortunate recipients.

Tony couldn't believe it had really happened. Mr. Brown called those of his department into his office to receive the bad news. He was sure it wouldn't be too long before they would all be called back, but most of them knew it would be a long time. All types of businesses in the city and in the country, for that matter, were either failing or about to. Tony and two other men were asked to stay for a few minutes after the others left Mr. Brown's office.

Mr. Brown said, "Men, you three are the newest employees in this department with the least seniority: therefore, I'm forced to let you go. But because I picked you people for the customer service team and took you from other departments, I certainly owe you as much consideration as possible. Now, I can keep you three on for another month doing special jobs for this department. While you are actually no longer employees of the Road, I have funds to pay you in cash during the next month."

There were smiles of relief from all three; At least they'd have something coming in for a short while. They all thanked him for the extra job they would have to start on Monday, then got up to leave.

"Just a minute men," Mr. Brown said, to their chairs, "all three of you have some seniority in the departments you left to come here. Now you are entitled to go back to your old office and request your previous job back. This is called "Bumping." You will keep the job until someone with more seniority bumps you."

Mr. Brown continued, "In fact, before this damned depression is over, I'm liable to be bumped back to a yard supervisor."

A very sober and thoughtful Tony drove home slowly this Saturday afternoon. Through, he had another month before he was unemployed, but after that, what? He thought about what Mr. Brown had said about bumping for his old office clerk job, but he also remembered the guy who now had the job was married and had a baby. Tony decided his situation would have to be pretty desperate before he would consider bumping another guy out of his job.

There wasn't much sense in telling his buddies the bad news for another month. Besides, he could get lucky, get another steady job, and work harder looking for nightclub stints. He was beginning to feel better already and looking forward to his date with the lovely Gladys.

On Monday morning, Tony reported to Mr. Brown and began the temporary job. He was assigned a desk, given pencils, a comptometer, a slide rule, and a map of the Milwaukee division of the railroad. It was explained his job was to figure out per diem costs for operating freight trains on the divisions assigned to him. It seemed the railroad bigwigs needed this information to affect expensive cuts and operating costs.

Tony knew he was in trouble right at the start. He began to wish he'd paid more attention to his fifth-grade math teacher. What might well have been a simple problem for an Einstein would prove to be a sizable headache for Tony and the railroad. Simply as possible, figuring per diem costs meant taking a given freight train, say fifty loaded cars and an engine, and crew from Chicago to Milwaukee. One had to figure the cost of coal, water and crew per mile, for the run. Also, to be included would be the cost of deadheading any empty cars on the same train, and the return run Chicago.

Each man assigned this task had several schedules to figure out and return in his reports at the end of the week. Being left handed made using a comptometer a problem and its proper use proved to be an unfathomable mystery to Tony, as his final reports for the week clearly showed. For a guy who had trouble getting two plus two to always come out to four, this is no job for Tony.

Tony faced a very unhappy Mr. Brown on Monday morning. Looking at Tony's report, Mr. Brown posed a question. "Tell me in your own words Tony, how you managed to figure running a freight train with a load of goods worth perhaps $25,000 to Milwaukee could cost us half a million dollars?"

Tony started to speak as Mr. Brown held up his hand. He continued, "And that kind of money didn't even get the damn train back to Chicago."

"Well Sir," answered Tony hopelessly, "I guess I must've let this slide rule slide too much."

Mr. Brown replied, "Tony unless I take you off this per diem job, the whole railroad will be a total loss in two weeks."

"I can't say I blame you Mr. Brown," Tony answered. "I'm sorry about messing up the job. I guess that's it for me," and got up to leave.

"Sit down son," Mr. Brown said with a smile. "I'll find something for you to do. I promised you a month's work and you'll get it."

The next three weeks, Tony spent tracing lost cars. Mr. Brown figured they couldn't suffer any more losses even if Tony were looking for them. With some luck he might even find a few.

The late summer months didn't offer much in the way of small nightclubs. Working lodges and dinner affairs wouldn't start until fall, providing some of the organizations still had enough money to afford entertainment. With only two week's salary in hand, plus what he earned for the month of August, Tony was really counting pennies. He realized the fun and games were over. Future dates would be held to coffee and doughnuts at the apartment rather than gin fests and fancy snacks.

By September Tony was scanning the want ads, willing to take any kind of job. There were very few that offered any salary. Most offered the opportunity to make all kinds of money but on commission only. All you had to do was become one hell of a salesman. Tony's first try at a sales job was with a famous name sewing team, selling door to door.

After a few days training, Tony was sent out with their top salesman who would break him in. Bob Faller was a fast talking, natty dresser with shifty eyes, who had the reputation of seldom losing the sale once in the prospect's house. The first day out Bob told Tony, "You let me do all the talking. I'll introduce you as my assistant, and you do everything I tell you. I'll show you how to sell this damn machine."

Tony answered, "Okay Bob, you're the boss."

They were working a middle-class neighborhood of neat houses on the Northwest side of Chicago. At the first few houses, they got a cold reception. This didn't seem to bother Bob. As he explained, "you have to play the law of averages."

The eighth door they knocked on was opened by a motherly lady in her sixties. Introducing himself and Tony with all the charm of a Baptist preacher at a pancake supper, he then asked, "Madame, do you have a sewing machine?"

"Why yes, I do," she answered. "Well now, this is your lucky day, " exclaimed Bob, getting one foot in the partially open door.

He continued, "For today only, I'm authorized to check your old machine free of charge. Why don't I just come in and check yours. Any adjustments I make are also free."

"Oh, that would be nice. Come in," she said, opening the door the rest of the way.

Stepping into the small hallway, Bob saw a religious picture on the hall wall. "Just look at that," he said, crossing himself, "this is truly a Christian home." Tony couldn't believe what he'd heard, but the lady did. "My, my." she smiled, "it's so nice to meet God fearing young men. My machine is upstairs," she said leading the way.

The old machine, covered with a dust cloth, was in the corner of a small bedroom. Whipping off the cloth, Bob exclaimed "Now, this is a real beauty." It was a 1892 model with a cast iron frame and a foot treadle.

Turning to the lady Bob said, "Why don't you go downstairs to the living room. My assistant and I will bring the machine down so I can give it a good look. She answered, "Very well, I'll just go down and make us some tea. Please be careful. This was my grandmother's machine," she cautioned and left the room.

Bob rolled the ancient machine to the doorway of the bedroom. "Look, I think we've got a sale here," he whispered to Tony. "Here's how we work this. You carry the front-end downstairs. When I say, "careful' you drop the damn thing, got it?"

Tony got it but doubted he'd do it right. No wonder this guy is such a hotshot salesman. He'll do anything for a sale. Bob interrupted his thoughts, "Hey, you ready?" He whispered again, "Let's go." Tony picked up his end of the machine. At about the third step Bob hollered, "careful" but Tony didn't let go.

"Drop it," hissed Bob, jerking the machine from Tony's grasp.

Leaping to one side of the stairs to avoid being run over, Tony let the 1892 machine go crashing down the stairs, and land in a crumpled heap of ironwork and wood in the living room. At the sound of the crash, a horrified Mrs. Watson ran in from the kitchen, spilling her tea along the way, to see the remains of her grandmother's machine.

As a tearful Mrs. Watson slumped into her favorite rocking chair, Bob heaped a tirade of abuse on Tony's head. "Of all the dumb clowns I've ever worked with, you're the worst. Just look at what you've done to Mrs. Watson's machine."

Tony couldn't believe this guy, and was about to lay hands on him, but then thought better of it. He just had to see how this good Christian peddler was going to dry Mrs. Watson tears after busting up her machine, and then sell her a new one to boot.

Tony listened in awe, and with some admiration at the guts of this character as he went to work on Mrs. Watson. Pulling out his handkerchief, he knelt in front of Mrs. Watson. Dabbing the tears on her cheeks "Dear Mrs. Watson," Bob said soothingly, "I'm so sorry this has happened, but don't cry anymore. I can't fix your old machine, but I can help you get a new one."

Tony could've sworn Bob had tears in his eyes, as he looked up sadly at Mrs. Watson. Cecil B. DeMille would love this guy, Tony thought.

Bob went on, "You see Mrs. Watson, because this accident was our fault, the company will reimburse you. The company will give you $25 for your old machine." Then pausing to take out his order book, he continued, "I'll just write this up, then we'll send you a nice new machine, and you'll send the company $3 a week, okay?" Scribbling he added, "now, I'm going to take your old machine back to the shop. Maybe, just maybe, we can fix it. If so, it won't cost you a dime. Please sign right here,"

Mrs. Watson stared through red rimmed eyes at the order form Bob thrust into her hand. All she saw was $25 allowance and three dollars per week. The actual cost of the new machine wasn't there, but it sure as hell would be on the contract she would receive in the mail. Hesitantly taking Bob's pre-offered pen, she signed the order form.

"There you are, dear lady," said a smiling Bob. "Now don't you feel a whole lot better?"

Gathering up the pieces of Mrs. Watson once proud machine and dumping them in the back of Bob's car, all Bob wanted to do now was wish Mrs. Watson a pleasant day and get the hell out of there. Stopping at a restaurant for coffee, Bob said, "You've been real quiet since we almost loused up my sale back there. What's biting you?"

Tony answered with a question of his own, "Tell me Bob, is that the way you make all your sales?" "Na," he replied, "I only use drastic methods when I have to. That old gal never would've bought the machine any other way, probably couldn't have afford it but now she's hooked."

Tony said heatedly, "Bob, to take an old lady like that, you've got to be the crookedest, most conniving salesman I've ever met." "Yeah," replied Bob. "You'll learn that in door-to-door selling, you've got to use every trick in the book or you ain't going to eat regular."

"How about the company," asked Tony, "do they go along with your dirty tricks?" Bob said, "look Buster, all they care about is selling their damn machines. They don't give a damn how I do it, just so I get the orders." He continued, "Anyhow, how often do you think anyone buys a sewing machine? Once I got an order, I never see them again."

Tony thought about Bob's remarks for a moment, then said, "Look, you can drop me off anywhere I can get a streetcar. Tell the sales manager that I ain't hungry enough to be a good salesman like you." A few minutes later, Tony stepped out of the car, leaving old hotshot Bob shaking his head.

CHAPTER 8

THE HEALTHMOOR SANITARY SYSTEM

Within a day or two after ending his short career as a sewing machine salesman, Tony again looked over the want ads. One ad which piqued his curiosity read,"MEN This is your chance to make big money in the worst of times. We need aggressive, reliant salesman to introduce the new Healthmoor Sanitary System to a waiting public. Generous compensation to the right man." After reading the ad a few times, Tony still had no idea what a Healthmoor Sanitary System was, but he wanted to find out.

The Healthmoor offices were located in a very respectable address on Wacker Drive near Wells Street. Several men were waiting to be interviewed when Tony arrived. When Tony's turn came to be interviewed, he was asked a couple of pertinent questions, such as his last employment and had he ever been a salesman. He evidently gave the right answers and looked like a potentially good salesman because the sales manager said he was just the type they were looking for. No mention was made of what he would sell or where. He was simply told he was hired and to report back at 8:00 AM sharp on Monday for sales training classes which would last for three days.

On Monday morning, Tony was greeted like a long-lost son by the sales manager who, over coffee and donuts, introduced him and two other new trainees to their team captain, an older man would conduct the training classes. A few minutes later, the new men were escorted into a private office where they were about to learn what they were supposed to sell and how to do it. The training manager, Mr. Johnson, first explained there were two teams, red and blue, and how lucky they were to have been chosen for the blue team which was currently breaking all sales records.

"Now gentlemen," said Mr. Johnson. "I'm going to introduce you to our marvelous sanitary system." With that he extracted from an oblong box what looked like a fairly large electric motor with a shining chrome casing and a short pipe-like extension on the back. "This," he announced, "is the heart of our sanitary system." Then attaching a round canister to the front of the unit, he flipped the switch, and the machine came alive with a roar, filling the room with the odor of chlorine. "This vapor will kill all sorts of germs and prevent cold and hay fever. In fact, if we had had it in 1918, there would not have been a flu epidemic." Tony believed him for it felt like his sinuses had been burned to a crisp.

Grabbing another canister from the box, Mr. Johnson took off the chlorine gadget, attached a second unit and turned on the machine. "Here we have the answer to moths and other household pests," he announced, as the room became saturated with the odor of mothballs. "Using the sanitary system in all closets, on upholstered furniture, and under rugs, will eliminate any more problems.".

The new men gagged a bit on the mothball fumes but were fascinated as Mr. Johnson again invaded the oversized Pandora's box, this time coming up with a small handle which was attached to the top of the machine. He wasn't through though, for next out of the box came a wide mouth unit which he clamped to the front of the machine. Then noting the small bag on the back "Why it's a damn vacuum cleaner!" Tony blurred out as the others stared at the transformation.

Mr. Johnson blared at Tony, "This is a sanitary system, and you'd better remember that young man." Tony felt severely rebuked and decided to keep his mouth shut for a while at least. Mr. Johnson continued, "We now have converted our system so the housewife may easily clean mattresses, furniture, closet shelves etc."

Removing the small bag and handle, he again rummaged in the box, this time coming up with a chromium wand and a large bag. Attaching these units, he hooked the electric cord to the handle. "Damn it", thought Tony, "it's got to be a vacuum cleaner now, but he said nothing.

Mr. Johnson, however, confirmed his mission, but in different terms as he said "Gentlemen, you now see the most well-designed rug sanitizer on the American market today."

Tony began to get the idea. Under no circumstances is the salesman to let the housewife know she was about to get stuck with a common vacuum cleaner, but rather about to purchase, of her own free will, the world's foremost home sanitary system.

Mr. Johnson was once more fishing in the inexhaustible box, coming up with a flexible hose, two funny looking nozzles, a couple of brushes, plus what he called a body massager. This gadget was flared around a flexible rubber unit with a fair-sized hole in the center.

By noon, Mr. Johnson had demonstrated all of the accessories. He then advised that for the afternoon and the next two days, they would practice a prepared sales pitch and complete demonstrations on each other until they were letter perfect. As he finished, Mr. Wilson, their blue team captain, came in and announced the lunch for today was on him.

During lunch he told them about the great opportunity they had to make real money, and how their top salesmen were living in luxury because of the Healthmoor system. He went on to say because of their newspaper ads, women all over Chicago were begging to have a salesman call, and how some women would literally steal to have this great system in their home.

"Just how do we get paid" asked Tony.

"Oh," answered Mr. Wilson, "Hasn't that been explained to you men yet?" He continued, as the men listen attentively, "You get a most generous commission on sales. The system itself is $65 and your commission is $22.50 for each sale. Men like you should be making $300 a week in no time at all."

This sounded a bit far-fetched to Tony, seeing the demonstration would take at least two hours. This was providing you got into the home and was able to convince the poor woman to sit through it. But he conceded the commission did sound fair enough. After lunch they went back to selling each other the system.

Tony marveled at how the dirty words 'vacuum cleaner', were never used at Healthmoor. Other greats like Electrolux had vacuum cleaners, but not Healthmoor. They had a System and that was gospel.

Finally, the training was over. Tony, who had a good memory and a fair gift of gab, felt ready to win over any reluctant housewife he met.

The 8:00 AM sales meetings were a must at Healthmoor. Tony attended his first one, and found it was a cross between a pitchman's convention and a Baptist revival meeting. Mr. Morris, the sales manager, open the meeting with a rousing speech.

"Is everybody happy this morning?" he asked. A chorus of "yes sir's" rattled the picture on the back wall.

"Do we love our system?" he roared. "Like a mother," the leather-bound salesmen roared back.

"Well now," he went on, lowering his voice to a conversational pitch, "We all know we have to be happy and love our product, right?"

A chorus of "Yeahs" greeted those words of wisdom. Tony wouldn't have been surprised if the response had been" amen."

Mr. Morris' voice suddenly took on a pleading tone as he continued, "Gentlemen, I'm not asking you to break your back for the Healthmoor Company. I'm asking you to sell this system for your own wives and children, for your own sake, and for the sake of those poor housewives struggling through life with a broom, mop, or a broken down vacuum cleaner! Am I right?"

"Right," they yelled with a religious fervor that shook the walls.

Mr. Morrison's voice changed back to an evangelical shout as he extorted "Now, I want

to see smiles and hear laughter, as you are about to hit the streets of this great city searching for those unfortunate women who don't have our wonderful sanitary system. Demonstrate the system right and they'll find the money. And don't you dare come back here without orders. Your wives and children will lose faith in you and so will I. Now let me hear laughter as you go."

A lot of backslapping and belly laughs echoed through the room as the troops filed out.

Tony noted some faces weren't exactly excited and the laughter sounded a bit hollow here and there. But he had to admit Brother Morris put on a good show.

Picking up his demonstration machine, Tony went down to his car to find he'd been given a ticket for illegal parking. What a way to start the day. He considered going back to ask Mr. Morris to get him laughing again.

Tony had the North Side residential area to start. He must have looked like a vacuum cleaner salesman, though he never mentioned the word. In any case, the rejection percentage was pretty high. By 3:00 PM Tony remembered Johnson had cautioned them about making calls too late in the day as husband were likely to be home. Husbands, he said, had a definite aversion to door-to-door salesman, and vacuum cleaner salesmen in particular.

Finally, a lady let him into her small house. He was sure she didn't understand what a sanitary system was, for the house looked as though sanitation was an unknown word.

Opening his carton, Tony extracted the motor unit and was about to go into his pitch when the woman peaked into the box, "why, that there's a damn vacuum cleaner!"

"Yes um," replied a cowed Tony, forgetting all the sales rules.

"Well, you can just get out of here with that thing. I don't need no vacuum cleaner!" she bellowed.

Tony finally gathered up enough courage to say, "I don't quite agree with you ma'am, but I'll leave."

Back in the car, Tony reviewed his day: parking ticket, a lot of calls, and no sales. He doubted Mr. Morris would get a laugh out him tomorrow. He'd have to be a lot funnier than he was this morning.

The second day's sales meeting went much like the first. Everybody was happy, or at least said they were and the sales litany of the day before was repeated with reasonable gusto. Eventually the sales manager gathered some reservations about just how happy his troops really were. After the cheers for good old Healthmoor died down, the manager moved a table to center stage. On it were three luscious looking blueberry pies topped with cream. There were napkins, but no forks. The pies had been cut into quarters. It began to look as though there was only pie for those salesmen who had made sales the day before. That wasn't the idea, however. Mr. Morris was smiling ear to ear as he announced there was going to be a pie eating contest.

"For this contest," he said, "partial dentures are out. Only those with complete uppers and lowers can compete. Now, eligible men, get up here.

Tony looked around the room as did the other younger men. He couldn't believe any of the older men would volunteer, but he was wrong. Five older men went up front and turning their backs, dropped their false teeth into handkerchiefs.

Tony decided this was indeed true loyalty to the Healthmoor system, and far beyond the call of duty. Even if he had them, he wouldn't take them out in public if Jehovah himself were to give the command. Either these guys really needed their jobs, or they absolutely loved Healthmoor.

The five sunken face men were ready. They didn't dare laugh or smile, as the results would've been too horrible.

"Ready now," bellowed Mr. Morris, as each man was handed two pieces of pie, each on a small paper plate. "On the count of three, go. The first one to finish both pieces of pie wins!"

Wins! What, Tony wondered, was winning? was it the everlasting ridicule of his fellow salesman?

"One, two, three, go!" yelled Mr. Morris.

Blueberries and whipped cream flew in all directions. With a great gnashing of gums, the five attacked the pies. They had pie in their eyes, hair and all over each other.

"The winner!" yelled Mr. Morris, holding up the hand of No. four as laughter and applause rang out.

While taking his bows, Tony noticed the winner only had one paper plate. In his zeal for dear old Healthmoor, he must've eaten the other paper plate along with the pie. Tony hoped he was blessed with good digestion.

"Now men", extorted Mr. Morris, as the five contestants headed for the washroom to repair the damage. "I want you all to go out and show the same determination our contest winner did. Go, be happy, and bring in the orders." Mr. Morris retreated to his office with the cheers of the happy men of Healthmoor ringing in his ears.

Tony's next three days on the street were no better than his first. All he heard were sad stories from dejected women. Husbands out of work no money coming in, and most of them were true. The next few sales meetings weren't nearly as much fun, and he certainly wasn't happy. So one morning after the sales meeting, he sought advice from the team captain, Mr. Wilson.

"Mr. Wilson," Tony began, "I'm not getting anywhere, I'm making a lot of calls, but I'm not getting into the houses to demonstrate the system. I think I need some help. Besides no sales, I got a parking ticket last week."

A sympathetic Mr. Wilson replied "You sure do need help. First give me your ticket. I think I can get that fixed." He continued, "Now, come with me, I want you to meet our top salesman, Jack Hartman. Tony followed Wilson into the main office.

"Jack," asked Mr. Wilson, "do you think you could take Tony with you today, and show him how you get into a home and how you demonstrate the system?" Jack answered, "sure, anytime."

Then turning to Tony asked, "Aren't you the guy who drives the yellow Oakland roadster?"

"Yeah, that's my car," replied Tony.

"Boy, I love that car; I'll take you out today if we can use your car." Jack said.

Tony grinned, "It's a deal. Teach me how to sell the machine and you can drive it all day."

They got into Tony's car, Jack at the wheel. He headed south on Wells Street, then turned west on Madison. Tony kept quiet while Jack got used to the car. He was acting like a kid with his first toy.

"Where are we headed?" Tony finally asked.

"Oh, out to the far west side." Jack answered, then said, "See, I don't make cold turkey calls if I can help it. Every night, I make a bunch of phone calls to a good neighbor and try to set up appointments. If I'm lucky and get three or four demonstrations set up, I usually sell at least one of them."

Tony agreed. "That makes sense. I'm learning something already."

"Yeah, and it saves time. Right now, we're going to make a demonstration I set up by phone last night. I'll do the demonstration; you hand me accessories when I ask for them."

Jack guided the car into a really nice area of fair sized homes, stopping in front of a pretty Dutch Colonial. It was a really hot day for September, so they had the top down and the system box in the rumble seat. Jack went up to the door and rang the doorbell. The door was answered by a very pretty young lady about twenty-five years old with the figure of a chorus girl.

"Are you Mrs. Larson?" Jack asked, then continued, "I spoke with you last night on the phone about our sanitary system, remember?"

She smiled, "oh yes, come in."

A light breeze molded the summer dress about her beautiful body, outlining every curve. Tony surmised she wasn't wearing much, if anything. under the dress. They went into an immaculate living room.

"What a lovely home you have here." exclaimed Jack. "Just look at this room, Tony, isn't it beautiful?"

"It certainly is," agreed Tony.

"Now" said Jack, "why don't you get real comfortable in this easy chair, while Tony and I show you our system." With the gallantry of a knight of old, Jack smiled and escorted her to a big chair.

"Tony, if you will hand me the sanitizing unit and plug in the cord, we'll get started."

Jack was a master. He made no unnecessary moves and, everything was done with precision and accompanied by a pleasant voice and smile while he demonstrated and explained the workings of the Healthmoor system. He even elicited a number of oohs and ahs from Mrs. Larson. In fact, she seemed to agree with every point he made, not even objecting when he dumped a bag of flour and cornmeal on the floor to demonstrate the awesome suction power of the machine.

Tony handled his part with skill, whipping out accessories with the precision of an operating room nurse. All had gone well up to now. Tony was sure she couldn't wait to get her hands on the marvelous piece of equipment. Jack then said to the gorgeous Mrs. Larson, "Now, so far we have shown you what the system will do for your lovely home, but it will also help you stay healthy and beautiful."

"Hand me the massager, Tony." he instructed.

Tony dived into the miracle box, found the odd-looking gadget, and handed it to Jack. Moving around to the back of Mrs. Larson's chair, Jack connected the massage unit to the hose.

"Okay Tony, turn it on," he said.

"Just relax and enjoy this," he told Mrs. Larson, moving the vibrator over her short curls, "doesn't this feel good?"

"Oh yes," she giggled.

Jack then slowly moved the massager down the back of her neck and back, next up and across her shoulders, while Mrs. Larson let out peels of perilous laughter. Then disaster struck when Jack moved the massager over her shoulders and across her chest. At this maneuver she stood straight up. Jack lost control and one beautiful breast went 'swoop' into the massager. At once the laughter died as the beautiful brown eyes looked down at the trapped breast. Her lips trembled for a moment, then emitted a scream which rattled the windows.

"Turn the damn thing off!" yelled Jack, tugging at the massager.

When Tony yanked the plug out of the socket, there was a flop sound like a cow pulling its foot out of the mud, as the wayward massager released its hold on the lovely mound of flesh.

Tony was sure Mrs. Larson felt much like Cleopatra when the asp bit her. While Jack tried his best to soothe the distraught Mrs. Larson, Tony was busy throwing the scattered parts of the system into its box. Tony picked up the box and ran to the car. Tony threw the box into the back and started the car as curious neighbors began gathering. Looking back Tony saw a no longer suave and debonair Jack come flying out of the house, followed by a very mad Mrs. Larson. She was beating him over the head with the stainless-steel handle of the machine.

Tony muttered, "Damn, I knew I forgot something."

She caught poor Jack with two solid blows to the head. "Don't you ever come back here", yelled the wild eyed, but still beautiful Mrs. Larson. Another well-placed blow caught Jack in the middle of his flying leap into the front seat; he cleared the closed door by a foot.

Tony jammed the car into gear and took off with a roar.

The rearview mirror showed an irate Mrs. Larson still brandishing the handle of the unsold Healthmoor sanitary system. As they headed for safer parts, a shaking Jack was nursing the lumps on his head.

"Want to go back for the handle?" Tony couldn't resist asking.

"Hell no!" Jack answered blaring at Tony, "you know damn well where she'd put it if she got another chance."

A few minutes later, they found sanctuary in the rear booth of a cafe and calmer nerves after two cups of coffee.

I won't forget the look on Mrs. Larson face if I live to be hundred." Tony said, laughing at the memory. "You'll never live that long if you ever mention this at the office." Jack scowled..

Tony answered with a grin, "Hell, I've got the great Jack Hartman to blackmail for life."

Jack said, "Seriously Tony, I'd be ruined if this story ever got out. Come to think of it, I may be ruined anyhow if that gal decides to sue the company."

Tony answered, "I don't think she'll do that. She was plenty mad, but I'm sure she wouldn't want to tell anyone, including her husband, what really happened. Besides, it was an accident, wasn't it?"

"Of course, it was." Jack said. "I don't louse up a sure sale just for laughs. Now let's go sell a damn machine." And that they did on the very next call.

The following morning, Mr. Wilson was looking for them. "Well, he asked, how did you two make out? Did Jack show you how to demonstrate our machine?"

Tony answered, "Mr. Wilson, I saw the greatest demonstration anyone's ever seen. I'll never forget it. This guy Jack is a killer; those women don't have a chance with him."

After their disastrous team venture, Tony and Jack became friends. In spite of what happened, Jack was one hell of a salesman and Tony learned a lot about door to door selling from him. By the second week, Tony had sold a few machines by following Jack's method of setting up appointments, and more importantly, by working in better class neighborhoods where people still had jobs and money.

After another two weeks Tony took a tour of the large summer homes in the Round Lake area and did even better. He wasn't doing too badly with the housewife's dream machine and could even laugh some at the terrible jokes of Mr. Morris, the guiding light of Healthmoor.

By October 1930, the depression was really showing its teeth. More and more people were out of jobs. Many were losing their homes to foreclosure, and their savings had folded with the banks. World War I veterans could be seen on most every corner in downtown Chicago selling apples for a nickel. Herbert Hoover was beginning to wish he'd never tackled the President's job; he was being blamed for everybody's troubles. Businesses were failing at an alarming rate. The Government slogan "Prosperity: Just Around the Corner," fell on unbelieving ears, and soup kitchens were set up to feed the more desperate people.

No one at the apartment on Kenmore was laughing much either. It began to look as though they would have to split up and find less expensive quarters. Bill Foy eased the burden somewhat by going to live with his folks. George, Tony, and Grover agreed to stick it out through October since the rent was already paid for that month.

Grover and George had taken a cut in salary, while Tony's sales future looked none too bright at the moment as people found more important things to buy than vacuum cleaners. The small clubs where Tony had some chance of getting Saturday night entertainment jobs were also closing up fast.

Tony returned to the apartment one afternoon to find a welcome visitor, Ellie. She had gotten a job as secretary to the minister of a large church on the south side.

"Let's go out and get a steak," said Ellie. "That would be great Ellie," answered Tony "only problem is, I'm broke."

"Come on, I'm working. The steak's on me. You can pay your share another way." She laughed.

Both ideas appeal to Tony, and they headed for a steakhouse on Broadway.

Following their steaks, they chatted for a while before going back to the apartment. When they did get back, they found Bill Foy was visiting with a girlfriend, and Grover had also brought a friend over, along with some gin. Seems like they all felt one last fling was in order. Ellie and Tony joined in, but it certainly didn't look as though they were going to have much privacy. About 10:00 PM Ellie was ready to go home; it would take an hour to drive to the South side where Ellie lived with her aunt and uncle who had fixed up a little apartment for her on the second floor of their house.

Driving away that night, Tony didn't know this would be the last time he would ever see Ellie. He called about two weeks later for a date, but she gently turned him down. She had joined the church and was teaching Sunday school. As she put it, she wanted to start a new life and perhaps get married again. In his own way, Tony did love Ellie but with no job to speak of marriage with anyone was out of the question. Wishing Ellie the best of everything for the future, Tony hung up the phone.

With prospects for the Healthmoor Sanitary System becoming fewer and fewer, and the winter months approaching, Tony decided he would have to find something which didn't require his car. So back to the want ads. This time he applied for a job with a firm offering a hot real estate deal. It turned out to be an almost legitimate swindle, if such as possible. The deal offered free city lots in the boondocks of Lombard, Illinois, about thirty miles west of the city, to a chosen few which turned out to be half the population of Chicago.

The real estate deal required a three-pronged sales effort. During the day, a crew of women covered a given neighborhood and passed out coupons to housewives who filled them out with name, address, etc. The saleswomen returned a carbon copy of the coupon to the office as a lead.

Starting at 4:00 in the afternoon, a sales crew of men went back to the same area to explain the deal to both husband and wife and tried to get them to take an option on the free lot. A payment of $5 or $10 was required if they signed for the option. This fee was the salesman's commission. After securing the signed option, the salesman would set up an appointment with the couple and be taken out to Lombard in a company car to see the free lot. If they didn't like the lot, they could get their option money back, but they seldom did. The company picked them up in a chauffeured Cadillac, Pierce Arrow, or Packard limousine, escorted by a high-pressure salesman who seldom missed a sale. They were shown an unimproved lot in a poor location of the tract and on wet days, they might need a boat get to the lot. The free lot is supposed to be worth $500. However, the salesman would just happen to have a few choice lots on improved property which he could let the parties have for $1,000 to $1,500, with an allowance of the $500 for the free lot they had turned down. It was amazing to Tony how many people went for this deal knowing it would be years before they could hope to build or even sell the lot. A good many would lose the down payment of $150 to $300 because they couldn't pay off the balance. Some of the lots were probably sold four or five times.

Each afternoon, Tony would leave the downtown office with five or ten coupons. The first two evenings he had no luck at all. On the third, he hit pay dirt, signing up a couple and collecting a $10 option fee. With barely enough carfare to cover the first three days, Tony had been skipping dinner at night. By the third night, he had never been hungrier in his. Holding tight to the $10, he grabbed a streetcar for downtown You could get off at Madison and Canal Streets and walk over to the L station for a train going north.

It was 10:00 PM when Tony got off the streetcar in front of a greasy looking café that catered to day laborers and the derelicts of West Madison Street. With his stomach rumbling like a pipe organ, he had to eat and now! A big platter of beef stew, a large, sweet roll and coffee cost him a total of $0.40. Food had never tasted as good. The two reeking derelicts who passed out at the table in front of him had no effect on his appetite.

The end of October was fast approaching when the boys would have to give up the apartment which had been their home for a year and a half. Grover had decided to take a room with his brother; George found a so-called one-room apartment on Sedgewick Street near North Avenue where he and Tony would hold up for a while. Twice Tony called the dealer where he bought his beloved roadster, advising them he could no longer meet the payments. In fact, he was already two months behind. Evidently, they were having cars returned every day and couldn't care less about his calls. It was another week before they towed it way. Tony felt sick watching it go, wondering when or if he would ever have another car like it.

When Tony first saw his new home at the end of October, he was really sick. The apartment, one large room with a bath, was on the ground floor of an old townhouse built in 1885, a time when this area of the near North Side was inhabited by the rich and mighty of old Chicago. For many years now, it had been a German neighborhood. The room was furnished with an old brass bed and a couple of well-worn chairs. The kitchen area consisted of a small cupboard, a two-burner gas plate, but no refrigerator. Tony decided George would have one hell of a time cooking gourmet meals with this sad equipment. Hamburgers and eggs would be more like it, and about all they could afford. They had indeed fallen on evil times.

Tony managed to stay afloat through the first two weeks of November with the real estate rip-offs, but it was getting too cold for him to prowl half the night. Besides, no one was willing to go to look at snow-covered lots, even in a Cadillac limousine. Tony decided to find something to pedal an apartment building and offices; at least he wouldn't freeze to death.

The answer proved to be Shaughnessy Silk Hose and Lingerie Company. Armed with an unattractive sales case containing sample silk hose, lingerie, and other unmentionables, Tony set out to snare young and old customers alike with his bag of goodies. At first, he felt a bit self-conscious discussing the advantages of the hose and lingerie with strange women, but soon got over it, since most of them seemed to enjoy it.

On one occasion, he became the recipient of one lovely ladies' anger at her wayward husband. He knocked on the door of an attractive home. The door opened quickly, and something very gooey was pushed in his face. It was a box full of chocolate creams. He looked like the end man in a minstrel show. The gift was given with a "Take that you misbegotten bastard!"

Wiping the mess from his face, Tony said, "You sure don't like salesmen much."

The pretty lady's s face went from rage to consternation. "Oh, I'm so sorry," she exclaimed, "Come in and let me clean you up."

"Is it safe?" Tony asked through the chocolate mask. His friendly grin must've been horrible to see.

Tony followed her into the bathroom, took off his coat and tie, and for the first time in years, had his face and ears washed by feminine hands. While she administered to him, he explained why his face has gotten in such a mess.

"My no-good philandering husband came home late last night with flowers and this damn box of cheap candy. This morning," she went on, "I found theatre ticket stubs and a bra belonging to his blonde secretary in his coat pocket. We had a good row before he left. When you knocked, I thought he was coming back for something, so I decided to give back the candy."

Tony laughed as she dried his ears, "It wasn't such bad candy, but a little much at one time."

The closeness of her warm and attractive body was getting to Tony; he'd better be about what he came for, as in getting a sale. Besides, she seemed to be enjoying the close contact in the bathroom. Tony decided he didn't want to be shot by an irate husband, and this one might just decide to come back to make amends with his wife.

Showing his wares in the living room and explaining he only had samples, and any goods she ordered would be sent parcel post, Tony was sure she would order something, and she did. Three pair of the most expensive stockings, two pair of silk panties, and a black negligee. She gave him the required 20% advance payment, which would be his commission, then said, "Give me your phone number. I'll call you when the order comes.

"I'll expect you to come back to make sure everything fits." The smile and suggestive look he got with her instructions was an invitation to more than a fitting of unmentionables.

Tony, "Lady, you can count on my coming back, and thanks for the candy." Then laughing, gave her a teasing pat as he started out the door.

Tony's prospects for the hose and lingerie lines were everywhere, even the waitresses in restaurants. While the commissions weren't that great, prospects were easy to come by. It was a good line for cold weather; one could spend a day in some large apartment buildings and there were no idiotic sales meetings. Tony only went into the office once a week for fresh samples as he mailed orders directly to the plant.

Over the next few weeks, Tony learned a lot more about door to door selling. He was amazed at the personal things women would tell a salesman that they wouldn't mention to relatives or friends. It could be anything from Aunt Minnie's moles to what lousy bed partners their husbands were. Listening to the lurid details of operations also took a good deal of his sales time, and he was usually invited to inspect scars, regardless of the location. Tony figured if he took advantage of all the invitations he got to bed down, he'd be walking on crutches three days a week.

Early November brought snow, cold winds, and Cabbage Willington to Chicago. The miserable weather was to be expected, Cabbage was not. But Tony should've known he was liable to pop up anywhere, at any time. Cabbage, George, and Oscar Olsen had all been at Avondale in the early years of the school when Tony's dad was the bandmaster.

Willington's weird nickname, "Cabbage", was given to him by the boys because his favorite answer when asked to repeat anything was "I don't chew my cabbage twice." And you didn't ask Willington the same question twice or you would get two completely different answers, both of them likely to be big fat lies. Cabbage in manhood became one of the greatest of salesman, and also the wildest of the Lotharios. His one-night stands and stories would have made any bestseller's list. It was rumored Cabbage once attended the wedding of a certain village lady of the evening to a local yokel, got the yokel drunk, and took the bride to bed. The only complaint heard from the bride was he neglected to leave the usual two bucks.

Cabbage was handsome, blonde, and blue-eyed with a winning smile which captivated the ladies. He was married to a very pretty girl but spent most of his time on the road selling a line of industrial sewing machines. Had it not been for Cabbage's mother-in-law, who he claimed had tongue-lashed two husbands to death and was working hard on him, he might have been more of a homebody.

George had called to warn Tony of Cabbage's impending visit. He was driving in from St. Paul, and probably broke, as he asked if he could stay with them a few nights.

Cabbage arrived on a Tuesday afternoon, frozen stiff. The heater in his Model A Ford had quit 200 miles from Chicago with the temperature at 10 below. Once thawed out with soup and coffee, Cabbage was his old self. Looking about the apartment he said, "Jeez you guys have slipped back a rung or two on the ladder of life."

Tony agreed, "Yeah, but it's more like the bottom rung right now." He then asked, "What happened to you, couldn't you go home?"

"I'm separated again," Cabbage explained, "And the Dragon moved in with my wife. I'm not about to make up with that old witch."

"Well, I can understand that, but what about your sales job?" Tony asked.

Cabbage laughed, "Oh, I've been fired again. I'll swear that damn sales manager must be related to my mother-in-law." He continued, "But, they'll hire me back in a couple weeks, I'm still their best salesman. What are you doing now? Cabbage asked.

Tony explained the hose and lingerie business, and said, "There ain't much money in it but I'm able to eat twice a day."

"Look Tony, Cabbage said, his sales juices bubbling up. "Show me the samples, I've got an idea. If you can scrape up a couple of bucks for gas, we could make a few bucks."

"Okay," Tony replied while getting the sales kit, and explaining how the deal worked.

"Hey, this is great," exclaimed Cabbage, "I know where we can work on fifty women at once."

"That sounds a little strenuous at your age, Cabbage," Tony said, grinning.

"Physically, perhaps," Cabbage answered, "but there's nothing wrong with my mouth. We'll sell 'em all tomorrow."

What Cabbage had in mind was a candy factory in Evanston, which a friend of his managed. Arriving at the plant at noon so as to catch the women during their lunch hour, Cabbage got the okay from his friend to sell anything he could to the girls, most of whom were in their 50s and 60s. It was a revelation to watch the master salesman at work.

If Tony had dared to make the remarks about the legs, busts, and other female attributes of those mothers and grandmothers, as Cabbage did, he would have been slapped into unconsciousness.

But from Cabbage, they ate it up. Tony wouldn't have been surprised to see Cabbage raped before his very eyes. If Don Juan had been able to see this action, he would've cut his throat.

Those ladies really loved Cabbage. For Tony it was hard to keep up with the orders.

Within an hour, he had collected $32 in commissions, and a 5-pound box of candy. Tony split the commission with Cabbage who had done most of the work.

Tony had not been to the Aragon ballroom in weeks. He had to make a choice between dancing and eating; somehow eating seemed to be more important. On Saturday night, Cabbage wanted to go to the Aragon. Tony said, "That's out, I can't afford it right now."

"Sure, you can," Cabbage answered, "I've got it all figured out so it won't cost us a dime." Tony wondered what nefarious scheme he was cooking up.

"Forget it Cabbage," Tony said. "There's no way you can get in there without money."

"Every hear of the power of the press?" Cabbage answered. "We'll borrow George's press card and tell them we're doing a story on the Aragon, and they'll beg us to come in."

"Yeah, if you talk George out of his press card, and they catch us, we'll be begging their bouncers not to throw us out on our ears." Tony suggested.

"You worry too much, "Cabbage grinned, "just leave everything to me."

George took a dim view of lending his press card to anyone, but Cabbage was persuasive. George finally gave in but told Cabbage if he got into trouble, George would swear he swiped the card.

Presenting themselves at the Aragon box office, Cabbage asked to see the manager while

Tony planned a fast exit in case of trouble. When the manager came out, Cabbage presented the press card, introduced himself as George Anderson, and said, "My assistant Mr. Harte, and I are here to do a story on the Aragon and the Wayne King band. We'll need a couple of passes and the cooperation of your staff."

The manager looked over the two imposters and with a gracious smile replied, "Why certainly, I'll get passes for you, and alert Mr. King."

Tony nudged Cabbage and whispered, "Quiet you dummy. Wayne King knows me, he knows I'm not a reporter." Cabbage grinned, "Relax, he knew you when you weren't a reporter, but now you are."

The manager returned with the passes." Enjoy yourselves and write a good story on us. We can use the publicity." he said.

Once in the ballroom, Cabbage said, "Look around and see if you know any of the girls."

"I hope I don't," answered Tony, "I'd hate to have them see me get arrested or thrown out on my ass."

Cabbage laughed and took off in search of ladies willing to dance and listen to his line. With one he'd be a doctor, another an actor, and yet another a banker. And there was always a ninety-five percent chance he'd be believed.

Tony went over to the bandstand to see Wayne King and Louie Henderson and alert them about Cabbage. Louie, who knew Cabbage, laughed and said, "He'll do anything to get a free ride. Wayne and I won't give you guys away, but we'll have some fun with old Cabbage. Get that rat over here and stick around."

A few minutes later, Tony found Cabbage promising the world to some blonde. He got him away from her and they went over to greet Wayne King which Cabbage had no intention of doing on his own.

"Mr. Anderson, it's a pleasure to meet you," said Wayne, "are you ready to take some pictures and interview me for your story?"

Cabbage stared at King open mouthed. For a guy seldom at a loss for words, he gulped a couple times before he found any. "Oh yes, the pictures. Sorry but my dumb cameraman forgot the film, but I can interview you anytime."

"How about me?" asked Louie Henderson, "You don't forget old buddies, do you?"

Cabbage hadn't seen Louie for years and probably didn't know he was in the band. "Should I know you, Sir?" With each bluff Cabbage gave Tony a panicked look.

"Come on, Cabbage," Louie said with a laugh, "you're still as big a conniver as you were at Avondale."

"Yeah, I guess I am, Louie." Cabbage answered with a grin. Then he asked, "Are we going to get thrown out, or can we go quietly?"

Go on with your dancing," Wayne said to Cabbage, "I'll square it with the manager.

Come to think of it, I ought to hire a guy with your guts to be my agent." Shaking hands with Wayne and Louie, the two went on with their dancing.

A few hours later, Cabbage told Tony he had lined up a couple of girls to take home.

"I told them we were in vaudeville and leaving town tomorrow. Come on let's go round them up."

The girls were strictly the Saturday night dance hall type, pretty, but not too bright, and naïve as hell. Tony could see Cabbage had really captivated them with his tale of vaudeville life; they hung on his every word. They both lived fairly near the same area as Tony. Stopping at a large Thompson restaurant for coffee and hamburgers, Cabbage apologized for the meager fare, explaining because of the depression, they were having trouble getting bookings. The girls were very sympathetic. Tony played along and tried to keep from laughing.

"You girls have probably lived a sheltered life," he began, "but you wouldn't believe the trouble we've had, right Tony?"

"That's right," agreed Tony, "no one gets into more trouble than we do."

"Yeah," Cabbage continued, "We had a great magic act. My wife traveled with us, but she didn't like the pigeons, they roosted in her hatbox. We were playing the Palace in New York two weeks ago where we followed Finley's mules. You had to be very careful after those mules were on stage. Anyway, one of the mules kicked my wife backstage while she was holding the pigeon cage. Two of the pigeons got loose and flew out into the audience. One of them landed on a guy's head, the other landed on a lady shoulder and had an accident."

The girls were laughing heartily, but Cabbage went on with a straight face. "I got the damn birds to come back but the one on the guy's head took off with his toupee, the other one got confused and flew into the base horn in the orchestra pit. With every note the guy played, feathers flew. My wife was so mad she took all our money and ran off with the drummer in the band!"

Cabbage paused to light a cigarette, then continued, "But worst of all, we ain't got a magic act anymore. We ate it, three pigeons and two rabbits on the way here from New York. Tony and I cried every time we had dinner."

Tony was never sure whether the girls believed Cabbage's story, but they certainly enjoyed it. Ready to leave the restaurant, Cabbage asked where they lived.

"Oh," one said, "We both live at my house, and my dad waits up for us. It's only a block from here. We'll walk."

Cabbage yelled, "What, you eat, listen to my sad story, and then we don't get to take you home?"

The girl answered, "I'm sorry, but my dad hates actors. Good night."

The girls left. As Tony and Cabbage got into his car, he growled, "I should've told the broads we were Baptist preachers."

True to his prediction, a week later, Cabbage's company forgave his transgressions in St. Paul and called him back to work. Through the years, Cabbage had problems with the bottle, and his mother-in-law, but he was one hell of a salesman, and he always left them laughing.

CHAPTER 9

THE GOING GETS TOUGHER

On November 10, 1930, Tony became a man. He turned twenty-one, though it was not the happiest birthday he could remember. All of the gang who should've been helping him celebrate were scattered. The depression had seen to that.

It had been months since he had seen Gladys or had a date with her. Calling her on her birthday, he learned she and her sister were leaving the next day to live with relatives in Ottumwa, Iowa.

"What the hell will you do in Ottumwa?" Tony asked.

"Hopefully, we'll get some sort of job, and have enough to eat." Gladys answered glumly.

"Cheer up honey," Tony replied. "You'll be the sexiest cornhuskers in the whole damn state! Just look out for those farmers, 'cause they're pretty wild."

Gladys managed a laugh as she said, "Why don't you stop by for a farewell drink tonight?"

"How come it took you so long to ask?" Tony replied.

Arriving at Gladys's apartment that evening with a $2 box of candy under his arm, Tony received a warm greeting. There were suitcases and boxes stacked all over the small living room. Tony wondered how they were going to get all that stuff on a bus. Over drinks, the guys wanted to know all about the Kenmore Avenue bunch and what had happened to them. "They're scattered from hell to breakfast.

This depression has messed up everything." Tony told her.

Gladys answered, "It's a shame, we all had such good times together, and now we'll be lucky if we ever see each other again."

Gladys's sister Suzanne said, "We're all going to start new lives. I just hope we can get along with our relatives. They already think we're lost souls after living in Chicago."

"Don't worry about it," Tony laughed, "you may have to watch your Chicago language and go to church once in a while, but two pretty girls like you will have the Ottumwa boys falling all over themselves. Besides, this is your chance to snag rich farmers."

"You can forget that idea," Gladys cried, "I'll look for a banker."

Suzanne excused herself saying, "I've got a date. I'm sure you two won't mind if I leave you alone. I got some goodbyes to take care of too."

A few minutes later, they were alone. Promptly Gladys pulled Tony down on the davenport beside her and burst into tears. She sobbed, "I hate to leave Chicago and friends like you. We hardly know the relatives in Iowa".

"Come on honey," Tony said, trying to soothe her. "You know how to charm people. I'm sure they will like you. After all, they are relatives not strangers."

Gladys replied, "Okay, let's forget about my relatives for now. Since this is our last day for a long time, I want to make it one we will remember."

With that she melted into Tony's arms for a passionate hour they both would remember for a long time.

The following morning, Tony helped Gladys and her sister to the bus. It was the last time he would ever see Gladys.

Going home after seeing the girls off to Iowa, Tony had never felt lonelier in his life. With the exception of Bill Foy, who he seldom saw anymore, and George Anderson, all of the other friends of the past three years had gone their separate ways.

This just about closed Tony's little black book of girlfriends, except for Bobby and Elaine. He'd only seen Bobby twice after their initial romp at the apartment as she had moved, he had no idea where. While Elaine is fun to be with, Tony decided she wouldn't be interested in a guy with no job and no car. She wanted to go places. It certainly was apparent if Tony wanted future female company, he would have to make some new friends, which wouldn't be easy in his present economic situation.

Right now, however, there was the problem of keeping body and soul together. Girls would have to wait. On reasonably good days after making twenty or thirty calls, he was lucky if he ended up with two or three dollars in commissions. This was little more than enough to eat on, and he felt guilty about not paying his share of the rent. The door to door hose and lingerie business was getting tougher since most lady's shops were having sales of some of the items at half the price of Tony's merchant.

Just before Christmas of 1930, Tony got a check for five dollars from his dad. With this windfall, he, George, and Bill Foy had a rather satisfying Christmas dinner downtown as George was working through the holiday.

On New Year's Eve of that year, the three spent the night nursing a pint of gin at George's office, watching a less than exuberant New Year's Eve crowd trying to be gay and happy about the arrival of 1931.

Tony spent New Year's Day alone in the cramped apartment. He was not much in the mood for company even though at this point in time, he had never felt lower in spirit. No job, most of his friends gone, and what with the severe depression, there seemed little to look forward to in the future. Getting up and putting on the kettle to make some instant George Washington coffee, which was pretty terrible as a coffee, he also found a couple of two-day old doughnuts. Setting down with this decidedly unattractive breakfast, he decided things couldn't get much worse in 1931.

George must have been gifted with ESP, because at 3:00 PM he called, "Hey kid, are you still moping around our luxurious apartment?"

Tony responded with a less than cheerful, "Yeah, what else?"

George, "Well get your ass down here. We can at least manage a small steak at Pixley's on New Year's Day."

"OK, George," he answered, "I'm on my way."

The week after New Year's, Tony received a phone call from his uncle Oscar.

"Hello son, how are things?" he said, "Seems like it's been a long time since we heard from you. Your aunt has been worried about you since you lost your railroad job."

Tony replied, "Well, the jobs I've had weren't anything to write home about. To be honest, I haven't made a decent living since I got terminated by the railroad."

"Well in any case Tony, why don't you come out to Waukegan and stay with us for awhile? You're more than welcome; besides, you might find something to do here. How about it?"

"Boy Unc, that's really nice of you. Are you sure there's plenty of room? I wouldn't want to be in the way," he replied.

"Nonsense," his uncle shot back, "Of course there's room. You know you're always welcome here, so get your bag packed and meet me at the Northwestern station tomorrow at 5:30, OK?"

"I'll be there," Tony agreed. "Only thing is I hate to leave George here alone, but I'm sure not much help to him now. Thanks a lot, and I'll see you tomorrow."

Tony hung up the phone and found it hard to take in the sudden turn of events. Maybe fate wasn't so unkind after all. Just maybe he could make a new start in Waukegan; he would certainly give it a try. A few minutes later he called George and gave him the news. George was happy about the idea but didn't seem too surprised. Tony had a hunch his uncle had talked to George before calling him.

After Tony explained the situation, George said, "Look Tony, you'll be a lot better off with the Olsen's for a while. I'm sure as hell goin' to miss you but you can always come back when this damn depression let's up a bit and there are decent jobs to be had, right?"

"Yeah George, I guess you're right, as usual. I just want to thank you for all you've done for me," Tony replied. Then added, "We sure had a hell of a lot of fun the last three years. I certainly will miss our gang of troublemakers in the apartment. Maybe someday we'll all get together again. In short, while I'm away, try staying clear of the law and bad gin."

George snorted, ", there's no one left to drink with, so I'll have to behave myself.

So long, kid."

The next day Tony packed and left before George got home from working a twenty-hour shift at the Hearst studio.

His aunt picked him up Friday evening at the station in Waukegan and greeted Tony with kisses and tears.

"What the hell are you crying about now? He's back with us," his uncle said.

"That's why I am," his aunt answered with her usual logic.

The following week, Tony started job hunting with little immediate success. Two possibilities were a clerk job at the downtown A & P store, and ushering weekends at the Genesee Theater, both types of jobs, he was experienced in. The only problem with jobs in Waukegan was transportation. Other than a streetcar running from the northern boundary of the city to downtown and the bus which made four trips a day from Zion City and back, there wasn't much choice.

Since his arrival, Tony hadn't seen his old Model T Ford. His uncle now had a 1930 Plymouth four-cylinder coupe. Tony had taken over chores of driving his uncle to catch the 7:20 AM train to Chicago and then Dorothy to high school at 8:15 AM. Dorothy had to be picked up at 3:00 PM in the afternoon, his uncle at 6:15 PM in the early evening.

One evening Tony asked, "Whatever happened to the Ford, did you sell it?"

His uncle replied, "No son, it's stored in the garage across the street. It needs tuning up or something. Amy hasn't been able to get it started all winter."

"Mind if I check it out? It shouldn't be too much of a problem." Tony suggested.

"Hell no, go to it. You may be needing wheels and we sure could use two cars again." he replied.

The next morning Tony went over to look at his old car. The temperature in the garage was about zero. Tony just hoped his aunt had remembered to put enough alcohol in radiator. Otherwise, the block could be cracked in this much cold.

Everything appeared to be okay except the battery was dead. Trying to crank the engine was tough as the oil had become like sludge. Tony remembered an old trick his dad taught him for hard to start Fords. Jack up the right rear wheel, switch the ignition to magneto, and crank like hell. The trick still worked. After a few spins, the engine roared to life. Tony let it run for a while to charge the battery, then checked the oil and gas. When his aunt heard her favorite car running, she came over to find out how Tony had worked a miracle.

She exclaimed, "Boy, I thought my little Ford had given up the ghost. Use the Ford to pick up Oscar tonight. He'll be happy to see this old car running again.

Tony was happy about the revived Ford himself. If his aunt was agreeable, he 'd have his little old car to use. It was a good thing he got it going again. The next three mornings, the Plymouth refused to start until Tony pushed it a mile or so with the faithful Model T which always started regardless of the temperature.

The next month, both the A&P store and Genesee theatre returned his previous phone calls. With both jobs, he would make about $20 a week which was certainly better than he had been doing with the hose and lingerie business in Chicago.

By the end of March, Tony was out of a job at the A&P as they decided to cut down on clerical help. But despite looking again it would be a couple of months before he got another break.

Since Tony's young cousin Dorothy attended Waukegan High School, Tony got to know a number of the younger females in the local area. He started dating Nina quite frequently. She was eighteen and had graduated from high school the previous June. She was a tall, well-proportioned browned eyed brunette. Besides being extremely pretty, she was intelligent and certainly more sophisticated than most girls her age. She was also an extremely passionate young lady, as Tony soon discovered. Believing if two people liked each other enough, making love was the natural thing to do, if done carefully. This was fine with Tony, so long as it was understood he was not to be hogtied and free to pursue other interests with no questions asked.

After a couple of more or less than permanent jobs, Tony got started in a new venture. Though not the most lucrative of businesses, it did prove to be interesting. Through his Uncle Oscar, he met Mrs. Houlihan, a widow in her late forties who operated two cut-rate dairy stands, along with sandwich shops in Kenosha. Wisconsin is noted for its fine dairy products and Mrs. Houlihan was assured Tony he could make good bucks in the Waukegan area.

Her Wisconsin suppliers would sell to Tony, and she would get a percentage from the dairy. Tony was enthused about the idea of having his own business, and started looking for a convenient location, preferably on Sheridan Road north of the Waukegan town line. The traffic flow both ways was considerable and should provide plenty of customers. He finally found just the spot, an abandoned enclosed stand on the old Lyon farm, only a half mile from the Olsen home with easy access from Sheridan Road.

It was October 1932 when he finally got it into operation, having made a deal with Mr. Lyon to rent the stand for $20 a month. Being quite ignorant about the dairy business in general, Tony was only vaguely aware when he opened his cut-rate shop that the legitimate dairies in Lake County were already engaged in a price war due to the depression.

Within a couple of weeks after the opening, certain dairymen learned he was selling milk for $.16 a quart, cream at $.25 a quart, ice cream at $.40 a quart, butter at $.25 a pound and eggs for $.20 a dozen. The local dairymen were bound to be upset, especially since he was importing Wisconsin products.

Shortly he was visited by a delegation of three local dairymen. These guys were already fighting with each other but appeared ready to call a temporary truce and concentrate on Tony, so they got right to the point.

"Mr. Harte," one of the three announced, "We sure hate to see you messing into our business. We're having enough trouble as it is. Besides, we don't like no one selling Wisconsin dairy stuff here in Illinois."

"Yeah," agreed number two delegate, "you just better look for a different business because you ain't gonna like this one for long!"

Sensing some effort to placate the irate men was in order, Tony said, "Gentlemen, I'm not looking for trouble. I'm just trying to make a living. If you're sore about me selling Wisconsin dairy products, I'd be happy to buy them from you three if the price is right. One thing for sure, I'm staying in business at this stand."

"That ain't the right answer," growled one of the delegates. "Only thing we want is you out of business. We ain't a bit interested in you selling our stuff at your crazy prices."

Tony answered, "Sorry, but I'm staying right here, so I guess we've got nothing more to talk about."

Tony's words were much braver than he felt, as he had a pretty good hunch these guys meant trouble. Some of the dairymen were already dumping each other's milk and their route men were having fistfights on a daily basis. The three men abruptly turned and headed for their car. Tony was about to breathe a sigh of relief when one of them turned and said, threateningly, "Maybe what you need in this dump of yours is a good ol' stink bomb. Them things can really mess up dairy products, and it takes three days to get rid of the smell."

Tony didn't answer as he figured there was no use in irritating these fellows any further. Maybe they just wanted to scare him out, meaning they weren't as mean as they looked.

At dinner that evening, he told the folks about the threats. His aunt was horrified and said, "You just better get out of the business. Those people could throw a real bomb in your shop!"

"Nonsense," interjected Oscar, "Tony's not going to let them scare him out, are you son?"

"No sir, I'm staying right there," he answered with more confidence than he felt.

Oscar replied, "Good, but just in case, you better take my revolver to the shop. It's good to have, especially after dark."

A phone call came for Tony and the old conversation ceased when Dorothy said, "Hey lover boy, Nina wants to talk to you."

Tony waited until Dorothy went back to the table to answer saying, "Hi honey, what's new with you?"

Her voice didn't sound very cheerful. In fact, she seemed close to tears when she answered, "I thought I'd better tell you my Aunt Agnes hasn't visited me this month."

"Who the hell is Aunt Agnes?" Tony asked.

"Boy are you dumb, I mean the curse, period, or that time of the month. Get the point?" she said with some sarcasm.

"Oh, that Aunt Agnes," he replied, peeking into the dining room to be sure Dorothy hadn't decided to listen in on the kitchen extension. "Just how late is old Aunt Agnes?"

"One week tomorrow, and I'm scared stiff. My dad will kill me if I'm in trouble." she sobbed. "He'll kill both of us, me first probably, but don't worry yet. I'll see you tonight and we'll figure out something, okay?"

"Dry your tears, I'm on my way." Tony answered in what he hoped was a soothing tone.

Hanging up the phone, Tony felt an emotion close to panic, what with the dairymen after his hide and a good possibility of Nina's father beating them to it. He wondered if it might be a good idea to see if his uncle's customers could get him aboard a ship to China or some other remote corner of the world. That would be the coward's way out, but right then he never felt more like a coward in his whole life.

Later that evening Tony was relieved to see Nina's parents had gone out before he arrived. She greeted him with her usual passionate kisses. Tony decided if she was slightly pregnant, she had never looked prettier.

Tony said, backing off a bit, "Well, are you feeling better now?"

"Yes honey, but nothing's changed since I called you. I think I was afraid you might not show up tonight, but I'm sure glad you're here," she answered.

"You didn't think I'd run out on you at a time like this, did you?" he continued.

"No honey," he said thoughtfully, "but a lot of guys would have been hopping a freight train by now."

Tony's conscience tugged at him at bit; he was glad she hadn't mentioned ships.

Nina's next question brought him up short, "Just what are we going to do?" she asked tearfully.

First of all, we'll wait another week. If Aunt Agnes hasn't shown up by then, you can

try pills, jumping off chairs, or praying for a crop failure. If all else fails, you'll just have to make an honest man of me!" he answered cheerfully.

Nina grinned, "That, seems like an awful lot of if's, but you get a big kiss for the last idea. Seriously though," she went on, "I sure hope something works, because I really don't want to get married, and neither do you. Besides, I'm going to college next year if we can get out of this mess."

"Yeah," said Tony laughing, "go to college now and we'll blame our problem on a

drunken senior or a befuddled professor."

"That's not very funny. If there's going to be a daddy around here, you're going to be it, Nina said with conviction.

"If that's the case, come closer Honey. We can't get into much more trouble than we are already," was Tony's reply as he wrapped his arms around her. Later that night, they both agreed another week would provide an answer, one way or the other.

The next day being Saturday, Tony was on his way to the dairy stand about 7:00 AM.

The dairy truck from Wisconsin would arrive about 7:30 AM. It was a beautiful fall day; business should be good. However, when he was about twenty yards from the stand, a horrible odor assailed his nostrils. It was not unlike a mixture of essence of skunk, and rotten eggs! "Damn," thought Tony, holding his nose, "those bastards weren't kidding around".

Fortunately, he remembered there were only a few quarts of milk in the ice chest.

Everything else was sold out on Friday. The stink bomb, thrown through the window, had rolled to the far end of the room before breaking. Still the awful smell made Tony's eyes water as he tried to keep from throwing up, which would have only added to the mess he already had to clean up. Opening doors and windows helped a bit but no customer would want to enter the shop. When the dairy truck arrived, Tony got the men to help him move the cooler outside to air. A few minutes later, the iceman showed up.

Tony borrowed a couple of tarps to cover the ice and set up with fresh products outdoors away from the shop. By 8:30 AM he was back in business and telling the customers they were painting the shop inside.

The iceman had said, "Boy you're lucky that's all they did. One of the dairies got a real

bomb last night. These guys are really at war. They even got a bunch of out-of-town goons to do the dirty work for them."

Tony hoped for a while at least, his dairy friends would be too busy bombing each other to bother with him.

Tony normally kept his stand open until 8:00 PM. When he got home the following

Thursday night, Dorothy said Nina had called him at least five times so far.

"What's with you two?" she said with a grin. "Is Nina in love with you or just pregnant?"

Startled by Dorothy's intuitive remark, Tony snapped, "You little wiseacre, whatever gave you an idea like that?" Pausing for a moment, he asked hopefully, "did she sound happy or sad? I had to break a date with her last Saturday."

"Well now," Dorothy answered thoughtfully, "Maybe a little of both. Anyway, you better call her and find out for yourself, Buster. I'd sure like to listen in if you don't mind."

"I sure as hell do mind; now beat it up to your room, so I can talk in peace." Tony growled.

Waiting until his nosy cousin went upstairs, Tony dialed Nina's number. With sweating palms and a heart of lead, Tony waited for her to answer. She didn't, her dad did.

"Hello, who's calling?" he asked.

It's me, Tony. "Is Nina home?" our hero stammered.

"Yes, but she doesn't feel too well. She's lying down but hang on and I'll call her," he answered.

"Oh boy," Tony muttered to himself, "is that good or bad?"

A few minutes later, Nina was on the line. "Hi honey", her voice was a little more than a whisper. Aunt Agnes arrived this morning, meaner than ever, but thank goodness she's here!"

Tony's leaden heart came back to life. Breathing freely for the first time in days, he made a mental note to visit the drugstore. There will be no more taking chances.

"Better late than never, honey," replied Tony happily. "We've got some celebrating to do. You get rested up for Saturday night, okay?"

Sensing good fortune and determining he would neither have to leave town suddenly nor get married, he could now concentrate on the dairy business which was beginning to show promise. Because of the dairymen's prices, and uncertainty of delivery, many Waukegan housewives were buying from Tony.

By the end of October, another bit of good fortune had come Tony's way. In the summer, a group had financed and built a large indoor miniature golf course. In addition, there were pinball machines and other games of chance, plus a snack bar. By September, the operation had gone broke; it simply didn't attract enough people. Another group took over, put in a large dance floor, a kitchen and real dining facilities, and reopened as a nightclub. Floor shows on Friday, Saturday, and Sunday nights would be featured, as well as live band music four nights a week. A professional club manager had been hired, and a good chef. The club was located on the north side. One of the new owners who had previously hired Tony for an Elk's dinner and dance contacted him to work as MC and entertainer at the new club.

Tony would produce shows with local talent and alternate with out-of-town entertainers every other week. On Friday and Saturday nights, the club imported waiters from Chicago. Most of them looked like members of the mob and were about as surly. After the third week, there were so many complaints about check padding and shortchanging, the manager added to Tony's chores, making him the captain of the waiters. This was hazardous duty since it was his job to seat customers, make sure the checks were correct, as well as making sure the service was good. The waiters were paid only $2 a night, plus train fare to Waukegan and back to Chicago. Thus, tips became their only source of other income, aside from trying to cheat the customers. Tony soon found keeping hungry waiters reasonably satisfied with their stations and clients was a thankless job. He seldom left the club at night until all the waiters were on the way home. There had also been a number of veiled threats directed his way.

While the nightclub job curtailed his social life to some extent, he found little to complain about. He was paid $15 and dinner the nights he was on duty, and he occasionally was able to wrangle a free dinner and an evening of entertainment for his girl of the moment.

By the end of October, everybody was excited about the upcoming presidential election.

The Republican Party of Lake County was busy damning the communists and Franklin D. Roosevelt, singly and together, claiming the two were practically bedfellows. Waukegan, at the time, was considered by many to be a hotbed of card-carrying communists because there were several ethnic groups of laborers working in the surrounding plants agitating for unions. There had already been several serious clashes between these workers, management, and the strike busting goons. The depression had spawned a great number of strange political and patriotic organizations which were determined to save the country in spite of what they believed was the nation's determination to end it all like lemmings marching to the sea and led by FDR as President.

One well-known patriotic organization of the period was the Paul Reveres. Headed by a strikingly beautiful redhead in her late thirties, Elizabeth Warren was death on communists, pinkos, and other Soviet sympathizers. She lectured tirelessly all over the country, her husband acting as her bodyguard. Tony had attended several of her meetings in Waukegan, two of which were held at the Olsen's home while she was organizing a Waukegan Chapter of the Paul Reveres. A Mrs. Sibley was elected president of the Waukegan Chapter. Tony's patriotic fervor for the organization rose considerably when he discovered Mrs. Sibley's most attractive niece lived with her.

Meetings attended by Tony and the lovely Adrian became much more interesting. In fact, they soon decided lovemaking and fighting communists, in that order, was a terrific way to spend an evening.

CHAPTER 10

BUSINESS IN WAUKEGAN

The winter months of 1933 went by quickly. The repeal of the noxious prohibition took place in February. Now anyone over the age of 21 could get themselves a happy or a mean drunk, depending on how booze affected them. While the repeal of prohibition cut into the mob activities somewhat, they rallied quickly by expanding their other rackets such as prostitution, drugs, numbers, loan sharking, and protection insurance for small businesses.

In June 1933, Tony gave serious consideration to obtaining a beer license, having expanded his operation at the dairy stands by opening the only access road which ran through the old Lyon farm to a secluded beach area on Lake Michigan. He agreed with the owner he would charge $.50 per car for people wanting to use the beach road, and he and Mr. Lyon would split the fees.

Figuring he could sell a lot of soft drinks and beer to the beach customers, Tony checked with a beer distributor he knew. After finding out what the dispensing equipment and a bar would cost him, plus the license, he was ready to give up on the beer idea. However, the distributor said there was no reason he couldn't keep a few cases in the shop for his own use, implying if he sold a few bottles on the weekends, who would care? It worked out quite well over the summer. His customers were discrete, and the cops never bothered him as long as they got a free beer occasionally.

Repeal of the Volstead Act served to increase business at the club; they put in a bar and were doing well, except on occasion Tony would have a few drunks to control. The Fourth of July weekend at the club was a great success. What with good food, an excellent band, and overflow crowds, the club appeared to be operating in the black for a change. There was only one unfortunate incident. On Sunday night of the glorious weekend, the trusted manager of the club cleaned the club safe of $4,000 and disappeared into the summer night. He was never found and the club closed the following week.

With no more entertainment job site, Tony decided to keep his stand open until midnight on Friday and Saturday nights and close the beach area at midnight. This added activity was made easier by sleeping at the stand on weekends. Most of Tony's customers were young couples looking for a place to picnic, swim, fish, and make love, not always in that order. It was always necessary to check the beach area before closing the entrance gate at midnight, as there were usually a few passionate couples who didn't keep track of the time.

One memorable Saturday night he was sure he had rousted out all the late couples, even waiting for a few to retrieve their clothes and dignity after he'd stumbled on their leafy love nest. Returning to the stand and locking the gate, Tony turned in. He was awakened shortly by someone knocking at stand's back door. Being a bit cautious at this time of night, he secured his thirty-eight and asked, "Who's out there, what you want?"

"Please Mr., I'm in real trouble." answered a quivering male voice.

Tony opened the door and there stood a shivering young man stark naked except for the oak branch he held in front of himself. Tony hoped he hadn't also picked up some poison oak. "Where in the hell have you come from?" Tony asked the naked and thoroughly chilled caller as he stepped into the stand.

"My girl and I were at the beach, and I pulled the dumbest stunt of my life," said the boy, busily wrapping the blanket Tony offered about his shivering body.

"Go on," urged Tony, "where's your girlfriend and how come you didn't leave the beach at midnight?"

"Like I said, I did a stupid thing." Pausing to accept a cigarette, he went on, "my girlfriend and I didn't have bathing suits so we were just going skinny-dipping. I took our clothes and locked them in the car trunk. The car keys were in my pants pocket. My girlfriend is still hiding in the bushes and freezing to death. You've got to help us, please."

Tony was sure he had never seen a more forlorn or frustrated young suitor. His girlfriend must be ready to kill him.

Grabbing another blanket, Tony said, "Come on, let's get your girl and then see if we can get your car trunk open."

Finding the half-frozen Venus of Waukegan Beach was no problem as her friend was reasonably sure of her location. Tony's flashlight beam soon focused on the scared face of a pretty girl peering out at them from a clump of bushes that hid this modern-day Eve. Her friend rushed to her with the blanket. Secure in the warm protection of Tony's blanket, she stepped out, red-faced, to face her rescuer. Tony tried to suppress a grin as he asked "Feel better now? You must have been freezing."

Managing a weak smile the girl replied, "Yes, thank you and for your blanket. God, I don't know what we would have done if Jack hadn't found you. I don't think I'll ever go swimming again. Boy, what a mess we're in."

"We ain't exactly out of it yet," Jack cut in. "If we can't open the damn trunk, we're still in trouble. I can't see me taking you home in a blanket."

"Let's get to the car," Tony urged. "Maybe we can get the trunk open with this hammer and screwdriver."

Fortunately, the car was an old Chevy with a simple trunk lock that responded to a prying screwdriver and a few well-placed whacks with the hammer. With subdued cries of joy and relief, the young couple grabbed their clothes and lost no time getting dressed. The old Chevy coughed and sputtered a bit but finally started. A couple of minutes later, Tony let two grateful young people out at the main gate. Tony decided between dairymen after his scalp and naked couples on the beach, this was proving to be one hell of a business he had gotten into.

Heck Aiken had been minding the stand while Tony did some shopping. It was almost 6:00 PM when he got back to relieve Heck.

"You got company at home," announced Heck. "Your cousin Harold and his girlfriend

were here with Dorothy looking for you."

"Oh boy," Tony groaned. "All I need at the club opening tonight is for weird cousin Harold to be in the audience."

Harold was a nephew of his Uncle Oscar. He was a tall blonde skinny Norwegian who looked as though he never had a square meal, but who could eat as much as three grown men in one sitting and still be hungry. He was the same age as Tony but there the resemblance stopped.

Harold's father was a stern and humorless man who had strictly raised his family according to old world customs. He maintained Harold, the youngest of three children, would never amount to anything, and because of his shenanigans, would probably spend a good part of his life in jail.

At times it appeared Harold was bound to prove his old man right. There was no doubt he had, particularly through his teen years, deeply resented his father's harsh discipline and deliberately set about doing anything which would infuriate his father. Despite his cocky attitude with people, his tendency to drink too much and innate ability to find trouble, or make it, Harold did have a great sense of humor, and could at times be quite likable. As they were locking up the stand, Tony asked Heck, "Are you and your girl coming to the club opening night?"

"You bet," replied Heck, "I wouldn't miss seeing old Harold in action, but Dorothy's already told me all about him."

Tony couldn't wait to get home. As far as he was concerned, Harold was no lover boy. He found it difficult to picture what Harold's girl might look like, but he was sure she'd be no raving beauty.

Tony arrived at home to find them in the living room with Harold and his girlfriend as the center of attention. Harold's girl was so beautiful even Oscar was impressed. She had waves of black hair, deep blue eyes, a saucy turned-up nose, a smiling mouth with perfect teeth, and that was only the beginning. Tony's eyes traveled over a near perfect body from her rounded breasts to chorus girl legs. A proud and grinning Harold introduced her to Tony.

"Mary, this is my notorious and lecherous cousin; I hope you don't like him" he said almost seriously.

"Is he really all that dangerous?" Mary asked, as she gave Tony her hand.

"Never mind my Nordic cousin, Mary. He lies a lot. I'm really a very sweet, charming fellow," Tony said defensively.

"Oh yeah!" replied Harold. "I'll bet half the fathers of Waukegan girls are looking for

you right now."

As the laughter died down, Amy called the group into dinner. During the meal, Dorothy explained that Tony was going to be M.C. later that night for the floor show at a new club and suggested Harold and Mary might like to stay over and see it.

"Oh, could we?" asked Mary with her blue eyes fastened on Tony.

"You bet we will," replied Harold. "Would be exciting if Tony gets run out of town and the club is raided." As an afterthought he added, "Aunt Amy, do you have any rotten eggs we could take a long?"

"You're awful, Harold. I'll have you know Tony puts on a good show," replied Amy.

After dinner Tony said, "Look kids, I've got to leave early to rehearse with the band. Heck and his girl will be stopping by here, so why don't you all come along about nine PM. Jimmy knows where the place is and will pick up Nina for me. I'm not sure they'll let Harold in, but Mary won't mind as long as I'm there."

"That'll be the day." Harold yelled after him, "I'll be there. I ain't about to let Mary go anywhere near you." Tony left to roars of laughter.

The five-piece band was already rehearsing when Tony arrived at the club, which was certainly the smallest one he had ever worked in. It couldn't seat more than sixty people including the bar, which would accommodate ten. Tony checked in with the owner, Mr. Finney, and was shown to a dressing room about the size of a large closet. Mr. Finney said the girl dancers from Chicago would show up around 8:30 PM. One was a tap dancer; the others did exotic routines.

Tony hung up his tuxedo and wondered how the hell all three of them would manage changes in this closet. It's sure to be cozy. By 8:30 PM, Tony had rehearsed his dance numbers with the band, but the other acts had not yet shown up. They wouldn't have time for rehearsals as patrons were already coming in. Remembering he would need a table for his group, he had a waitress reserve one near the small dance floor.

At 9:15, his group showed up. He heard Harold's loud voice before they even got inside. Tony decided he had been hitting Oscar's beer before they left home, or else had been nipping from his flask on the way. They had barely gotten seated when Harold, after a fast look around, announced, "This ain't exactly the Green Mill is it!" He was referring to a posh Chicago club. Mary gave him an elbow in the ribs, as nearby patrons shot dirty looks in his direction. Tony decided old Harold might become a problem.

Tony ordered a round of drinks as Mr. Finley approached their table and was introduced to the group. He then advised Tony the other two acts hadn't shown up yet, and was afraid they might not make it in time for the first show at 10:00 PM, if at all.

"Well, don't worry Mr. Finley. I'll just have to do longer routines and hope they get here for the second show," Tony assured him.

Tony's group was generally having a good time, the small band was doing an excellent job, other patrons seemed to be enjoying themselves and kept the three waitresses busy. At 10:00 PM, a fanfare from the band announced the first floor show. Tony, as MC, received a good hand as many of the patrons had seen him before at the Waukegan Club.

Tony stepped into the green baby spotlight. "My God, I've mildewed!" That got an opening laugh, then as they switched to soft white light, Tony continued his opening monologue with, "Ladies and those you brought with you," pointing at Harold, "Our first show this evening is going to be a bit short on talent."

"You can say that again!" yelled Cousin Harold.

As the laughter died down, Tony went on, "That, ladies and gentlemen, was my uncouth cousin. At times he tries to get both feet in his mouth at once and usually does! We were to have other acts here tonight, but they are late so we'll bring them on later, okay?" Tony signaled the band and went into a tap routine.

Halfway through the number, Harold piped up again, "And just think," he told the crowd, "That guy never had a lesson in his life. Ain't it about time he did?"

This time he got a few boos for his trouble and instructions to shut up from Mary. Tony just grinned and thumbed his nose at his personal heckler. He finished the first show with a couple of dialect stories and another tap routine. The crowd liked his act, as their applause brought him back for three bows."

Rejoining his group, Tony said, "Keep it up Harold, you're making me look good!"

"If he doesn't stop heckling, I'm going to crown him!" Mary cried, "I think you're great!"

"Oh boy," Harold groaned sadly, "I knew I shouldn't have let Mary meet the old Don Juan of Broadway."

"Hey Tony," Jimmy asked as they laughed at Harold remark, "What are you going to do if those other acts don't show?"

"Don't worry," Dorothy said. "Tony will think of something."

Nina added, "That's right. I've seen Tony carry a show alone in bigger places than this."

"He may just have to do it again this time" said Mr. Finley who had just stepped over to their table and heard Nina's remark. "Those damn girls from Chicago haven't shown up yet. I'm about to give up on them." Tony grinned, "Well, how can I miss with loyal fans like these? Maybe I can get some help from the band."

Tony got up and went over to talk to the band leader. "You guys have any specialty or novelty acts the group can do to help me out?" he asked, then added, "Two of our acts haven't shown up."

Jack, the bandleader, answered, "Yeah, no problem. We do a little German band number where we march around the room. Then two of our guys do a comedy skit. Just say when and we'll be ready."

"That's great, and thanks a lot. I'll stick your numbers in after my Jewish monologue, which will give me time to change for my drunk act."

Greatly relieved he would have some help with the late show, Tony returned to the table and another hour of dancing. The club stayed open until 1:00 AM, with the last show starting at midnight. Tony was welcomed back with a nice round of applause.

Tony was just about ready to announce the dancing girls hadn't made it when irrepressible Harold hollered, "Hey Tony, where're the broads you promised?"

Tony shot back, "Sorry Harold, but they saw you were in the audience and refused to come."

"Want I should throw ole bigmouth out on his ear?" asked a burley half-soused patron as the crowd roared with laughter.

"Not yet," answered Tony. "Wait till he pays his bill, then we'll both throw him out."

The rather rough crowd loved the exchange, but Harold looked a bit worried when Mary gave him a cold stare.

Tony performed his Jewish stories, then introduced the band members and said they would entertain while he made a costume change.

According to the applause he heard while dressing, they did a good job. Then the band leader announced there was a guy backstage who was insisting on doing a number for them. Tony staggered onto stage carrying a rubber lamppost as the band broke into the *St. Louie Blues*. His oversized tuxedo plus the battered derby resting on his ears fooled even his friends for a couple of minutes. Tony did some sliding, slipping soft shoe steps, just barely saving himself from falling down by making it back to the rubber lamppost in time.

By now the crowd was in good condition to appreciate this type of comedy. Tony ended the number by straying too far from lamppost, and did a prat fall to the crash of the drummer's cymbals. The audience really appreciated this number and as Tony took his last bow, Harold rose steadily and said loudly, "That was not an act; he's like this every Saturday night!"

He was promptly pulled down by Heck and Jimmy as the burley drunk headed for their table, yelling, "He's done it again! I'm gonna throw the bum out on his ass!"

Tony hurried over to his table where his number one fan looked as though he meant to do just that.

Intercepting the irate customer before he could lay hands on Harold, Tony grabbed his arm and said, "Come on friend, he's part of my act. How about you buy me a drink?"

The huge inebriate, weaving on unsteady legs, glared at poor Harold saying, "Ish that so? Ought to throw him out anyhow 'cause he's a very disrespectful person. Let's have that drink old buddy."

The small crowd burst into applause as Tony and his self-appointed protector headed to the bar. A little later, Tony got back to the table, joining his friend for steak sandwiches and a nightcap.

"Thanks Tony," said a subdued Harold, "that big clown could've killed me. He was really mad!"

"That's okay Hal," Tony grinned, "maybe I should keep you in the act. Your cracks really put the audience in my pocket."

Mary was still a bit miffed at Harold, "I still don't think you were very funny, but I'll forgive you if Tony does," she said planting a kiss on Tony's cheek.

"Isn't he just the greatest. Didn't I tell you Tony could handle the show by himself?" Nina asked the group.

"Heck," said Jimmy, "Ain't it getting' a little thick around your feet? These gals can sure shovel it out."

"That'll be enough out of you, Jimmy. You're just jealous," Dorothy cried. Tony, being a true ham, loved the attention, and drank it in like a rare wine.

They were about ready to leave when Mr. Finney came over to the table with Tony's check. "Tony sure got us out of the spot tonight, thanks a lot. There will be no charge for your friends' drinks and the foods on the house. Now, can you come back in two weeks?"

"You're more than generous, Mr. Finley. My friends and I thank you, and you can bet I'll be back," Tony assured him.

After they got their coats, it was agreed Heck would see the other two couples got home to the Olsen.

"I'll see you guys tomorrow. Nina and I are going to be busy for couple of hours," Tony grinned as they headed for their cars. As an afterthought, he added, "Mary, don't let my beloved cousin get in any more trouble tonight. You and Dorothy tuck him in bed, okay?"

"Don't worry about me," Harold shouted back as he gave Mary a lecherous grin, "I can go to bed alone if I have to."

"You better believe you'll be alone." Mary advised.

At dinner on Sunday, Harold for once wasn't very hungry. He'd had a bad night. His blue eyes appeared to be nested in pools of ketchup.

"It looks like you can't take Waukegan nightlife, Harold," Oscar observed.

Harold answered, wincing with the effort, "I got in with a bad crowd last night."

A short time later, Harold and Mary were headed back home to Chicago. As they all waved goodbye, Tony decided at some future time, he was going to get to know Mary a whole lot better.

On October 21, Tony was getting ready to close the stand. It was already dark, and he was about to go out to his display table. The display consisted of milk and cream bottles and empty butter, egg, and cheese cartons. When he saw a car driving slowly in front of the stand, he thought it was a late customer so Tony waited. Suddenly a mean looking character in the back seat of the car reached out with a rake and cleared the table. As the bottles crashed in all directions, the guy yelled, "Close this damn store by Friday night or we're going to blow it to hell."

Furious, Tony turned, grabbed his thirty-eight and fired three shots over their heads, as the car roared away.

Shaken by the incident, Tony sat down to regain his composure, and gave serious thought about this latest raid by the dairymen's goons. This was a Wednesday night, and he was sure these guys wouldn't dare pull anything in the daylight. Besides, they know now from the shots he fired that he is armed and will use the gun if necessary. It seemed quite evident the dairy price war was really heating up if the goons were so desperate as to attack a small operation like his.

Deciding to say nothing to the family about this latest threat, Tony went home. Each morning through Saturday he searched the stand carefully before opening for business but found no indication his dairy friends had been back. Perhaps, he thought, they will back off for a while.

Closing the stand on Saturday night, Tony, for some reason he could not explain, took home the few personal things he at the stand. As he locked up, he had an eerie feeling this might be his last day in the dairy business. However, thoughts of his date with Nina and his appearance at Mr. Finley's club later that night soon dispelled his uneasiness about the stand.

Arriving home about 2:00AM, Tony was about to put the car in the garage when he heard a dull boom. Looking in the direction the sound came from and seeing flames and smoke, he was sure the dairy goons had carried out their threat. Jumping back in the car, he raced up the road to find his stand blown apart and burning furiously. No doubt about it, he sure as hell was out of the dairy business.

Discussing the situation at breakfast with his uncle and a tearful, slightly hysterical Aunt Amy, the consensus of opinion was for the money he was making, the cut rate dairy business was just too dangerous. On Monday, Tony paid off his creditors, and advised Mr. Lyon of the demise of the stand. After all his debts were settled, Tony had about $75 left over from the operation.

Tony spent the following week scouring the city of Waukegan in search of gainful employment but found nothing.

After four years of acute depression, it appeared 1934 was not going to be any better. Prosperity was still around the corner, and likely to stay there for some time.

Early in November, Oscar announced he had found a job for Tony and Jimmy at a steel plant in Chicago. With everyone at dinner that evening his announcement even caused Jimmy to stop eating, which wasn't easy to do.

"What kind of job, Unc?" asked Tony.

"We've decided to repaint all the steel superstructure at the warehouse so we'll need your help for about three months." Oscar replied.

"That sounds like dangerous work for the boys!" objected Amy, as Jimmy got busy with second helpings.

"Amy," laughed Oscar, "you'd worry if the two took up knitting. Come to think of it, you should."

"Let's hear more about how you're going to put these two clowns to work, Daddy, " Dorothy suggested, ignoring the icy stares from Jimmy and Tony.

Oscar said, "Well, they'll simply paint steel from 8 to 5, for $20 a week. Of course, they'll have to commute taking the same train I do. They can start work on Monday."

"Suits me fine. How about you Jimmy?" Tony asked as Jimmy reached for more meat.

"I guess so," Jimmy mumbled with very little enthusiasm for the idea.

The Castle Steel Company warehouse was located in an old industrial area on Goose Island. Very few Chicagoans had ever heard of the place as the island was formed by the Chicago River and its North branch. The boys found the warehouse large and cold. Cranes rumbled back and forth across four huge bays carrying steel beams, flat sheets, and all types of construction steel to the shearing, sawing, and torch cutting machines which cut the products to the customers' specifications.

After changing into overalls, Joseph, the head painter, took Jimmy and Tony to the No. 1 Bay where they would start work. The upper steel structure holding the roof was 45 feet above the floor and 20 feet below the crane tracks. Joe explained they would first steel brush the rust off, then re-lead the structure. Later on, it would get a coat of aluminum paint. Loaded with wire brushes, paint brushes, and a bucket of red lead paint, the boys stared up at the grimy structure.

"You know Tony," said Jimmy, "we're nuts to climb up there. It looks like a good way to get killed." Tony agreed, "Yeah, but we've got to eat, so just take it easy and be careful."

Within a few days they got used to the height and scrambled about the superstructure like monkeys. It was dirty work, and by five o'clock each evening, they both looked like paint smeared chimney sweeps. Changing clothes and washing up enough to be allowed aboard the train, the two wanted no more than a hot meal and a soft bed when they got home about 7:00 PM. Neither one was exactly an exciting date on Saturday night. Dorothy and Nina complained bitterly about their tendency to fall asleep in movies and even on the dance floor.

Jimmy never did work up enthusiasm for his painting career. One morning after two months on the job, Tony saw him climb down, place his paint bucket and brushes by the ladder, and disappear into the washroom. A few minutes later he emerged, dressed for the street, and headed out of the warehouse.

"Hey Jimmy," Tony yelled, "Where the hell are you going?" Jimmy never looked back; he was gone.

When Tony and Oscar got home that night, Jimmy and Dorothy were nervously waiting for her dad's reaction to Jimmy's sudden departure from the job he had gotten him. They didn't have to wait long. Oscar was angry with Jimmy but waited until dinner was over before bringing up the subject.

"Jimmy," Oscar said as they left the table, "How come you just walked off the job. Were you sick or what?"

"No sir," Jimmy tried to explain, "not sick, sick. Just sick of painting. I'm sorry, but I ain't going back."

Oscar replied "I see, it's your decision, but it's the last time I'll try to get you a job."

"Daddy," Dorothy said, putting a protective arm around Jimmy, "he can't help it, he hates the warehouse. I bet you wouldn't do that kind of work." Her last remark didn't do anything to calm the stormy water.

"That's right," replied Oscar, "but I'm not the one who needs a job, he does."

This ended the discussion. Jimmy and Dorothy left to find a more congenial climate. Jimmy made himself scarce around the Olsen house for a few days until Oscar got over his anger.

Two weeks later, Jimmy who was crazy about electronics, got a job assembling small radios at a local plant. Tony had to admit he wasn't so dumb after all.

Castle management had totally underestimated the time it would take to paint the warehouse. It went from April 1 to the end of June before the job was finished, even with three additional painters added to the crew of six. Since the weather was getting warmer, the bay doors where the steel trucks were loaded were kept open most of the day. But with spring came the horrible smell of animal hides being processed at the tanning factory across the street. At times the odor was overpowering and reminded Tony of the stink bomb at the dairy stand. In time, like everyone else, he got used to it, and was thankful he didn't have to work in that smelly place.

The painting job was completed in early June, but Oscar got the warehouse manager to keep Tony on as a catcher on the steel sheer at $0.47 an hour. This machine was used to cut angle iron up to 6' x 6' x 1' and also flat bar steel and reinforcing rods. It would catch and pile the steel in lifts for the crane to carry to trucks. This was heavy and tricky work, but Tony caught on quickly. The shearing machine required a crew of three, the shearman who was boss, the stockman, and the catcher. Sam, a fairly congenial Italian, was the shearman. Ivan, a miniature Russian, was the stockman, and Nick, a Croatian, was the crane operator.

For the first couple of weeks, Tony had trouble understanding any of his fellow workers. They each had their own version of the English language, which they mixed freely with words of their own languages. Within a month, Tony could cuss fluently in four languages. He also found he was much more likely to be understood if he spoke to them in the same fractured English they used, plus the derogatory phrases of each national tongue he was learning.

CHAPTER 11

FINDING THE RIGHT GIRL

By May 1935, Tony was fed up with commuting. Between the cold weather and long hours, it was very tiring. Nina had gone off to college last September; the North Shore club had closed, as well as the Serio-Comic Club, so there was little to hold his interest in Waukegan.

The Olsen's home had become a bit more crowded since Oscar's older sister, Marie, had moved in. Aunt Marie, separated from her husband, tended to enjoy her ill health. Her favorite remedy for a headache was a washcloth soaked in vinegar on her forehead. This cure made the living room smell like a salad.

Aunt Marie had been a very pretty girl in her youth and still retained the blonde hair and good features which had gotten her in a few chorus lines of good musical comedies. She used to tell Dorothy and Tony about her narrow escapes from Stage Door Johnny who she claimed was only after one thing. At times, they were sure Aunt Marie was disappointed some of them had given up so easily. One of her warnings to Dorothy about boys on the make was, "Honey, don't ever let them young fellows put cigarette ashes in your beer 'cause it'll make you easy to take advantage of."

Taking Aunt Marie at her word, Tony tried this surefire method of seduction a couple of times himself. All it got him were rebukes for being so clumsy and the cost of extra beers.

Aunt Marie, at fifty-five, had little to look forward to in life, and in spite of her ailments and sometimes weird advice, Tony and Dorothy were quite fond of her.

Tony finally decided it was time for him to move back to Chicago. His job at the steel company seemed reasonably secure and he was quite sure George Anderson would welcome him back as an apartment mate. He knew George, Gus Kneve, and Gus' brother had a nice apartment on Lincoln Avenue near Ogden, and that Gus had recently gotten married.

Tony called George one evening. "Hi kid, what's new with you?" Was George's cheerful greeting.

"Well, I called to see if you could use another roommate." Tony explained. "I'm working at Castle steel and tired of commuting. So, I've decided to come back to town."

"Sure, you can move back with me," replied George. Gus and his bride have a flat on Bryn Mawr now, so there's just Gus' brother Lee with me. How soon do you want to move in?"

"How about Friday? I'll come over after work, if that's okay."

George answered "Good, I'm off Friday night so I'll have dinner ready. See you then."

Tony hung up the phone to find Dorothy at his elbow. "So, you're running out on me. I guess you tired of this old folk's home" she said with mock sadness.

"Shhh, they'll hear you. Your Aunt Marie's not so old, just frustrated, Tony answered. He added, "Besides, how come you've always got big ears when I'm on the phone?"

"I never know when I might hear something spicy like when Nina thought she was pregnant!" whispered a grinning Dorothy.

"I just wish I could get out of this town," she confided. "I'm seventeen now and ready for some real excitement. Can I come and visit you and George soon?"

"I guess so," Tony answered, then asked "how the hell did you find out about Nina, nosy cousin?"

"When a guy walks around with a worried look for two weeks, and jumps three feet every time the phone rings, I just put two and two together," replied Dorothy with the age-old wisdom of her sex.

On Thursday night, Tony packed his clothes and went directly from work on Friday to George's apartment. He had already explained his reasons for leaving to his aunt and uncle, who understood his decision. Finished with packing, Tony went downstairs to say goodbye to his grandparents, the Hannington's, and Aunt Marie, as he would be gone before they were up the next morning. Tony and Oscar were having their usual fast breakfast at 6:30AM Friday when a sleepy-eyed Dorothy made an unexpected appearance. For one who never opens her eyes before 8:00 AM, this was a shock.

"What happened, did you fall out of bed, or haven't you been there yet?" asked her suspicious father.

"If I fell out of bed, at least it will be my own, I'm sorry to say!" replied Dorothy, grinning at Tony.

"Lippy damn kid!" muttered her dad.

"I'm up," said Dorothy, juggling a cup of coffee, "because I wanted to see Tony off."

"That's sweet of you Cousin, but I'll get back to see you all often." Amy was calling, "Come on, you'll miss you train."

As Tony kissed Dorothy goodbye, she whispered, "Don't forget about my visit, and I'll expect a wild time, right?"

Tony pondered this remark all the way to the station. His little cousin was sure growing up.

On the drive to the station, Amy wiped away tears. "For Christ's sake Amy, quit crying, or you'll run into something!" exclaimed Oscar.

"I can't help it," said Amy. Tony's going back to that awful city and I'm afraid he'll get into trouble."

"Not anymore trouble than he almost got into in Waukegan," Oscar replied, winking at Tony.

Tony's face reddened a bit, but he decided to let the remark alone. A few minutes later he was boarding the commuter train for the last time.

George's apartment was a fairly good size, except for the tiny kitchen which was sufficient but with only enough room for one person to work. When George was at the stove, his butt was jammed against the refrigerator door. He fried on one side and froze on the other.

When Tony arrived at 6:00 PM, George was busy cooking a delicious stew which would feed five, but George usually ate enough for at least two.

"Good to have you back, kid." George said. "Kinda lonesome here. I was about to look for another roommate when you called. I seldom see Lee since he's out all day."

The apartment hotel was only about six blocks from the old place on Sedgwick Street, so Tony was in the familiar neighborhood of North Avenue and Clark Street. It was only two blocks to the Division streetcar line which took him right to the Castle plant in a matter of twenty minutes. He could now sleep until seven, have plenty of time for breakfast, and still get to work on time.

George had acquired a 1928 Buick coupe in fair condition. Tony was free to use it whenever he wished, as George preferred the streetcar or L for traveling to work. George, who still worked the night shift, was asleep when Tony left in the morning, and was gone by the time he got home at 6:00 PM. With this kind of schedule, the three had plenty of privacy.

Tony, after the first few weeks, decided it was time to meet some new girls. He began spending most Sunday evenings back at his favorite but not for fun and romance, the Aragon ballroom. Occasionally he would run into old friends and dancing partners from previous years. The job at Castle was by now a routine of heavy work with occasional overtime which was always a welcome addition to his rather meager salary. Appreciating the fact, he was lucky to have a job at all, Tony managed quite well.

On a Sunday visit to the Olsens in February 1936, Tony learned Dorothy would soon be moving to Chicago to attend beauty operator school. Her mother had arranged for her to live with an old friend while in the city, but she would go home on the weekends. Dorothy wasn't happy with this arrangement, but it sure put her friend Jimmy's mind at ease. During the week when she stayed in town, she managed to visit and have dinner a couple nights a week with Tony and Lee.

Shortly after Dorothy started her beauty course, Heck Aiken decided to seek his fortune in Chicago and was looking for a place to live. At the same time, Gus' mother retired and wanted to live in Chicago with her younger son Lee, who was still living with George and Tony. Later on, Gus and his sister would join George's new family. Tony got a smaller apartment nearby and Heck moved in with him.

On a visit to Waukegan in the summer of 1936, Tony discovered two new houseguests at the Olsen's, Ciele Armbaugh and her little boy Sonny. Tony had known Ciele since the Grayslake years. She was a very pretty girl with blue eyes and long ash blonde hair. Recently she had started a secretarial job in Waukegan. Amy Olsen and Ciele's mother had been friends for years.

After dinner one Saturday night, Tony called an old girlfriend for a date but got turned down. Oscar, noting Tony's dejected look said, "Why the sad look Tony? We've got the prettiest girl in town right here! You two should go somewhere with Dorothy and Jimmy. They need a chaperone."

Tony turned to a blushing Ciele saying gallantly, "I didn't intend for you to play second fiddle Ciele. I just wasn't sure you were ready to start dating again, but how about it?"

"I'm fully recovered," smiled Ciele, "I'd love to go out."

"Well, it's settled then," Dorothy cut in, eyeing her dad, "but we ain't going far on Jimmy's bicycle."

"Tonight, the car is yours as long as Tony drives," replied Oscar.

After an evening of dancing and a few beers, they dropped Jimmy off at his house. Ciele and Tony had a few minutes alone while waiting for Jimmy and Dorothy to say good night. Tony leaned over and kissed Ciele saying, "I bet you can't remember the first time I did that."

"Oh yes I can," she replied with a grin, "1926 at the movie in Grayslake."

This first date with Ciele started a series of visits to Waukegan every other weekend for almost a year. On occasion, Ciele would meet Tony in town for dinner and a show. As their relationship occasionally became intimate, Tony found her to be a very select complex person. She could at times be quite passionate, but other times cold and distant and often in a world of her own. After several months, Tony really believed he was in love with Ciele and certainly very fond of her boy Sonny. He could see she had accepted his proposal with some reservation, and she insisted on a long engagement. Tony presumed her reluctance was due to her first unsuccessful marriage. Every two weeks wasn't very conducive to a successful romance. Tony was sure that during their so-called engagement period, she was having other dates. He didn't make an issue of it as he was doing the same thing, so he could hardly complain about it.

By October, Dorothy had become fed up with beauty school and had gotten a typist job. Dropping out of school upset her mother and friend Mrs. Green considerably though she stayed on with Mrs. Green.

A couple of weeks later, Tony received a phone call from his uncle who was, to put it mildly, terribly angry. "Why the hell didn't you tell me what those dumb kids were up to?" he yelled Tony.

"Just a minute," Tony said, "Calm down, what have they done now?"

"Done! You don't know? Dammit, Dorothy and Jimmy ran off and got married, that's what they've done!" Oscar replied as if he still didn't believe it himself.

"Gee Unc', I didn't know anything about this. They sure never let me in on it that they were up to any stunt like getting married." Tony answered, then asked, "How is Aunt Amy taking this?"

"You know your aunt. She thinks it's beautiful, just two lovebirds flying away to nest," Oscar replied sourly, then continued, "Wait till they have to eat like birds! You can tell him this feeding station is closed."

"Come on," Tony said laughing, "you don't really mean that. Anyway, I bet those kids are too scared to call. If I see them, should I tell them all is forgiven and to come on home?"

"Yeah, I guess so," Oscar replied, "I just hope Dorothy isn't pregnant, another Jimmy around here would be just too much."

Tony had a hardly hung up the phone when Dorothy called. She asked, "Tony, have you heard from Daddy yet? Did he tell you about Jimmy and me?"

"I have, and he did," answered Tony. "I don't know why he used the phone; I could've heard him without it. He thought I knew all about you characters."

"Oh, he must be pretty mad at us. I'm sorry he hollered at you though." Dorothy giggled.

"I think you could say he's a bit upset with you, but you'd better call him. If you aren't pregnant yet, you could take a chance on going home, but throw Jimmy's hat in first," laughed Tony.

"Pregnant!" cried Dorothy, "I'm not that dumb. We took off to Crown Point and got married because I just couldn't take the house full of people any longer. Living with Mrs. Green during the week wasn't a barrel of laughs either."

"Yes, I'd have to agree with you on both counts, but maybe you better talk to the folks soon." Tony said sympathetically.

"We'll call them tonight," replied Dorothy, "but I won't be moving back. Jimmy and I have a one room apartment and he's looking for a job in town."

"Okay cousin, good luck to the both of you. Poor ole Heck will probably be broken-hearted when he finds out you're married.

I'll come to see you soon. Bye for now" Tony said, hanging up the phone just as Heck came in.

He didn't seem too surprised at Tony's news. "I thought those two were acting goofy," Heck said, putting on a brave but sickly grin. "It's too bad but the best man didn't win."

A few weeks later, Heck lost his job in Chicago and went home to Winthrop Harbor to take charge of his family's business. This left Tony with an apartment he couldn't afford alone. He then moved into a smaller apartment in the 1500 block of Clark Street. His leisure hours were mostly spent next door at the Rendezvous Bar.

Making trips to Waukegan every other week to visit Ciele were less then reassuring as far as their relationship was concerned. Ciele acted more like a friend than a lover, and avoided, when possible, any ardent advances by Tony. Hoping to revive their romance, he invited Ciele to come to town one Saturday night for the play, *Idiots Delight*. Ciele made a number of excuses, but then agreed to come. Tony had expected her to stay overnight with Dorothy, but she had no overnight bag when he met her train.

Ciele broke the news to Tony that she wanted out of their so-called engagement during the second act, which was sad enough to begin with. He really wasn't ready to cope with her ultimatum, as he sat through the rest of the play.

During their after the play supper, he asked, "What's with you Ciele? I thought you loved her., What's changed, another guy?"

Ciele's answer was both honest and to the point. "That's right Tony, there is someone else. He has a lot to offer, and I've got to look out for me and Sonny."

Tony exploded angrily, "Boy, you sound like you're choosing a prize bull. Where does the love, come in?"

"That wasn't very kind," she replied, her eyes filling with tears. "Do we have to fight?"

"I'm sorry, Ciele. It's just that I thought we had a lot going for us," Tony apologized.

"You see Tony," explained Ciele, my first marriage was really a mess. I'm not going to get into another one like that. I want more than just a bare existence the next time, if there is one. I am sure sorry about us, but I don't think it would work out. Anyway, I'm in no hurry and I'm not sure I love this other man either."

Later when he put Ciele aboard the train to Waukegan, he said, "I guess this is it for us Ciele. Goodbye and good luck!"

It was February 7, 1937, the temperature at about 5° above zero, with a chilling wind coming off Lake Michigan in 30 mile an hour gusts. This made it feel like 30 below. Not the most pleasant afternoon to go dancing, but then the Aragon ballroom would be cozy, and there would be plenty of pretty girls to warm a man's heart.

The cold streetcar bumped and screeched its way north on Clark Street to Lawrence Avenue and the Aragon. Even if he thought hard about it, Tony couldn't remember how many Sundays he had spent dancing at the Aragon, but for some reason, he felt this would be a special evening. By the time he got to the ballroom, he was freezing. A stop for hot chocolate at the soda bar and once inside the music of Freddie Martin's great band warmed him quickly. A fast check of the corner of the ballroom to the right of the bandstand where he usually found friends and dancing partners showed a few were there already.

Loosing no time, Tony got himself listed on the dance card of three of the regular partners, spent some time chatting with members of the 400 club, then sat out a couple of dances to have a cigarette. Tony's ever alert eyes studied the couples dancing on his side of the floor, particularly noting the really good dancers who would warrant his attention later on. Freddie Martin was playing a dreamy waltz when suddenly Tony saw a vision in a white scarf floating by in the arms of a good-looking young fellow. Going to the end of the floor for a better look at this dream, he caught glimpses of a beautiful face, large brown laughing eyes, a cute nose, luscious lips, a smile exposing beautiful teeth, all framed by shoulder length wavy dark hair with glints of bronze, all this and a gorgeous figure which curved in all the right places. Tony's heart jumped as he feasted his eyes on this lovely girl. He noticed he wasn't the only one eyeing this young lady as she came off the dance floor to rejoin her friends, as several would be swains were edging closer to her. If he was to meet and dance with this dream, and he certainly intended to, he'd better be about it.

To Tony's somewhat conceited mind, there was no question he would dance with her. It never occurred to him he might get refused for any reason whatsoever. Gallantly he sallied forth to win her hand for at least the next dance.

With all the savior-faire he could muster, he asked, "May I please have the next dance?" "I'm sorry," replied Brown Eyes, smiling, "but my card is full."

"Perhaps a little later than. I'll be back," answered Tony, his disappointment quite evident. Never in his years at the Aragon had this ever happened to Tony Harte. Girls so favored had always found the place on their card for him, even if they had to drop some other poor joker. A couple of dances later, Tony approached Miss Dream Boat again with no better results.

"You are the best dancer here," he pleaded, "I've just got to dance with you!"

"Oh, I'm sorry," she said sweetly, "but I'm still booked up."

"Maybe," replied Tony hopefully, "one of your partners will break a leg, or go home early. I'll be back."

As he walked away, Tony thought, "why with all the girls here who I can dance with do I keep asking her? But I'm not about to give up. I've just got to dance with her.

An hour or two of pleading requests later, Tony got his wish. She said yes, and they moved onto the floor to the waltz *Sorrento*. Tony's ego was restored as she said with a smile,

"My dance card really was filled, but one of my partners left. You sure are persistent. I didn't think you would come back."

"I've been watching you dance," Tony answered grinning, "this is the first time I've ever had to ask four times for a dance, but honey, it was worth it! I'm Tony, what is your name?"

"Regina," she replied, as he waltzed her to the opposite side of the ballroom. "Regina means Queen, doesn't it?" he asked, adding, "They sure gave you the perfect name."

When the waltz ended, Tony suggested they stay on the floor. "Regina," he pleaded, "stay here. We can sneak in two more dances before intermission."

She protested, "Oh, I can't do that. What about all the boys I promised dances to?"

"Sure, you can," argued Tony, "maybe they'll just think you went home. We'll go

upstairs during intermission for a soda. Besides, I'm not going to let you get away now."

Before she could protest further, the band started another set, and they went right on dancing.

At intermission, Tony steered her through the crowd and upstairs. In doing so they brushed past three young men who glared at both of them.

"Oh golly," Regina whispered, trying to avoid their gaze. "Those are the three I had booked dances with, and they're mad."

"They'll get over it," replied Tony. "There maybe a few more mad ones around, because I'm taking the rest of your dances for the night."

"How did you get that idea? What if I say no?" asked Regina, a bit angry.

"I hope you won't say no," Tony grinned. "Can I help it if you're my favorite dance partner and I want to keep you all to myself? Besides, you'll never see those fellas again, but me, you will!"

Back on the dance floor a few minutes later she said with a smile, "Tony, you sure are the most stubborn man I've ever met. Do you always get your way?"

"Not always honey, but I try." he replied.

At midnight, Tony and Regina had danced every dance since the intermission. Tony felt lucky he hadn't gotten hit in the chops by one or more of the disappointed guys he had cheated out of dances with her.

As they were leaving the floor, Tony said to her, "I don't want to say good night yet. Let's go across the street and have some Chop Suey. Then I'd like to take you home, okay?"

"Well, if my girlfriend doesn't mind my leaving her, I guess we could," she smiled. "I'll go find Ann."

While Regina looked for her friend Ann, Tony went to the check room to get their coats. What was he doing? Taking a girl home from Aragon was practically unheard of for him. Besides, he was thinking of taking a cab and he didn't know yet where she lived. There was certainly something about this lovely girl that had Tony breaking his own ironclad rules about dancing with the same girl more than twice or taking her home. Coming back with their coats, Tony found Regina saying goodnight to her friend who had a date, so her feelings were not hurt. A minute later, Tony and Regina hurried across the street to the restaurant. It was bitter cold outside, so Chop Suey and hot tea really hit the spot.

During the meal, Tony learned Regina lived with her folks and her brother, and worked for a large food manufacturer, Reid Murdoch Company, near the loop. He told her a bit about himself, being sure to mention he wasn't married.

Finishing their meal, Tony helped her with her coat. Outside the cold wind was biting as he hailed a cab. Regina looked surprised, as she said, "We could take a streetcar you know, it's not too far to my home."

"A streetcar is okay for me," he replied gallantly, "but the Queen of the Aragon rides in a warm cab on a night like this. Besides, what else could I do after stealing most of your dances?"

"You sure did that", she said smiling, "but I enjoyed our dances and the nice supper.

Thank you."

Regina lived on the Northwest side of town, about a half hour trip by cab. Tony sat with his arm around her shoulder as they chatted about their evening together. He occasionally managed to nuzzle her ear which she didn't seem to mind, but when his hands slipped down to caress her lovely breasts, he got a warning look from flashing brown eyes, and his hands firmly pushed away. Looking up, Tony noticed a grinning reflection of the cabdriver in the rearview mirror.

Angrily Tony growled, "Maybe you better watch the road instead of us, Buster!"

"I don't have no problem doing both. But you better watch it buddy." he laughed, as Regina blushed and hid her face in her fur collar.

A few minutes later, they pulled up to Regina's house. "Want me to wait?" asked the cabbie. "I can see you ain't gonna be too long."

"On your way, wise guy!" he answered. An embarrassed Tony paid him as Regina ran, laughing, to her door.

As he joined her he said, "Are you going to let me come in for a minute, Regina?"

"Okay, for a few minutes," she grinned, "but remember what the cabbie said."

"Yeah," Tony agreed, adding, "I wonder how many times a week that smart-aleck gets punched in the mouth and no tip?"

Tony was quite sure Regina meant what she said, so a few minutes later he left, having secured her phone number and a friendly good night kiss. He promised to phone her for a date soon.

It had been almost two weeks since Tony met Regina. On Friday night, he phoned her. Hearing her voice, he said, "Hi Regina, this is Tony. How about a movie Saturday night if you're not busy."

"Tony who?" she asked, seeming puzzled.

"Tony Harte, Aragon, Chop Suey, taxi," he answered. "Boy I must've really impressed you." What girl, he thought, waiting for her reply, could forget old Don Juan Harte that quickly?

"Oh, I'm sorry," she apologized, "I just didn't hear the name clearly. It usually takes longer than two weeks for me to forget someone."

Tony thought her remarks made him feel a little better, but he wasn't sure. "Well now, since that got me recognized, how about a movie?" he asked hopefully. "Sure," she laughed, "I remember, you never give up, so I might as well say yes."

Tony replied, "Fine, I'll call for you about 7:30 PM, and thanks."

Saturday night Tony arrived at Regina's house and had time to meet her family before leaving for the movie. Her mother was tall and had black hair with sharp but rather pretty features. She was polite, but quite reserved. Tony could tell she was looking him over very carefully. Regina's father was a short stocky man with a ready smile. He immediately offered a drink or coffee which made Tony feel quite welcome. Her brother, Ted, was tall and thin with curly black hair, brown eyes, and handsome features. He was friendly but somewhat reserved like his mother. Both men were engrossed in Western story magazines when Tony came in. After having coffee with Tony and Regina, they both went back to reading.

A few minutes later, Tony & Regina left for the movie. On the way to the Belmont Theatre, Tony observed, "I can see why you're so pretty, Regina. Your family are all good looking, especially your brother. He must have to carry a baseball bat to keep the girls off."

"Thank you," she said smiling, "Ted usually doesn't date much, he rather be with his buddy's drinking beer. He's had his share of problems with girls already."

The movie was a Fred Astaire musical, always good entertainment. Tony was satisfied with handholding and an occasional peck on her cheek. Remembering her firm action during their earlier car ride, he'd better behave, though it was a difficult and unusual decision for Tony. After the movie, they stopped for a snack, and were back at Regina's home by 11:00 PM. Her folks had already gone to bed, and Ted had gone out, so they had the living room all to themselves. She was no prude, and, like most girls of that era, allowed some mild necking, but was on guard against roaming hands. To Tony's credit, he managed to stick to good behavior, knowing if he wished to continue seeing this lovely girl, he'd have to earn her respect. He intended to do just that!

In May, Regina invited Tony to a party at her home. Most of her close friends were people she worked with. The party was fun, and Tony even enjoyed himself during the inevitable kissing games. He also felt a twinge of jealousy as Regina was taken off to be kissed by some other lucky fella. While mixed drinks and beer were served, no one got smashed. When after party refreshments were served at 1:00 AM, everyone was quite sober. By 3:00AM, all the guests had left except Regina's cousin Isabel who was staying the night. Tony hung around to help the girls straighten up. Before he realized it, it was 4:00 AM and high time he left, but Regina had another idea.

"Why don't you stay awhile longer Tony," she suggested, "You can take Isabel and me to mass at five AM."

"But I'm not a Catholic honey." Tony explained, "I doubt they'll let me in."

"Don't worry," she laughed, "Isabel and I won't tell the priest you're a heathen. Will you

go with us?"

Tony grinned at her and said, "Boy, I must be in love when I let a girl talk me into going to church at five in the morning. Sure, I'll go."

On the streetcar ride home, Tony fell asleep and missed three stops past his hotel. The walk back in the fresh air revived him a bit, but he was only concerned with a hearty breakfast and a good day in bed. Then he remembered this Sunday Heck Aiken and his mother were spending the day in town and had invited him to join them for an early dinner and a show. Breakfast and a shower he would get, but bed was out of the question. He was to meet them downtown at 10:00 AM.

The day with Heck and his mother, who chatted on and on, kept Tony awake while they were on the move, but at dinner, he almost fell asleep at the table.

"Boy, you must have had a bad night." Hecht commented.

"Yes, Tony does look tired," agreed Mrs. Aiken. Were you out late?" she asked.

He explained, "Well yes, I was at my girl's house for a party, then at five this morning we went to church."

"Was her father carrying a shotgun?" asked Heck, grinning. "It's about the only way anyone could get you to church. That's some story."

"It's as good as the one about you and the snake charmer at the Liberty Inn," Tony said defensively.

"Oh, I'd love to hear about that, Heck. What were you doing with a snake charmer?" Mrs. Aiken asked. "It's nothing mom," replied Heck, glaring at Tony, "Just one of Tony's jokes."

This ended the discussion about Tony's weariness. He managed to sleep through most of the movie and couldn't wait to see them off at the station when they finally left for home. He was in bed by 8:00.

The second weekend in June, Tony borrowed George's car and invited Regina to join him for a visit to the Olsens in Waukegan. He knew Dorothy and Jimmy would be there for the day, so this was a good chance to show off Regina and introduce her to his local relatives. She seemed pleased to be asked, but Tony was sure she must have had some qualms about meeting his relatives, having only known him for a short time.

All of the Olsen family treated Regina graciously and made her feel at home. Dorothy and Jimmy thought she was a gorgeous girl and just right for Tony. Grandpa Hannington who is 89 years old, had not dimmed his sharp eye for a beautiful woman; he promptly fell in love with Regina. As usual they all stayed for one of Amy's excellent dinners. When she called them to the table, Regina was chatting with Grandpa who was sitting in a deep chair with his feet crossed. As everyone took off for the dining room. Tony looked back to see poor Regina desperately hanging onto a sagging grandpa, who was about to fall on his face. He had forgotten to uncross his feet, and it looked as though both he and Regina would end up on the floor. Tony ran back just in time to save them both saying, "Gramps, you would do anything to hang on to a pretty girl."

"Yeah," he agreed smiling at Regina, "I don't have much time left, so I hang on while I still can."

At dinner Oscar asked Regina, "Have you and Tony been going together very long? It's about time he settled down with one girl. I think you just might be the right one"

"Oh, we've only known each other a few months," Regina answered blushing.

"I agree with daddy," Dorothy said. "It's about time somebody hogtied old Tony before

he gets too old and feeble."

"Just like you hogtied me?" grunted Jimmy.

"It would be nice," Amy said, "if you all would mind your own business. Regina and Tony don't need your help."

Tony agreed, putting his arm around Regina, "Yeah, right now we're just dating. If it gets serious, we'll let you know."

On the ride back to town, she said, "All your relatives are nice and I enjoyed the day, but they sure seem anxious to get you married off."

"Not really," Tony grinned at her, "they just worry about the lecherous life they think I lead."

Tony was now twenty-seven and up to this point in his life he had never spent much time on self-analysis, nor had he been particularly concerned with where he wanted to go in life except for show business. So far, he had too much fun just living to worry about what the future might hold.

In the past couple of months, he had become aware of the fact he wanted more out of life than just fun and games, particularly, like those at the Rendezvous Bar. The people he had been associating with were goodhearted for the most part but were leading hopeless lives in a hopeless environment which they would probably never escape. This, he decided, was not the life for him.

He thought for quite a while about his and Regina's visit to the Olsens and the impression she had made on them and their collective acceptance of her as the right girl for him, a fact he had, so far, not even admitted to himself. He was in love with her. Not only that, but he also wanted to marry her if she would have him. He just hoped she felt the same way. Only one way to find out, ask.

The following Saturday night, they had gone to a show, then stopped at the Rendezvous Bar for a drink. Regina seemed to sense Tony was nervous and much quieter than usual, though she said nothing. She seemed to get a kick out of the weird assortment of people in the bar. The bartender was making every effort to make her feel at home and comfortable.

Finally, Tony said nervously, "Regina, let's get out of here. I want to talk to you alone, so let's go to my room next door."

They said good night to the gang and went into the hotel. If Regina was worried about his intentions, she didn't show it.

"You've been acting funny all evening, what's wrong?" she asked, as they sat down in Tony's room.

"Nothing honey," he replied, kissing her. "Except those big brown eyes have done me in. Honey, I'm in love with you. Will you marry me?"

Regina stared unbelievingly at him. She wouldn't have been more shocked if he'd ask her to jump off the Michigan Avenue bridge. It took a few seconds for her to get over her shock, then she gave her answer. "Yes, I'll marry you. I love you too Tony." A moment later, they were in each other's arms. Tony still couldn't believe he had won this beautiful girl.

"Honey," he whispered, "you're wonderful, I'll always love you. Can we set the date for October 7? Remember, we met on February 7?"

"So soon? That's only four months from now," replied Regina.

"As soon as possible, beautiful. You might change your mind if we wait any longer and I'm not about to lose you." Tony grinned.

"Okay honey," she replied, giving him a kiss. "You better come over for dinner tomorrow so we can tell my folks."

"Oh boy," Tony said, "I'm not worried about your father, but I'm not sure about your mother. I don't think she is exactly crazy about me."

Regina replied, "Don't worry, she won't bite you."

A few minutes and many kisses later, Tony took Regina home. He didn't stay very long, because he would see her tomorrow and there were plans to make. One thing worried him a bit, though. Regina being a Catholic would present some problems. Tony had been raised Episcopalian and, well, was not an active church member; he wasn't ready to change unless it became absolutely necessary.

At dinner on Sunday, the two lovers announced their decision to get married to Regina's family. No one seemed overly surprised and her father appeared genuinely pleased. Not a connoisseur of liquor, as he didn't drink, he handed out a bottle of old Tiger Spit, which had been aged at least four days and poured drinks for Ted and Tony. For himself, he got a Coke. Regina and her mother responded to his toast for their happiness with coffee, while Ted and Tony bravely choked down the whiskey.

"I hope," said Ted, still gasping, "your marriage goes smoother than this booze. Where the hell did you get this stuff?"

"How soon are you going to get married, Regina?" her father asked, ignoring Ted's question.

"Tony wants to set the date for October 7, which isn't too far off," she replied.

"That soon?" asked her mother. "I don't see how we can have a wedding that fast," she finished.

"Well, my dear, we don't have to have a big church wedding; besides, I can't invite any of my friends from work. The company won't let me keep my job if they find out I'm married and we'll sure need the money I make," Regina replied.

Tony understood some of the problems involved and why Regina's mother objected to the date they had set. Her father owned a garage, but business was slow. A church wedding would cost money they really couldn't afford to spend, especially now. Then there was the problem Regina had raised about her job. In any case, they would have to be secretive about the wedding, no matter when they had it. "I've got an idea," said Tony. "Maybe we can have a real nice wedding that won't be very expensive and won't be in a Catholic or Episcopal Church."

Regina's father and mother both looked slightly horrified.

"Let me explain," Tony hastened to add. "I'm sure we can have a beautiful wedding in

the chapel at Avondale where I went to school, and where my mother and father were married. My uncle is the Methodist minister in Antioch, and he'd be happy to marry us. What do you all think of this idea?"

"Regina should get married in her own church," objected her mother.

Regina said, "We can't do that. The priest is strictly against marrying anybody out of our faith. Besides, my friends would know about it right away. I think Tony's idea is the best. Anyway, I will still be a Catholic. What you say?"

"Well," said her father. "Being married by a minister is better than a Justice of the

Peace. Perhaps later on they can have a Catholic service."

"All right, if that's what they want," her mother said reluctantly. "Just be sure our relatives and friends don't find out. What are Methodists anyway?"

"Oh, they're good God-fearing people." Tony hastened to assure her. "In fact, they have more strict rules about some things than Catholics do."

Tony was relieved Regina had been reasonable about his ideas. He had really expected serious problems later when they are alone, and Tony told Regina what all they had to accomplish. "By next Sunday honey," he said, "we will have to visit Cap' Bagley at Avondale and see if we can get married on the date we want, then go see my Uncle Sam and get his okay to marry us. If we have time on our way back, we'll stop at the Olsens and tell them our plans."

"Sounds like we're going to have a busy day," she replied.

CHAPTER 12

THE CHASE

Leaving town early the following Sunday, Tony and Regina made Avondale their first stop. Cap' Bagley, was delighted to meet Regina and even more delighted with the reason for the visit.

"Wonderful!" he exclaimed. "Of course you can be married here. It's about time we tied this young fella down. He's been running lose far too long."

"We both thank you. We'd like to have the wedding on October 7. Is that okay?" Cap' Bagley's broad smile faded as he replied, "Golly, Aunt Maude and I won't be here then. I'm retiring the end of August and we're moving to California. Can you to make it sooner?"

"Gee, I don't know. That's two months earlier." Then turning to Regina, he asked, "What do you think honey? It just wouldn't be an Avondale wedding without Cap' and Aunt Maude." He continued, "Do you think we could move it up to August 7?"

Regina looked at both of them, and realizing how disappointed they were, she smiled and replied, "You know it will take some doing, but I guess we can manage. I know Tony would feel terrible if you aren't at the wedding."

"By golly, that's great!" beamed Cap', then added, "You certainly picked the right girl. Now you two are going to stay for chapel service and lunch, right?" They spent the next hour meeting Aunt Maude, a couple of Tony's old teachers and touring the school grounds. After chapel and a good lunch, they left for Antioch to see Uncle Sam.

As they drove off, Tony said, "Honey, you sure have made Cap' and me happy. I just hope your mother won't be too upset about our change of plans."

Regina laughed saying, "I don't think she'll mind too much, but it sure doesn't give me much time to get to know you before we're married."

"Maybe that's just as well." he said, grinning at her. "You might change your mind."

Tony hadn't seen Uncle Sam, his dad's brother, for several years. Sam Harte was a tall heavy-set man with a ready smile. He was well-liked and respected by his Methodist flock having been their minister for 25 years. He also operated a greenhouse business and had once been mayor of the town. He often joked about his various activities saying, "I marry 'em, preach to 'em, bury 'em, tax 'em, and sell 'em flowers for all those occasions."

The Reverend Sam was busy in his greenhouse when Tony and Regina arrived. Greeting them with his usual good nature, he said, "Boy, it's about time you got around to visiting your old uncle. And, who's this beautiful girl?"

Introducing his uncle to Regina, Tony said, winking at her, "I see there's nothing wrong with your eyes, Uncle."

"Well," he said, grinning at them, "there is nothing in the Good Book that says I can't look or appreciate what I see."

"We hope you're going to get a chance to look at both of us over the Good Book," replied Tony, "We'd like you to marry us in August."

"That would be a pleasure. It's about time you settle down. "Just tell me when and where. You've sure picked a lovely girl. Congratulations," he said as he finished giving Regina a hug and a kiss on her blushing cheek.

"Capt. Bagley said the same thing about settling down. We've picked August 7 as the date and the Avondale Chapel as the place." Tony explained.

"No better spot on earth. That's where I married your dad and mother back in 1907. I hope your dad will be there for your wedding." he said, smiling at them.

"Thanks Sam. We'll see you again to work out the details, but now we've got to talk to the Olsen's," Tony replied.

While they were talking, Sam had picked s huge bouquet of flowers which he handed to Regina as they left. "Here's a pre-wedding bouquet for my new niece to be. I'll take care of the flowers for your wedding too."

"Thank you, Uncle Sam," replied Regina, kissing him goodbye.

"Boy!" said Tony as they drove off. "I better not let anything happen to you or our wedding after the hit you made with Cap' and Uncle Sam. They'd have my scalp for sure."

"Don't worry honey," Regina answered, smiling, and sniffing her flowers. "I don't intend to let you get away now. Those two are wonderful people; they must think a lot of you."

Arriving at the Olsen's an hour later, they were pleased to see Dorothy and Jimmy were also there.

Dorothy greeted them, "Hi guys, didn't expect to see you two so soon. Not having any trouble, I hope."

"No," Tony replied, putting his arm around Regina. "We just stopped by to tell the family we're getting married."

"You don't call that trouble?" Jimmy grinned.

"Oh, shut up Jimmy, you don't know how lucky you are," Dorothy said.

Turning to Regina, she gave her a hug. "Well, that's great! I'm glad my wild cousin finally got lassoed. Let's go tell mother and daddy. They'll be happy to hear your good news."

"We've just come from seeing Cap' Bagley and Tony's Uncle Sam," Regina told her as the two girls headed for the house. "We'd planned the wedding for October, but we've had to set the date for August 7 as Cap' is retiring."

Tony's aunt, uncle, and grandfather were all excited about the coming event.

"It's about time," Oscar observed, "now at least we'll know where he is nights."

"You be sure to take good care of each other," said Amy, then inevitable tears rolled down her cheeks.

"Well," chuckled Grandpa, "maybe now I'll get a great grandson, seeing as Dorothy and Jamie ain't doing anything about it."

Regina blushed as they all laughed at Grandpa's remark.

At dinner that evening, Dorothy's question startled Regina and Tony a bit. "Have you two picked your best man and bridesmaid yet?" she asked.

"We've done everything but that." Tony declared. Turning to Regina he asked, "What are you going to do honey? If we keep our wedding a secret from your company, where will you get a bridesmaid? I sure wouldn't ask any of the characters I know to be best man," he added.

"Maybe Dorothy and Jimmy would like to help us out," suggested Regina. "They would suit me fine, if they're willing."

"Oh, we'd love to." cried Dorothy.

George agreed, "Yeah, being the best man is a lot safer than being the bridegroom."

"You're already a bridegroom, dummy, and don't forget it!" Dorothy said with a grin.

"Good, thanks a lot kids. We sure are going to keep this wedding a family affair. I'm glad that's settled. Now all we have to do is get the license, right honey?" Tony answered, hugging Regina.

Later as they drove back to Chicago with Regina snuggling close to him, Tony asked, "Tired honey? This has been a long busy day."

"Yes sweetheart," she replied, but we've certainly gotten our wedding pretty well arranged. "I think it's been a wonderful day!"

The next day being a Monday, Regina went to her boss and requested two weeks' vacation, starting on Wednesday August 4th.

This would give her a couple days to do some final preparations before the wedding on Saturday. Even though they didn't have much money for a honeymoon, they planned to go to the Wisconsin Dells for a couple of days and then return to Chicago and spend some time together at Tony's apartment before they both had to return to work.

Regina's friends at work noticed how cheerful she had been recently. They even asked some leading questions, but Regina kept her secret. A couple of the older, more worldly women declared she must be having an affair to be that cheery. Regina just smiled at them and maintained her composure.

The Reid-Murdoch building was on the Chicago River two blocks east of the Merchandise Mart. It spanned the block between LaSalle and Clark Streets. An eight-story building with an impressive clock tower in the middle of its south side which housed the freight elevators. On the upper floors were offices where Regina worked as a clerk in the Accounting Department. The lower floors had food processing lines. Different vegetables were canned at different times of the year depending on what was being harvested. The production floors were hot places to work, with odors changing along with the products being canned. One department usually providing a pleasant smell was the coffee line, where coffee beans were roasted before being ground and canned.

The bottom floor was at dock level along the Chicago River. This served as the warehouse, which was divided in two areas, shipping of finished products and receiving of raw materials. The warehouse was serviced by two rail sidings, one each serving shipping and receiving. There were also two shipping docks for incoming and outgoing trucks.

On August 4th, Regina was busy all day trying to clean up her work before being gone for two weeks. Knowing she would be there a bit late; she and Tony had agreed to meet on the north side of the building, the corner of Kinzie and LaSalle streets, at about 6:00 PM.

As she was cleaning off her desk and preparing to leave, her boss came up with a thick manila envelope. He said, "Regina, I know you're about to leave, but can you drop these vouchers on Mr. Budinski's desk on your way out."

She responded, "Yes sir, I'd be happy to."

To accomplish this mission, instead of taking the main elevators on the north side of the building, she had to take the freight elevator which was on the river side. It went all the way to the warehouse level and then across the warehouse to the office area between the shipping docks on the north side of the building.

She was doing her duty, but really didn't like visiting the production or warehouse areas. There were large wharf rats and roaches as big as dates which made their homes in these venues.

Walking through the dimly lit warehouse, she found Mr. Budinski's desk and deposited the envelope, along with a note.

She proceeded to the shipping dock to take the stairs to Kinzie Street, but there were two trucks with their half-unloaded cargo blocking the dock. Rather than trying to work her way around the cargo, she proceeded back through the warehouse to the river side of the building where they were stairs to the LaSalle Street bridge. She exited the building and was at the base of the stairs when she saw, under the bridge, three or four figures in suits and one in a police captain's uniform. One of the men was handing a package to the police officer. She gasped a bit at what she was seeing.

One of the men saw her and hollered, "Get her!"

As the men turned to pursue her, she ran up the stairs to the bridge level. Pulling off her shoes she ran towards Kinzie Street. She could see over the side there was a car with a couple of other men who were exiting the car to pursue her.

Seeing Tony waiting on the corner, as she got closer she hollered "Tony Run!"

Tony responded, "What the hell?"

She grabbed him as she turned the corner onto Kinzie Street and yelled "just run!"

Seeing the pursuing men, Tony did as asked. As they ran east towards Clark Street, the pursuers were getting closer. At Clark Street there was a cop directing traffic in the midst of a huge jam. Several horns and jeering drivers could be heard. A taxi blocked the crosswalk with its front end sticking out into the intersection. Tony grabbed Regina's hand while opening the left rear door of the taxi. He pulled her into the cab and closed the door behind them.

The driver said, "Hey buddy, where do you want to go?" as Tony opened the right-side door and pulled Regina out the other side. They ran through the stalled traffic until they were on the other side of Clark Street.

Tony looked back as their pursuers reached the other side of the street. The policeman waved on the Clark Street traffic, stopping the pursuers in their tracks. Tony and Regina continued to run toward State Street, where Tony pulled Regina into a coffee shop and led her to the farthest booth from the entrance.

Catching their breaths, Tony ordered coffee and asked, "What the hell is this about?" Regina responded she'd only gotten a glimpse, but thinks she witnessed a police payoff, and when they saw her, they began chasing her. As she finished, she slid down in the booth as she saw two of the men walking down the sidewalk looking into coffee shop windows.

Tony said, "Crap, this isn't good. Did they see your face?"

"If they did, it was only for a second, cause I ran up the stairs to the bridge."

Tony thought a minute, "OK, but you're the only girl downtown without shoes. So, we have to do something about that. What size do you wear? I'll have to find some."

She told him her size and then added, "Low heels or no heels in case we have to run again and something in a medium brown would be nice."

Tony responded, "Oh Please! You stay here and eat something, and I'll find some shoes. If those bastards happen to come in here, the kitchen is right behind us, so make a run for it and I'll try to catch up to you."

Finding a shoe store just before it closed, Tony went in and bought the first pair of low-heeled shoes he saw. Twenty minutes later, he was back with a package.

Regina tried on the shoes, "Oh, they're not the best fit, but they'll have to do.

She had eaten half a sandwich while Tony was gone and left the other half for him. Tony went up to the register to pay and scanned the street before waving to Regina to come forward.

Looking around he didn't see any of the goons who had chased them. He was not sure but it seemed as if there was a larger than normal police presence on the street. Could the captain have the police looking for her too? There was no way of telling.

They headed north on State Street, trying to mingle with the crowds of people out for the evening. Since there were police on the corner, they crossed Kinzie in the middle of a group. Tony instructed, "Let's go north another couple blocks and then go over to Canal and take the streetcar to my place."

They crossed Hubbard Street and proceeded north. The next street was Illinois. As they were mid-block toward Illinois Street, a Cadillac sedan turned north from Hubbard. Regina exclaimed, "That looks like the car which was under the bridge!"

As Tony grabbed her arm and hustled her into the alley, they heard the Cadillac screech to a stop. They had been seen. As they ran down the alley, the Cadillac turned into the alley, giving chase.

Seeing a truck blocking the alley up ahead, Tony pulled Regina with him toward the side of the truck and a possible escape. As they reached the rear corner of the box van, Tony stopped after seeing a large, shadowy figure on the side of the truck coming their way and fast.

Turning back toward the Cadillac, its lights almost blinded them. But they could see figures getting out of each side of the car with guns in hand. Tony threw Regina against the rear of the truck and instinctively threw his body in front of her for protection. He took a deep breath, waiting for the inevitable pain of being shot.

After a couple of seconds which seemed like forever, he heard the loud report of two shots. He exhaled, feeling no wounds. Turning around he saw the two assailants from the car lying in pools of blood in the alley. Next to him stood a large man with a smoking weapon.

"Get in the car," directed the stranger, waiving his.45 automatic. "Get in back, we need to get the hell out of here!"

Since he could not object to a man with a gun, Tony, holding a shaking Regina by the shoulders, guided her into the back seat of the car. He shielded her eyes as much as he could from the grizzly scene at their feet.

The sound of gun shots had attracted some on-lookers at the street end of the alley. Two policemen also came running. The stranger jumped into the driver's seat, gunned the car and shot backward out of the alley, almost hitting some on-lookers who shouted their displeasure. The two policemen pulled their revolvers, but in the crowd of people, they didn't have room to fire.

The stranger squealed the tires in first gear as he sped north on State Street. He turned left on Illinois Street and then right on Canal Street where there was less traffic to dodge.

Tony and Regina flopped back and forth on the rear seat as the car made its sharp turns. When the car straightened out and headed in one direction, Tony could see with the light one side of the stranger's face and the scar on the right side of his neck.

Tony stammered, "You're the guy."

Before he could finish the sentence, the stranger broke in, "Yeah kid, I always felt I owed you for saving my ass at that school, back when."

Tony stammered again, "Those guys back there?"

The stranger responded, "Yeah I couldn't let them shoot you, and I never liked those two bastards anyway." He directed "We're out of the Loop; you can sit up now."

Tony and Regina sat up and he put his arm around her shoulders. She was quiet and still shaking.

The stranger asked, "So what are your names?" Tony answered with their names.

The stranger responded, "My friends call me Duke." He went on, "I need to get you two out of Chicago for sure and most likely out of Illinois for awhile. All of a sudden Regina stopped shaking and sat up straight. She said, "We can't leave Illinois. We're getting married on Saturday."

Duke asked, "So where are you getting married?"

Tony replied, "The chapel at the school where we first met." Regina interjected, "And I plan to be there."

Duke, understanding he had just been overruled, responded, "I don't know how bad they'll be looking for you, young lady, but they'll be hunting around downtown for awhile. Do you have any place out of the city to stay until the wedding?"

Tony replied, "I'm sure we can stay with my aunt and uncle in Waukegan."

"OK, I'll drop you at your homes for you to pack up your stuff and then I'll pick you up for the trip to Waukegan." He added, "Do you have a gun, kid?"

Tony responded, "Yes, a Smith& Wesson.38."

Duke, "Good, bring it with you in case this gets ugly."

Duke dropped Regina in front of her parent's house. As she left the car, Duke called to her, "For now, don't say anything more than necessary to your folks.."

He then drove to Tony's apartment and parked in the alley behind the Rendezvous Bar.

Twenty minutes later, Tony returned to the car with his suitcase and what didn't fit in it was in a pillowcase.

After putting his stuff in the trunk, Duke motioned for Tony to get in the front seat. Then they drove off to retrieve Regina.

Duke said, "I been thinkin' about it. You invite me to your wedding, and I'll show up with a different car and be your chauffer.

After the wedding is over, I'll take you where you'll be safe." Then asked, "Where are you going on your honeymoon?"

Tony replied, "We don't have much money, so we were going to the Dells for a couple days and then back to my apartment until we have to go back to work."

Duke said, "That's not far enough. You guys need to be gone for awhile until its safe around here. I'll come up with something better."

They picked up Regina and slid her to the middle of the wide bench seat. Duke drove them to Waukegan, getting to the Olsen's home at 11:30PM. Tony banged on the brass door knocker until Oscar was aroused and came downstairs to let them in.

As he opened the door, the Cadillac departed after depositing Regina, Tony, and their bags on the doorstep.

Oscar, "What the hell are you guys doing here, did you run away from home?"

Tony responded, "Unc' it's a long story and we're dead tired. If the guest rooms are available, I'll tell you in the morning."

Oscar pointed to the stairs and followed them to their rooms.

Tony had a fitful night's sleep, being exhausted from the evening's activities. When he slept, he slept soundly, but kept waking up and rolling around for long periods. At a little after 6:00AM, he heard Oscar getting ready for work.

Going downstairs as quietly as possible so he wouldn't wake Regina or anyone else in the house, Tony proceeded to the kitchen. Oscar was there in his pajamas getting coffee before cleaning up for work.

"Unc' we've got a talk," Tony said.

"You startled me," Oscar said. "Get some coffee and we'll talk."

Tony had to confide in someone, and no one was more reliable than his uncle. He explained the happenings of the previous evening and that Duke was going to protect them until they could leave town.

Oscar listened quietly, then asked, "Do you think you can trust this sleazy bastard?"

Tony replied, "I thought about that off and on all night. At this point he's killed two people while saving us. If he wanted to turn us over to the mob or the police, he could have done so as soon as he got us in the car."

"Do you know this guy?" Oscar asked.

Tony told him about the encounter many years before in the Avondale kitchen. He added, "So the guy says he owes me."

Oscar replied, "Sounds like a strange sense of loyalty. So, what happens next?"

"He wanted to take us out of state last night, but Regina objected saying she wasn't going to miss her wedding. We came here last night to get out of Chicago and be in place for the wedding on Saturday. Duke said he would attend the wedding and show up as our chauffeur. After the wedding and the festivities, he's going to take us someplace out of state where we'll be safe."

Oscar responded, "Well this is a hell of a mess." He went on, "so you don't know where you're going or for how long?"

"That's about right. I also don't know how bad the mob and the police want to find Regina. So, guess I'm stuck with the situation. I'll try to contact you, but if you don't hear from us in a week or so, please give my resignation to my boss at Castle and, I guess, try to do the same for Regina at Reid Murdoch."

"To hell with going to work. I'll call them and stay here today. I was going to take tomorrow off anyway to get ready for the wedding. Do you have a gun?"

Tony replied, "I have the old.38 revolver you gave me when I had the dairy stand."

Oscar opinionated, "Well you might keep it with you after the wedding on Saturday. I've never taken a gun to a wedding. Maybe I thought about a shotgun when Dorothy and Jimmy were getting all hot and heavy, but this may be the first time for real."

The discussion lightened up after Amy came into the kitchen. She was happy Oscar was planning to stay home for the day, and because Tony and Regina were there for her to fuss over. She immediately set about making breakfast for the whole clan.

Regina came downstairs an hour later, also having had a fitful night. She looked at Tony quizzically as he took her hand, gave her a peck on the cheek and whispered, "Everything will be all right."

After breakfast Dorothy arrived and was surprised to see Regina there a day early. Since the bride is not supposed to see the groom before the wedding, it had already been decided Regina was going to stay with Dorothy and Jimmy on Friday night and Saturday morning before the wedding. So, Regina's arrival a day early was no big thing. They would just do girl things for an extra day. By the same token, Tony was to spend Friday and Saturday morning with the Olsen's. As far as Dorothy was concerned, Regina was just there a day early.

Regina did tell Dorothy a little bit of what had transpired the evening before but didn't go into great detail. Enjoying each other's company, the girls spent the rest of the day window shopping and doing girly things. This eased the stress of the potential danger she and Tony were in.

Later in the morning Amy went looking for Oscar and found him and Tony in the garage cleaning their.38 revolvers. She said, "What the heck are you boys doing? Seems like a strange thing to do when preparing for a wedding."

Oscar replied, "The kid and I have plenty of time to worry about the wedding. This is just one of those maintenance things we usually forget about." Amy went back in the house shaking her head in disbelief.

Friday went fast what with pressing clothes and other wedding preparations. In the late afternoon everyone met at the Avondale Chapel for the wedding rehearsal. Uncle Sam, as the presiding minister, led everyone to the service and told them where to be and when. Amy prepared a formal dinner for the family where the wine flowed and everyone was in a jovial mood in anticipation of the big event.

After dinner when Regina had Tony alone. She asked, "Have you thought anymore about the mess we're in?"

Tony, "Yes. At this point, I think we just have to follow Duke's lead." Nervously,

Regina said, "What if he doesn't show up tomorrow?"

"I still have reservations in the Dells. I guess we'll go on our honeymoon and then decide if we have to leave town or not. Whatever happens, know I'll always love you and we are a team, assured Tony."

Saturday morning there was action at both houses as the bride and groom prepared for their one o'clock service. Amy and Aunt Maude left for the chapel at 9:00 AM to put the flowers in place and the bows on the pews.

A nervous Tony arrived at the Chapel at 11:30 AM. Cap' Bagley was already practicing for his duties as organist.

By noon some of the early guests started showing up. Tony was out in front welcoming everyone, while keeping one eye out at the school's entrance for Duke. At 12:45 PM Tony saw a shiny blue 12-cylinder Packard turn into the driveway.

Tony hustled over to greet Duke who parked at the outside edge of the parking area. He stepped out of the Packard, resplendent in a wide pinstriped charcoal gray suit and an ill-fitting little black cap on his head.

Duke said, "Sorry I'm so late. Borrowing the car was no big deal but finding this chauffer's hat was tough." Tony responded, "I'm happy to see you. Would you like to meet some folks?"

Duke, "Nah, it's probably best if I just stay on the outskirts and act as your chauffer."

Tony asked, "So where are you taking Regina and me?"

Duke replied, "I've got a train trip for you two. It should be a much better honeymoon than the Wisconsin Dells."

Being almost time for the service, Tony went to the back of the chapel to make his entrance. Meanwhile Duke, sitting in the rear of the chapel, kept an eye on the door. His arms, folded on his lap, covered up the bulge in his coat.

The service did not come off without a hitch. First the back door to the chapel was locked and Tony had to knock on it until his Uncle Sam came to let him in. Meanwhile, the organist, Cap' Bagley, got tired of listening to the people babbling in the pews, so he turned off his hearing aid. The bride and her father entered at the back of the chapel and the organist began playing, "Here Comes the Bride." The bride stood waiting for the music to begin. Halfway through the second round of "Here Comes the Bride," someone near the organ flipped the switch, turning it on, and the ceremony continued without a hitch.

Photographs of the wedding party were taken out on the lawn after the service. The wedding party then moved to their vehicles to go for lunch at the Karcher Hotel. Duke pulled the Packard behind Oscar's car and put Tony's bag in the trunk. He then moved on to Jimmy's car and did the same with Regina's bag.

Regina's father, Stanley, kept an eye on Duke from the time he arrived. Stanley owned an auto repair shop and over the years had fixed the cars of several disreputable characters in Chicago. To Stanley this guy certainly seemed to fit the mold. A couple of the other guests may have also felt Duke looked like an awful tough character for this event, but if so, they didn't say anything.

At the luncheon, Tony made sure Duke was served along with everyone else. Again, Duke sat in the rear of the room and played the role of a hired chauffeur.

As four o'clock rapidly approached Duke began looking worried and gestured to Tony to come see him. "We have to leave here soon if you're to make the train I told you about."

"Okay, Tony replied. I think the toasting is almost over. I'll round up my bride and meet you out front of the hotel."

Tony went back to table and announced to everyone that he and Regina would be departing for their honeymoon. He then ushered her through the lobby and out the front door, followed by the cheering wedding party. The Packard was waiting with Duke at the wheel still wearing his little black hat. Rice was thrown, the bouquet was thrown, and everyone shouted well wishes as the Packard sped off.

Duke said, "Sorry kids, but we have a train to catch."

Duke sped into Chicago through the loop and to the end of Northwestern Station. He handed Tony an envelope. "In there are tickets for the streamliner to Denver which leaves at 6:20 PM. I put a little money in it to help you out and the phone number for my cousin Mikey who lives there and can help you get established. Keep an eye on the Chicago papers. If that crooked cop O'Rourke gets caught, it will be safe to come back to Chicago. If for some other reason things cool down here, I'll put an ad in the notices section of the Tribune looking for a lost cat named Gus."

Duke passed the suitcases to a Redcap and handed him a tip up front as Tony showed him their tickets.

Tony grabbed and shook Duke's right hand heartily with both of his and said, "Thanks Duke, this has been really great."

Regina stepped up on her tiptoes, hugged Duke and gave him a kiss on the cheek. "Bless you. I don't know what we would've done without you."

The big guy blushed as he waved goodbye to them.

The Redcap led them to their compartment on the train. Tony commented about the first-class accommodations while looking in the envelope and finding $200.00.

At exactly 6:20 PM, the final "All aboard" was announced and the Union Pacific streamliner began to roll south out of the coach yard and to safety for Tony and Regina.

www.ingramcontent.com/pod-product-compliance
Lightning Source LLC
Chambersburg PA
CBHW061258210726
48293CB00003B/1015